THE FISHER MEN X MY HEART

Fisher Men series Book I.

Rebel Nicks
O'Dey

You need to crack before you Roar

xoxo Rebel Nicks O'Dey

Dedicated to the girl who never knew me. I was your first responder. A voice on the phone you never even heard. You were in a field. Discarded. Your pants were inside out, your appearance disheveled, and your underwear was missing. You couldn't remember what happened, but I will never forget. I had two beautiful girls your age. They were safe at home in their beds. I made sure of it the moment you were safe, too. I was nobody of consequence to you, but I have grieved the loss of your innocence every day. I wrote the happily ever after you should have had. I hope you don't mind.

To my daughters that lived the consequences of a night, they were not a part of. I became overbearing, nosey, and intrusive. It was because I loved you. I dealt with the horrors of humanity day in and day out, my only wish was that you would never know those horrors yourself.

To my real-life Fisher Men. The guys that surrounded me in my teen years. PaPa's Pizza, Riverwalk nights, and Sunday family dinners, made me feel invincible as your young friend. Some of my best times were in the passenger seat of your cars. I was off limits because only one of you had my heart. Thirty years later, he still does.

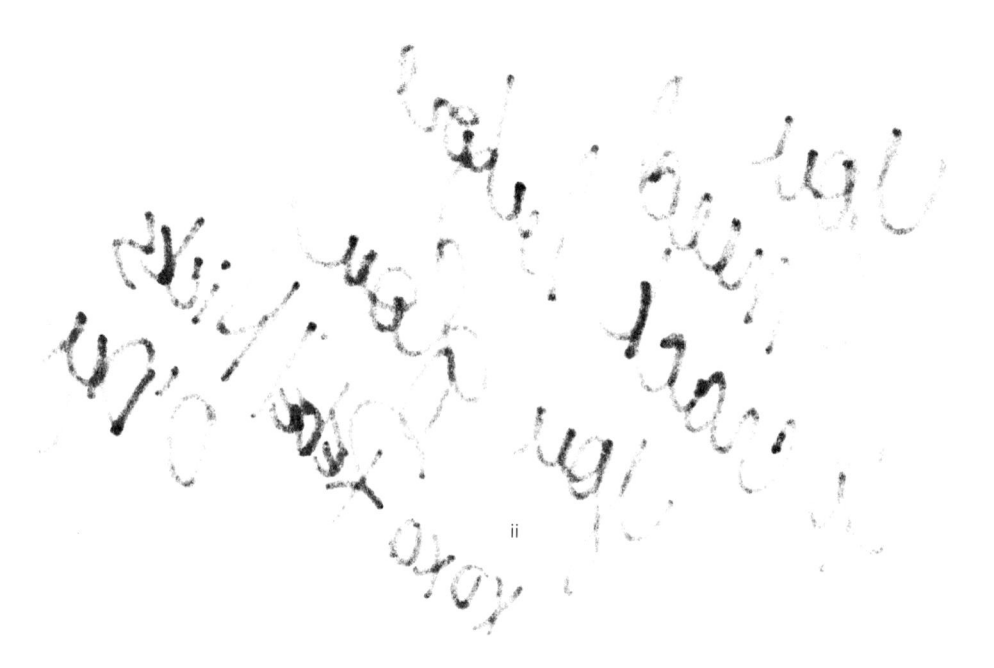

Fisher Men X My Heart © 2019 by Rebel Nicks O'Dey All Rights Reserved.

All rights reserved. No part of this book may be reproduced in any form or by any electronic or mechanical means including information storage and retrieval systems, without permission in writing from the author. The only exception is by a reviewer, who may quote short excerpts in a review.

Cover designed by Bel Books

This book is a work of fiction. Names, characters, places, and incidents either are products of the author's imagination or are used fictitiously. Any resemblance to actual persons, living or dead, events, or locales is entirely coincidental.

Rebel Nicks O'Dey
Visit my website at www.RebelNicksODeyAuthor.com

Printed in the United States of America

Touch of Nature Font (Front cover): Type features the creations of Ben McGehee bmcgehee@mis.net

Prologue

Blog Entry:

From the diary of a Casual Observer,

It's been a slow news week in the city, so today, how about a little gossip? Rumor has it that Champagne Falls long lost daughter, Samantha Reynolds, is coming home. It's been a long four years, hasn't it? With four single Fisher Men to greet her, one has to wonder, how long will they will remain just friends? Which one will she choose? Should we start a poll?

After everything the girl has been through, coming home can't be easy. She is a much stronger woman than I am. If I had been treated like she was, I would have left on the first bus with my shiny ass hanging out the window. It would be an open invitation for all of you to kiss it goodbye.

She endured six months of outraged hashtags trending her demise. It was a solid year for "justice" to be slapped on the wrist. It took two years for everyone to stop the hushed whispers in her wake. Even after eight long years, the twenty somethings of Champagne Falls look at her with either guilt or sorrow.

I, for one, hope that she settles in for a happily ever after with the eerily perfect Fisher family. I would love to know that not only did this town not break her, but we gave her everything she ever wanted. Even though my money is on her high-tailing it right back out of here, I'd love to see her stay and be happy.

So, Casual Observers, cast your vote. Who will she choose?

1.) Morgan Fisher
2.) Connor Fisher
3.) Xander Fisher
4.) Zack Fisher
5.) Fuck you Champagne Falls she's out.

Stay tuned to find out who everyone is rooting for.

Trigger Warning

***

My heroine is saved from a near sexual assault. During this scene, we are in her point of view where everything is very real, very scary, and based on the thoughts, feelings, and instincts of a woman in her position. While the attack is interrupted, the thoughts and feelings are explored vividly. If you are not comfortable exploring or reliving that moment. Look for the above and below asterisk separators. You can skip everything in between them, without missing the story. This is a tale of how she overcame the trauma of an ill-fated night. The character and story will not wallow in that despair, it is part of her well rooted back story.

***

CHAPTER 1

It all began with Kateri.

Sam

Jumping my whole five feet four inches of nothing self, down on my suitcase is comical. It's not any closer to closing.

"Rika help me!"

My roommate enters my room flushed from hauling her own stuff down the stairs and into my pick-up truck. "I can't get it closed. Sit on it with me." Between the two of us, we smash everything in as tightly as we can, jumping and sitting on the hard plastic until the suitcase is finally latched, and then we fall backwards collapsing on my bed.

"Sam, can you believe we are going home? We're leaving New York and heading back to Champagne Falls," she waves her hand in a sweeping motion above us, "with degrees and dreams."

I nod. "It's unreal. I'm nervous. It's time to be a grown up now, you know?"

Rika leans up on one elbow and pats my head reassuringly but gives me a condescending look. "You get to live with your dad, find a job, and then be a grown up." She mocks pouting. "I'm moving in with a stranger and half a plan."

I slap her playfully. "Connor isn't a stranger, he's one of my best friends, just like you."

"You mean one of the men in your harem."

I roll my eyes. *Like I haven't heard that joke a million times or more.*

"No, you mean reverse harem, and that isn't what it is. They are just... my Fisher Men." I shrug my shoulders, sitting up from the bed. "Look, a really terrible thing happened right before high school. The Fisher brothers took it upon themselves to change my circumstances. All four of them picked me up every morning for school, and all four of them brought me home. All four were my homecoming dates, and whoever aligned in age took me to prom. We hung out every day, all day until I went to college."

Grabbing my suitcase, I take one last look around the room. This has been my home for the last two years. After the first year in the dorms, Rika's friend invited us to live here. We got affordable rent and in exchange, we checked in on her friend's mom downstairs. Mrs. Flannigan is a nice lady and a great landlord. We picked up groceries for her, and at least once a week she made us dinner.

We graduated a month ago but couldn't find jobs in our field. Journalism isn't what it used to be. It's hard to get into, even at smaller Newspapers. Between my high school AP classes, skipping summer breaks, and accelerated curriculum classes, I graduated a year and a half early, making me too young for news outlets to take seriously.

We are both done being proof readers and book editors. We've done that throughout college, I don't mind it, but it's not what I feel like I should be doing. I did that without the degree I have, but can't afford.

Rika got a job at our local newspaper back in Champagne Falls after a prison interview she did with a famed serial rapist. She tried to ride that train straight into a job in New York City, but things didn't go as she had hoped. She won't be writing big city cutting-edge investigative pieces as she envisioned, but she'll have a real job. I don't know what I'm going to do yet.

Turning to leave, Rika grabs a box off the kitchen table and follows me out.

"You never, not even once, developed feelings for one of the Fisher men?" she asks with a side eyed glance.

"I developed feelings for all of them, but I fell in love with only one of them." Heading down the stairs, I knock on Mrs. Flannigan's door and hand over the key. "Bye. Mrs. Flannigan." *I'm going to miss her soda bread.* "We hired a cleaning crew to come in tomorrow, be sure to let them in."

"Yes, yes. We will miss you girls. You drive safe and do keep in touch." She hugs and kisses us on both our cheeks.

"Yes, Mrs. Flannigan," we answer in unison.

I feel nostalgic as we climb down the cement stairs to the street one last time.

Rika picks up her pace to match my stride to the truck. "Um, excuse me, Samantha, you can't drop a bomb like that and walk away. You're in love? With one of the Fisher Brothers?"

"Since the beginning, there has always been one. Pursuing it would have damaged our dynamic, and I needed the dynamic. I had been labeled strictly hands off, and each brother agreed to abide in the pact."

"So, you're never going to do anything about it? Ever?"

"I needed the dynamic to survive high school. Now, I'm an adult. I think it's time to get what I want."

Balancing the box on her hip she offers her hand up to slap. "Yeah, it is!" I return her high five and snort a laugh.

After throwing the last of our things into the pick-up truck, I button down the tarp. I pull my long brown hair up into a ponytail, throw on my trucker hat, and slide into the front seat. "So, which Fisher man are you in love with?" Rika chirps.

"To understand that, you have to understand the dynamic. You have to know how it all began. It started before the 'incident we are never to speak of.'" Turning the key in the ignition, my truck rumbles to life. Pulling out into minimal traffic, pushing the memory from the back of my mind, the forgotten words tumble out of my mouth. "It all began with Kateri."

CHAPTER 2

The moment I saw the Fisher Boys, my heart raced and dropped all at once. My cheeks pinked and my throat went dry.
-Samantha Reynolds

Sam's journal entry:

Ugh! My parents are ruining my life! Dad and I just moved in next door to the Fisher family. I no longer live across town in a large home, in a gated community, nor do I live with two parents.

My new house is described as quaint, charming even. Those are poetic words for saying small and old. The only thing I like about this house is the view. Sitting a foot away from my window so I can't be seen, I watch four shirtless, gorgeous boys a little older than me, playing catch with a football.

Everyone knows the Fisher Brothers. There is a blog devoted to all things Fisher Brothers. I admit it, I am a loyal subscriber to The Diary of a Casual Observer. I am the casual observer today. It sounds better than stalker. Leaning slightly forward, my mouth goes dry when sweat beads on their sun kissed skin. All four of them are sizzling freaks of nature. Seriously, it is unfair how genetically unflawed they are. Even though I'm on the A squad of popularity, they are out of my league. I mean, I'm but a mere mortal spying on the celestial.

I go to St. Mary's, they go to East Falls. I am starting eighth grade, they're in high school. I'm watching them drink water from the hose; while laughing and rough housing, they don't even know I exist. And because they don't know I exist, they don't know my bedroom window faces the side of their house. They don't know that their secret little make out spot, the patch of grass between the generator and the utility box hidden by hedges is right below my bedroom window.

I have their schedule down now. See the graph on page one. They go in order. Big Brother Morgan, a junior in high school, gets use of the spot every Monday. Connor the Sophomore gets the spot each Tuesday. Now the Freshman twins, Zack and Xander, are a little fuzzy. I don't know which one is which. I call them dark broody boy and cute artist boy. Not because it describes them, but because it describes their type. I voyeuristically watch them; my back to the wall perched from my loft bed. Up here I can see down with perfect clarity, but they need to angle to look for me. They don't even know I'm here. I keep notes and schedules. I don't know why, other than because I'm thirteen and curious.

Monday

Today, like every Monday night, Morgan has Ashley Aniston in his arms. She's a blonde cheerleader type, she giggles annoyingly while talking with and kissing Morgan. I have a feeling he keeps his mouth pretty firmly on hers so she'll be quiet. Her voice is annoying, her laugh is annoying, she's annoying. If she didn't look like a real-life Barbie doll, I can't imagine why anyone would want to be around her. She's a sophomore at my school; she's a snob.

Each time I watch, he takes things just a bit further with her. Today he lifts her shirt up and brings it down over his head. His face is probably on her bare skin because she squeals with delight. All I can see is the shape of his head stretching her t-shirt. She throws her head back and I get a clear view straight down the neckline. He unclasped the front closure on her bra. I didn't even know bras came like that. I can see his tongue flick at her nipple causing her hips to squirm on his lap where she's straddling him. When her breathing becomes ragged and her hips maintain a steady movement on his lap, He closes his mouth over her nipple and she springs forward blocking my view.

I've heard the term dry humping before, now I see what that is. It stirs strange new feelings and desires in me. His kiss looks harsh, passionate maybe? It looks almost painful. She leaves every Monday with swollen lips and starry eyes. Today she will leave with wet nipples. I wonder what it would be like to have a mouth on my nipples. Especially one belonging to a Fisher boy. Each time Morgan grabs Miss Perky Priss by her butt and pulls her down harder on him, I want to know what that feels like, too. I secretly wish it was me.

Tuesday

Connor prefers librarian looking girls. Unlike Morgan, it is a different girl every Tuesday. This one goes to my school, too. I recognize the uniform. As per his type, her hair is in a ponytail and she's wearing huge black framed glasses. Her body is lanky. She's all knobby knees and freckles. He plays it cool at first. They read. Laying side by side, holding hands, they look for and point out cloud formations. The looks he gives her suggests she is the most beautiful creature he has ever laid eyes on. Pushing a loose strand of hair behind her ear, he locks eyes with her. Slowly, he brings his mouth to hers but stops a breath from her lips, then he waits for her to fill the empty space between them. As he always does, he ends up on top of her in the throes of a sensuous kiss. I wondered what it would be like to have my face cupped, and my hair smoothed, with the deep slow passion that Connor prefers. Every Tuesday, I wish it was me being adored.

Wednesday

Its Dark broody twin day. Both twins have the blonde-hair, blue-eyed, boy-next-door look of their brothers, but Dark twin prefers goth girls. A stark contrast to the previous night. Dark twin holds his girlfriend by her neck when he kisses her. He sucks and bites on her bottom lip, and he also enjoys being bitten. He's wearing a black shirt and dark jeans, she's wearing a black leather dress and combat boots. They look dangerous.

He pulls the neckline of her shirt to the side, biting and sucking along her collarbone leaving bruises and marks. He leaves them where they can be covered easily by her shirt or hair. Today he spins her around and holds her back to his front. Brushing her unnaturally black hair to the side he sucks down her shoulder while the other hand travels up and down the smooth leather. She turns her head to resume the kiss and he cups her breast running his thumb back and forth over her nipple until it beads. She raises her arm over her head and to the back of his head, pulling him in for a deeper kiss. His hands travel down, lifting the front of her dress, and sliding his hands into her black panties. Gently he rubs her as she moans and squirms. Yikes, the sight makes my insides flutter. He progressed faster than big brother. Maybe he's had this girlfriend longer than Morgan had Ashley? A heat spreads inside me, and I want to be touched like that. It's such a naughty thought to have, I know, but the quake in my core doesn't care. I wonder if I would like biting, sucking harsh kissing more than the tender kisses Connor prefers.

Thursday

The other twin like his brother is an artist, but his girl is cute with unnaturally bright colored hair like pink or green. She wears pin-up style clothes. He always brings a set of markers on their dates. He likes to draw on her. He draws elaborate murals on her hands and across her fingers. At some point, he stops drawing and they start kissing. The soft felt tip of the marker is like erotic foreplay to her. She closes her eyes and sometimes even moans. They are usually rolling in the grass making out twenty minutes into his masterpiece.

Today cute artist girl is wearing a 1950's swing dress. It's white with little cherries and a halter top. Her hair is colored the same bright red as the cherries on her dress as well as her painted lips. She assumes her relaxed position in the grass and I find myself anticipating what he might draw. He takes her hand and writes a note on it. She reads it and her eyes grow wide. He kisses her. She threads her fingers through his hair. No artwork today?

As he lay beside her kissing her, his hand travels down her dress. Like his twin, he reaches under it and begins rubbing her. The twins are bad boys. Turns out the sweet twin is naughtier then all his brothers. Cute artist girl unties her halter top and her ample chest is bare. Totally bare. I have a full view of his mouth on her boobs, his hand up her dress, and she has her hand down his pants. Holy Smokes. I'm enthralled. Note to self, make popcorn on Thursday.

I wonder what a boy feels like, you know, down there. I keep my eyes trained on her hand. I want to know what you're supposed to do when you do get to touch it. It is so wrong how bad I want to touch a dick, but not as bad as I want to be touched, and licked, and sucked like the lucky girls that hide in the hedges with the Fisher brothers.

Friday

I don't know what the Fisher brothers do on Friday because I live with my mom on the weekends. She doesn't bring it up, but I know it hurts. I chose to primarily live with my dad. I love both of my parents, but my dad is a man of routine, structure, and dependability. In short, he's boring, and that's probably why they're divorced.

My mother is a poet, an artist, a musician, and frankly, a bit flighty. It's great to have a parent that fancies a little whimsy in life. We read salacious romance novels on the beach, discuss Jane Eyre over dinner, and read Shakespeare at bed time.

She's the one that fostered my obsession of reading and writing. She takes me on spur of the moment road trips, museums, and shopping sprees. Once she signed me out of school and took me downtown to watch the Transformers movie being filmed. I was a gigantic Shia Labeouf fan, so my mother batted her eyes, smiled her beautiful smile, and got us window seating at the bakery alongside the set where they were filming. We were right behind the director and stars chairs. I was close enough to wave, and Shia waved back. For a young girl with a big crush, it was HUGE!

When it comes to big surprises, she rocks, but day to day stuff, well… I started making my own breakfast at three and have self-sufficiently been awake, dressed, and off to school every day since the third week of Kindergarten on my own. It's not that my mom doesn't care, she just doesn't do the whole grown up thing really well. She's a terrible cook, she doesn't spend a lot of time cleaning, she's atrocious with money, but she always has a smile on her face and the kindest heart in all things.

I knew what I was doing. Dad will make sure I get good grades, go to college, teach me life skills, and Mom will take me to concerts, inappropriate movies, and beach vacations that she can't actually afford. She's a much better weekend parent.

I'm adapting to this new life, but yes, I'm angry. As angry as any teenage girl who discovers she isn't the center of her parent's universe anymore. I mean how dare my parents not stick it out for five more years, for me. I would be away at college, and not keeping journals like this to discuss in therapy. They have lived two separate lives for as long as I can remember. Why not continue for five more years? How could they not see how embarrassing this is? I am captain of the Champagne Falls competitive cheer squad. I am a company dancer at my dance studio, and I'm first chair flute at St. Mary's. I have a life and an image to maintain, and they don't see my position in all of this. Not. At. All.

If I have to live this so-called-life for four more years, at least I get to watch boys so hot my eyes melt.

CHAPTER 3

I guess I'll be letting my demons out to play this road trip.

Sam

I don't think you leave New York, so much as escape it. I will miss the noise, the crowd, and the chaos of this city. It is the only place where I can be alone while surrounded by people. In my small town, everybody knows everybody, and they all want to know about everyone else's business.

Sadly, they all know my business. Everyone knows.

Rika interrupts my musing. "So, get on with it girl. Is it Connor. Are you jealous of my new roomie?"

I am.

Connor is the passionate sculptor and my late-night movie buddy.

Rika pushes her glasses up her nose and ties her long, sandy blonde hair into a messy bun on top of her head.

I smile at her expectant look and blurt the memory that was dancing in my thoughts just a moment ago.

"Before Connor and the rest of the Fisher Men were in my life, there was Kateri."

Rika snaps her attention to me. "Who?"

I lick my lips and check my mirrors before merging on the highway.

"Kateri Fisher and I went to the same school. I was the cheerleader, and she was the pariah. I was her nemesis, and I was awful to her." I lose myself for a moment. How she ever forgave me... Swallowing hard, I glance briefly at Rika before I continue; guilt wrenching my gut.

"In grade school, she went by Kat. Needless to say, the name Kat Fisher made her the butt of every joke. Some boys teased that she was named after her smell. The kids would pull her hair, dump her books, and even sprayed some fish smelling spray in her locker."

"Oh my god, that's terrible. You did that?"

"No, but I didn't stop it either. I could have. I did nothing, then. When I did do something, it was far worse than anything they had done."

A tear falls down my face, and for a moment, I consider not telling her what an awful troll I was. I haven't spoken about it since I was thirteen. How could I know that Kateri was the girl who would change me? She changed everything when she saved me.

"In junior high, the schools were split. One sixth through twelfth grade school for boys, and one for girls. A very Catholic school thing to do. You know, because Jesus wouldn't want us to be curious." I roll my eyes and Rika chuckles. "Kateri grew boobs in junior high, and that caused a wave of white hot jealousy through the other girls. Myself included. I picked up where the boys left off. I spread rumors of promiscuity and had her all but shunned by our clique. The more she buried her face in her computer and ignored our taunts, the more I stepped up the bullying. I wanted to matter, and the fact that I couldn't affect her made me feel like I didn't matter to her."

"I cannot believe what I am hearing!" I glance at Rika; her genuine shock evident. "You are the kindest girl I know. Why were you such a bitch?"

I love Rika. She calls it as she sees it, and she is seeing exactly who I was.

"I was angry. I wanted everyone else to be angry, too. My mother had me working at her store every moment I wasn't at school, and tension was rising between my parents. Honestly, there is no excuse, and nobody in my life influenced or encouraged me to change."

"How does this get back to the Fisher Men."

"Kateri is the youngest Fisher. The only girl."

"Wow." Rika deadpans.

"Two things changed for her at the top of our eighth-grade year. First, Morgan Fisher in all of his glory walked across the cafeteria in our all-girls school. He stopped at the table where Kat sat alone every day and began helping her with her things. We quickly discovered he was her brother, and he was gorgeous. The next day, sophomore Ashley Aniston left our table to sit with Kateri. They became inseparable until Ashley began dating Morgan a week or two later.

"Second, around that same time, I got saddled with her on a project. As we spent long hours in the library together, I came to realize that she was really nice. She was smart without a doubt, but even though I was terrible to her in the past, she didn't let it affect how she interacted with me. I genuinely liked her. I continued chatting with her after our project was done. We would go to the mall and hang out sometimes, she even helped me close my mother's shop. The last of the final clearance sales were difficult for me. I grew up in Rocky Mudds, I couldn't imagine not going there every day.

"I miss Rocky Mudds, too. Remember how we would sit in the back and make jewelry with your mom? Oh, and that little boy from the tattoo shop next door brought us ice cream."

How could I forget Colton BaddStone? We started playing together when we were six, each of us at work with our parents. He was my first kiss. I was so nervous when our lips touched. We both looked surprised it happened. Our faces were as red as his hair, and the giggling that ensued got some unwanted attention.

"He died that summer when we were only ten in a freak drowning accident. I cried for months. He was my future husband you know."

Rika pats my leg in a comforting gesture. "He was really sweet on you." I glance at her and smile before returning my eyes to the road. I think of him from time to time and wonder what he would look like today. Rika's voice raises a pitch. It's something she does when she's nervous.

"What happened between the nine-year-old sweet girl I left at Rocky Mudds and the teen bully that made life miserable for Kat Fisher?"

I think about that for a moment.

Everything.

And in hindsight, nothing.

"Your dad got a new job in the city, so you left, the boy from the tattoo shop died, and my parents began arguing in front of me rather than hiding behind closed doors. I was a selfish teenager, and my life wasn't going the direction I had planned."

Rika giggles. "Work that out in therapy, did you?"

I hated therapy. She knows that. I reach over and awkwardly punch her arm.

"No, Morgan Fisher called me out on it. The Fisher Men were all the therapy I needed." It hurt at the time, but now I can smile fondly on the strong woman they had a hand in molding.

"My boys had help. Nonna Fisher, the matriarch of the family, runs a nonprofit that supports victims of domestic abuse. Safe Spaces provides safe houses, counseling, court advocacy, and more. Mr. Fisher is a teen substance abuse counselor. The two have been married forever and are still in love like newlyweds."

"Aww," Rika mews.

"The Fisher brothers had a wonderful example on how people should be treated. They are natural protectors and love with their whole soul." I glance to Rika quickly, "Rest area in five miles."

She shakes her head, "I'm good. So, with protective older brothers, it's a wonder Kateri ever had a date."

"You would think," I laugh. "At first they treated her like a brother. She played football with them. They didn't care if she dated, but as the St. Mary's pariah, she never did. After the incident, they didn't know how to protect her. The new lines drawn were confusing. Eventually, she became more discerning than they ever were."

Rika swallows hard and begins twisting her hands in her lap. "Sam, I want to disclose something to you in confidence, something huge."

Rika has been secretive for about a month. There is a story behind us going back to our hometown. I'm going back because I can't afford New York without Rika's connection to our apartment. She's going back to start working at a job she didn't apply for. The journalist in me has wanted to dig into Rika's reasons for going back since I spotted her uncharacteristic deception. She sucks at secret keeping.

I answer without hesitation. "You have my word. You know that."

She takes a deep breath and looks around. *Like someone is going to eavesdrop?*

"I'm writing a novel based on Liam Lancaster, the Rohipnol Rapist. He was my former classmate. After the prison interview, some really bizarre truths came out of his mad ramblings. I have been following the bread crumbs further and further down the rabbit hole. I pitched my idea and a hint of my discoveries to a publisher in New York. I got a cash advancement to finish my research. I'm not returning to Champagne Falls to work at the paper, I do have a job there as a columnist, but I will be in town and traveling all over to interview his connections for my book."

I slap my steering wheel and scream, "Oh my god, that's awesome!"

"I know." She smiles and a faint blush creeps up her neck. "I need to practice keeping an emotionless face and asking very few questions. I was such a noob when I interviewed Liam. I blurted, I gasped, I even let a tear fall."

"You did?" I ask; surprised.

"Yeah, the story of his childhood was heart-wrenching, but then he grabbed the tear from my face and put it in his mouth. He told me 'a woman's tears taste like her pussy and fear-based tears are sweeter.'"

I give her the disgusted look that response deserves. "Ew."

"I know! One minute I'm crying for him and the next, I threw up in my mouth a little."

"Creepy," I say, shaking the words off me.

Rika sighs, "I need to focus on the right questions, and not the million or more that pop in my head. I need to not cry when emotions get high, and not get angry when the details are upsetting. I can't throw up when I interview his victims. I need practice." Her pitch raises. "May I interview you about the incident?"

My insides plummet. I can't do that. *Can I?* I don't speak of the incident. After all this time, the scars still bleed. I want to help my friend, but this? Why does it have to be this? This isn't ripping off a band-aid. It's unwinding a tourniquet. My throat goes dry. My raspy words are barely a whisper.

"Not while I'm driving."

It looks like I'll be letting my demons out to play this road trip.

CHAPTER 4

We determine our worth, and we always stick ourselves in the $0.99 clearance bin.

Sam's Diary Entry:

Today is the first day of our final semester in junior high. I have speech this semester. I like writing. Speaking in front of people is no big deal. I was happy to have a class that guaranteed an easy A. My U.S. Constitution class, on the other hand, is killing me. So, bring on the public speaking.

My hopes for an easy A went downhill when Sister Mary Kate handed me the syllabus. She isn't as staunch as the few other nuns who are also teachers. She's kind and helpful, and apparently challenging. In addition to our weekly speeches highlighting the week's lessons, we also have to give an eight-minute speech citing statistics, sources, the whole shebang with the theme *What God Gave Us*. It's our final exam worth seventy percent of our grade! Kateri is in my class. We immediately partnered up.

Kateri comes to my house sometimes. I never go to hers. My mom will come to take us on shopping sprees at the mall or to the movies. Today it's strictly brainstorming day. We will have the kitchen table to ourselves.

I'm weirdly afraid to meet her family. Her brothers are so beautiful, I fear I'll be a bumbling idiot in front of them and after the whole losing her only friend Ashley to her brother thing. Kateri isn't really anxious to bring me around either.

Kateri is sweet. When cute boys notice her, she blushes and crosses her arms over her chest. If I had her breasts, I'd show those suckers off every chance afforded to me. I'm noticing that girls, in general, are not comfortable in their own skin. We are never happy with what we have.

Changing what we look like is a multi-billion-dollar a year industry. I chose the subject as my final exam speech. So, to answer, *What God Gave Us*. My speech is called *Why It Isn't Enough*.

We've been watching you tube videos of plastic surgery. Why would any woman or person subject themselves to that kind of pain? I discussed it with Kateri. She says I feel that way because I'm perfect, and suggests that I would feel differently if I wasn't. I'm not perfect, I don't feel perfect. Neither does she.

I am looking for studies on how much of our opinions are determined by how others make us feel. I had a big part in making Kateri feel worthless. When are we going to realize that other people's actions or inactions do not determine our worth? We determine our worth, and we always stick ourselves in the $0.99 clearance bin.

All of that is neither here nor there. The important part of today happened when our study session was coming to a close and my doorbell rang. I left Kateri to go answer it.

There in front of me was a well over six-foot-tall angel with an honest to goodness halo. I had to strain my neck to see all the way to his face. The sun behind him made him look like the ethereal paintings adorning our school hallways. I remember thinking I might have died on my way to the door.

No need to pass those pearly gates, because the archangel Michael was the prettiest thing I ever laid eyes on and heaven surely couldn't compare. He reached out, hooked his finger under my chin and closed my gaping mouth. Literally! I could die. Then he winked at me and I felt like the Wicked Witch when she was met with a bucket of water; melting to the floor in a smoking hot mess.

His voice was that of a man, not of the boys I usually speak to. My heart did flip flops when he said: "Hi, I'm Morgan Fisher." He shook my hand and the touch made my insides goo.

Thank goodness Kateri began speaking because my mouth was a dessert. He came into the kitchen to help her round up her things. Morgan Freaking Fisher was standing in my kitchen. I may have laid my cheek on the spot where he stood once he left. If my grandchildren are reading this. Don't judge me, you would have, too.

Recording from Rika's Interview with Morgan Fisher:

"Do I remember the first time I met Sam?" He laughs out loud. "She was so stinking adorable!" I knocked on her door to get my sister. She was so shy she froze and just stared at me open-mouthed. She was at a complete loss. She didn't say two words to me the whole fifteen minutes I stood in her house. I couldn't believe she was Kat's bully. I swear if I blew on her she would have fallen over. I wish she could have stayed that innocent forever."

Sam's diary entry:

I was washing the dishes, my earbuds were blaring Panic! At the Disco. I was dancing in my kitchen when a finger tapped my shoulder. I screamed, turned, and jumped all at once. I dropped the glass I was washing and it shattered on the floor. I was clasping my chest and nearly passed out at the look of concern on his face.

Cute artist twin! I thought it in my head, but I didn't realize it came out of my mouth until he smiled and repeated, "Cute artist twin?" Oh my god. What is wrong with me? He asked if he was the cute artist twin and I could feel the heat rise in my face. My whole body flushed.

Do you know what I said to him?

"No."

I said no. Then I rambled barely coherently.

"Your girlfriend is the cute artist. Your brother's girlfriend is dark and scary. I can't tell you two apart." He may have been holding his sides with laughter, but I wanted to die. Why couldn't I have just stayed silent as I did with Morgan? I'm a complete toad, and the minute I opened my mouth I confirmed it.

He explained that he broke a window upstairs. He tried ringing the doorbell and knocking, but when nobody answered he became concerned he hurt someone. The door was unlocked and he heard me singing. Could it be worse? I can't sing. Nobody should listen to me sing. Well, unless it was punishment. Hand me a flute and I'm your girl, but sing? No.

I stared at him becoming more aware of my messy bun, my sleep shorts, my tank top, and worst of all, the "I've been doing dishes" wet spot across my belly. Speech needed to happen. It took intense braining to make the words go.

I unwrapped my hands from the towel and offered my left hand in introduction. He stared at it unsure of my intention. Ugh! Our society shakes with the right. I switched the positions of my toweled hand and extended hand for a second attempt.

"I'm Sam." He smiled while taking my hand in his. Holy hot, I might melt from his touch. He pulled a felt tip pen from his back pocket and wrote Xander on my arm. It wasn't a signature, it was art. It was the most stunning name I'd seen and chills broke out across my flesh. It was a unique calligraphy. I had to drag my eyes away from it to look at him. He winked and reminded me out loud "the cute artist dater" has a name. He's never going to let me forget that. He also reminded me that since he came alone, I can clearly tell he and his brother Zack apart.

He was still holding my hand, so he guided me to the stairs. As he led me up, he laced his fingers with mine. I nearly lost my mind. Xander Freaking Fisher was holding my hand. My heart fluttered at the intimate feel of being led upstairs when I realized… No! We can't go upstairs. If he sees the window in my room, he will know I can see him. No, no, no, this can't happen.

I was so alarmed I yelled at him. "What are you doing?" I startled him as much as I startled myself. He gave me a *what the heck* look before yelling back at me. "Checking the window. Duh!" He smiled and continued walking. I prayed it wasn't my window. Thankfully, it wasn't. His piece of metal went through the bathroom window and landed in the bathtub.

Connor is learning to weld and sculpt. He likes to sculpt with clay and other mediums, but now he is trying his hand at metal.

Xander was intrigued by his new piece so he picked up a small sculpture not realizing it was still searing hot. He flung it away with more force than intended and now what looks like a balloon animal made out of metal is in my bathtub.

He put the plug in the drain and began running the water. He explained that he didn't know if it was still hot. As we stood in my tiny bathroom waiting for the bathtub to fill. I stared at him. He is so hot. Morgan may have the innocent good looks, but Xander looks like he has a secret. There is a quiet mystery surrounding him.

He took a step closer to me and took my hand again. Wordlessly he continued his artwork on my arm. He asked if it bothered me. I secretly loved it. His proximity to me was dizzying. He smelled so good, I wanted to bury my face in his white t-shirt. I could pull his open flannel up like the covers and sleep on his beautiful chest.

While he looked intently at his art, I got to take in the smooth skin of his face, the dark lashes that hooded his insanely blue eyes, and the heat of his hands on my skin. The atmosphere between us was intense. I was tempted to lean my body into his. I told him I liked it as nonchalantly as the lump in my throat would allow and he smiled.

He drew an elaborate XOF up my arm. "Do you know what it means?" I looked at it carefully, I hoped I was right, but maybe I'm not bold enough to find out. "Go on, take a guess." He urged.

I still cringe. I said it out loud. "Um, hugs and kisses forever?"

He burst out laughing, and replied a simple, "Okay. Are you sure you like being inked?" I nodded furiously and told him I love it.

He said his girlfriend hates it. I wanted to argue. I've seen how much she enjoys being drawn on. I also wanted to suggest he get a new girlfriend, but I've crossed my limit of bold comments for one day.

In the time it took for the bathtub to fill, he inked my arm up to my elbow into a masterpiece. It was amazing. If it were socially acceptable to not bathe, I would have this ink work on my arm at my nursing home when I'm ninety.

Xander called a window repair place and made arrangements to have the window replaced. Morgan and Mr. Fisher boarded it up, and Xander stayed with me until my dad came home so he could explain and apologize. He is kinder than I anticipated. Talking to him about little things was easier than it was with Morgan.

He liked to touch me. Holding my hand, inking my skin, and patting my knee when he stood. He even hugged me when he left. He looked deep in my eyes, inches from my face and just when I thought he would kiss me, he apologized for breaking the window and headed home.

Turning to leave he spoke over his shoulder. "Kisses and hugs forever are my initials. Xander Oliver Fisher." He smirked as he closed the door and I slumped to the floor begging the earth to swallow me whole.

Recording from Rika's interview with Xander Fisher:

He laughs. Yes, the first time I met Sam was memorable. I broke her window and tagged her.

I saw her walking home with Kat and I wanted to know more about her. I threw Connor's sculpture through her window so I would have an excuse to meet her.

I marked her. She didn't understand what I was doing. She told me she liked it. Man, she was so innocent. I guess we all were. If not for the fact I had a girlfriend, I would have kissed her in that tiny bathroom, I was pretty damn close when I hugged her goodbye, but Fisher men don't cheat. She was really cute, I instantly liked her.

"What do you mean you tagged her?"

"Like a gangbanger tags a railroad trellis, I tagged her with hugs and kisses forever, it was my way of claiming her as mine. It's what led to my being a tattoo artist. I thought she was cute. She liked being marked. I had a girlfriend who didn't. Bethanie and I were so different, I could plainly see who I wanted to be with. Plans to leave Bethanie formed in my head when I walked home with Connor's sculpture that day."

"Did it work?"

"Meh, my brothers always wanted what I tagged first."

CHAPTER 5

We don't speak of the incident because that night already holds too much power

Sam

Taking a deep breath, I sit on the hotel bed and try desperately to still my shaky hands. "I wanted to be a journalist because words are powerful. We don't speak of the incident because that night already holds too much power." I shudder and shake out my hands.

"My newfound acceptance of Kateri elevated her socially. Soon, in addition to all of my friends, she began making her own friends. Enter Ashley Aniston. I told you how she befriended Kateri with a motive. Imagine how well that went over when Morgan broke up with her. In my garage." I raise my eyes to meet Rika's. "With his face between my legs."

Rika's mouth drops and she slaps the bed. "Shut up!"

I pinch the rubber band I put around her wrist earlier and pull. It snaps her when I let go and she jumps.

"I'll snap you every time you react. This is an interview remember."

She clears her throat. Folds her hands in her lap. And tilts her head in my direction. "Continue."

"The people that owned our house before us left a bunch of junk in the attic of the garage. Connor and Morgan were interested in seeing if any of it was salvageable. Connor wanted metal, Morgan was looking for lumber. I had suggested he take some old furniture instead. Restoring something could be just as beautiful as building it from scratch. He had never considered it before and was anxious to see what I had up there."

"Morgan restores furniture because of you?"

I shrug, I don't know if that's true. I snap her band for the unnecessary question and continue.

"When I pulled the rope to let down the drop stairs, the rope broke landing across my head. I looked at them and winced. Apologizing for the necessary change of plans. They offered to repair the stairs for me instead. I agreed. So, the boys lifted me to pull by the handle.

"Connor lifted me around my knees and Morgan held one of my hands to steady me. It took a few swipes of my other hand before I connected with the handle. Morgan dropped his support to my waist so I could use two hands to pull. The plan was simple, pull down the staircase, reattach a rope that hadn't been weakened by time, and then see what treasures the attic held. The brothers were such gentlemen, they kept their eyes averted to the ground the whole time we staggered back and forth so they didn't see up my skirt."

The memories of that day warm my chest. It was a chilly winter day, and the normally cold garage was warm and felt inviting.

I am silent for a moment, lost in the memories. Rika pats my knee gently. It snaps me from my better times, and we each smile as the tension of silence subsides.

"Connor and I were in the attic and Morgan threw us the rope. He closed the stairs so we could reattach it. Once it was attached, I tried to push the stairs down again, but they were stuck. Morgan thought the hinges might just be rusting. He told me to push, while he pulled. After a few tugs, bangs, and force, the stairs swung down with unexpected swiftness, and I tumbled out head first."

Rika sucked in a sharp breath. "Clearly you were okay, but wow, how scary. Were you hurt?" She winced as I pinched the rubber band. I tilted my head apologetically as it snapped her wrist.

"Morgan caught me around the waist. My face was in his crotch and I can only imagine where my crotch was. Probably in the vicinity of his face." I motion to my face with my whole hand. "Since my skirt was across my chin, still, I'm guessing he was face to face with a sequined Victoria's Secret puppy."

Rika tries hard to suppress a giggle, but not hard enough. *Snap!*

"His laughter confirmed my suspicions. A brief discussion on how we would right the situation without dropping me on my head happened. He tried to flip me around, but he lost his footing on some hardware that fell off the ladder. My ass slammed hard on a stair. My skirt still up to my chin, my legs on his shoulders and his face on my Victoria's Secret puppy. The more he tried to get up, the more the ball bearings under his feet moved, and what Ashley walked into was… compromising. To say the least."

Rika smashes her lips together her dimples give away her amusement. I glare at her and make a pinching motion at her. She composes herself and clears her throat. "So, they broke up?"

I giggle at the recollection of her face. "She screamed then started yelling all kinds of obscenities at him. He tried explaining, he even yelled I don't violate twelve-year-olds! I turned fourteen that November and was totally wounded! I had the good sense to keep my mouth shut though."

Rika gives me a sympathetic look.

"Everything changed when she said, 'I became friends with your creepy weird little sister for *this*?' Her hand wildly gesticulating between Morgan and me. Connor flew down to the garage floor to defend his sister. A screaming match roused the neighborhood. All four Fisher Men, Kateri, and even their adopted sister Sue, whom I didn't even know existed until that point, were in my garage."

Rika holds up a finger, "We'll revisit the other sister soon."

Nodding, I continue. "As things escalated, the Fisher brothers were holding back us girls because Ashley became more volatile and hurtful as the screaming continued. Morgan had Kateri, Connor had Sue, and the twins had me." I giggle picturing it.

"Zack whispered in my ear. 'If I let you go, do you promise to get one good punch straight to her face before you get broken up?' Zack was a bad boy." I wink at Rika. "He yanked me out of Xander's grasp and threw me at Ashley I landed on top of her on the ground. and as promised, I punched her in the nose."

Throwing myself backward on the bed I sigh, "I had never done that before, and I was alarmed at the feel of cartilage giving way beneath my fist." Even today the thought makes my stomach clench. "Xander yanked me off of her and carried me kicking and fighting unproductively all the way into my house. He carried me up the stairs. Tossed me into the bathtub and turned the shower on me. Every time I tried to get up, he shoved me back down telling me to cool off." I sat up and looked solemnly at Rika. "Eventually, I sat crying and shaking on the bathtub floor. I was soaked and still in my school uniform."

Rika moves to sit over on my bed next to me. She silently drapes an arm over my shoulder.

"He wrapped me in a towel, scooped me out of the bathtub and held me until I was done crying. Once I had stilled, he let me up to get dressed. I don't even know why I was crying."

Rika gives my shoulder a squeeze reassuringly at the sound of my voice cracking.

"In short, that is how we got on the wrong side of Ashley Aniston and the first time the police came to my house. I was in huge trouble. It was the beginning of a series of life-altering events."

From the Diary of a Casual Observer,

It would appear that the reigning queen of Champagne Falls, Ashley Aniston, has been replaced. Oh, how the mighty fall. In one afternoon, she lost Morgan Fisher, her perfect nose, and her crown. Rumor has it that the Fisher family's tiny girl next door took her out, then took her man.

CHAPTER 6

I guess we've all been officially friend zoned.

Sam's Diary Entry:

Dad and I sat at my kitchen table with two police officers last night. I explained that since Ashley was blocking the exit door I felt violence was the only viable option. It's my story, and I'm sticking to it.

The truth is, when the argument broke out my blood began pumping, the angrier everyone was, the higher the temperature climbed, and when the Fisher twins held me, something primal unlocked inside of me. I understand how mob mentality works now. It was exhilarating, but looking back, it was also terrifying.

I am so grounded; my grandchildren might never leave this house. I earned some of it. The police didn't take any action because it was too difficult to determine fault. I broke her nose, but she was in my garage. The Fishers backed up my story. It wasn't that helpful; my dad is still super pissed.

After school, the Fisher brothers came over. My dad wasn't home from work yet, so I let them in. Morgan asked me if Ashley was mean to Kateri at school and if so, when had it stopped. I told him the truth. I told him how Kat was really treated at school.

The first friend she had made since I've known her was Ashley and it was only to get closer to Morgan. He dropped his head and I felt terrible for being so honest. Connor suggested that they make a pact to never date one of Kat's friends ever again. My heart sank because I am Kat's friend.

Zack, in his cheeky manner, put his arm around me and asked if he was friends with a girl before Kat was her friend, could he date her? Xander yanked me away and sat me in his lap and said I think, in that case, our previous brother rules of dibs comes into play.

Connor took my head gently pulling me back from Xander to face him upside down. He kissed me Spiderman style. He then smiled at his brothers, "If you recall, dibs are called with a kiss." We all stared at him open-mouthed. Holy mother of Mary! The Fisher brothers were fighting over me and Connor won. He freaking kissed me! His victory was cut short when Morgan explained that he met me first. Morgan and I met when he came over to get Kateri and bring her home for dinner. I am Kateri's friend and I was her friend first. Xander squeezed me in a hug before he released me. I guess we've all been officially friend zoned.

Everyone was sure to clear out before my Dad got home. Just as I was about to write and go to bed, Connor tapped on my bedroom window. He scared the Bejesus out of me. I opened it and he tumbled inside. Once we were certain my dad wasn't going to investigate the sound, he whispered an apology in my ear. He explained that the four of them can get fiercely competitive, and he hadn't considered how kissing me without permission would make me feel. He also explained that it was easy to forget how young I actually am.

I get that a lot. I am often told I seem older. My mom says that I could read at three years old. My parents talked to me like an adult, and as an independent only child, I grew up quicker than my peers. It makes sense I suppose, but I think I blend well with my friends, so I don't see it. I thanked him for the apology.

He pulled a portable DVD player out of his backpack and asked if I wanted to watch a movie. He even brought popcorn. His reason was that I had a rough couple of days. Before I could respond he climbed up into my loft bed. When I joined him, he was staring at my view of the make-out spot. I was busted. The only way to avoid embarrassment was sarcasm.

"Yep, I know and have seen all your moves. Don't bother, player."

His face reddened and he didn't make a single move while we lay in my bed watching Harry Potter.

Recording from Rika's interview with Connor Fisher

I don't actually remember the details of the first time we met. My mom picked me up from somewhere, and then we got Kat and Sam from school. I already knew who she was when we met. She was gorgeous, and I could see why Morgan and Xander tried to keep her from me. Assholes.

The details are fuzzy, but I do remember with perfect clarity the first time I kissed her. I didn't even use my tongue. Still, she was all pink cheeks and wide eyes. I laid in her bed that night watching a movie. I hid an old wooden ladder behind the trellis under her window, fully intending to be a regular. I was certain I would be the one to break the rules. I had a plan to kiss her for real. She called me out. It wasn't the last time I kissed her, but that was the first of many movie nights."

Sam's diary entry:

Zack is who I have the most fun with. He has an edgier lifestyle. He likes dark music, dark clothes, and dark girls. I am not his type. It doesn't stop him from flirting with me every opportunity he has. He meets me at the bus stop when I stay late for band or cheerleading. He holds my hand when he walks me home. We play elaborate games of would you rather. He wants his tongue pierced. It is strictly forbidden by his parents.

Last weekend while I was with my mom, I had him meet me at Stone tattoo. It hurt to see Rocky Mudds is now an insurance agency.

I introduced Zack to Mr. Stone. He was like another parent to me, Colton and I spent most of our summers, weekends, and school breaks in Stone tattoo and Rocky Mudds.

Zack bounced on his feet like he always does, enthralled with the entire idea of piercing. Mr. Stone taught him all about needles, gauges, and being clean and safe. He even offered his first piercing for free since he was a friend of mine. With Mr. Stone's direction, I let Zack pierce my ears. They were pierced when I was younger but had since closed up. I even let him pick out the studs I should wear. He was so thrilled he picked me up in a hug and spun me around.

A girl I don't know was working in Matt's room today. Matt is Mr. Stone's other son, Colton's brother. Matt isn't old enough to be a tattoo artist yet, but he has plenty of customers on the down low. Once he is old enough, he is supposed to work with his dad. The room across from Matt's was going to be Colton's room. I wonder what's in there now.

The girl I don't know came out of Matt's room and said she was wanting to get her nipples pierced. She offered to let Zack watch. He was on board and probably was turned on at the suggestion, but Mr. Stone wasn't interested in piercing his son's underage girlfriend.

That was my cue to suggest leaving and perhaps coming back with Xander sometime. I think Xander would love to see skin artwork since he does it all the time with his markers. Zack nodded quietly. I think he liked having me all to himself. He didn't want Xander to come with us, so next time, I'll probably bring Xander alone, too.

Recording from Rika's interview with Zack Fisher

"I remember the first time I saw her. We didn't actually meet. See, I would take my girl on the side of the house in a hidden spot to, you know, spend some alone time. I saw her reflection on Jillian's dog collar. She had a hidden view of the spot. I could see her watching us. I decided to give her a show. I became rougher and more aggressive with Jillian. Sucking, biting, licking, she watched every moment. I got excited by the audience. I mean, who doesn't like a little closet freak? Then I made it blatant. I turned my girl toward the window and felt her up, finger fucked her in plain view, you name it. Sam's eyes were so glued to my hands, she never once noticed me, watching her, watching me. It was hot!"

"She said you were bad."

"You're as adorable as she is when your cheeks are pink. I'm supposed to snap that rubber band on your wrist."

CHAPTER 7

They loved me differently.

Sam

Sitting in the restaurant, I look over the menu at Rika. "Sorry I forced you into a break. I need to eat, and maybe have a few shots before I continue."

She smiles and pats my hand.

"Eating isn't exactly a bad idea." She shrugs and glances back to the menu.

I absentmindedly ordered food and an Amaretto Stone Sour. I am so lost in my head I'm surprised when the food arrives.

"Have I been quiet that long?"

Rika lifts a shoulder then butters her potato. "I figured you have a lot of thoughts to organize before we continue." She sets down her utensils. "Let's start with something easy to talk about."

She's not wrong. I have so much to get through, maybe easy is the best way to start.

"Okay?" I answer.

"Tell me about this other sister. Sue?"

I feel the warmth of a smile relax my face. "Nonna Fisher's best friend was in an abusive relationship. Every time she tried to leave the situation became more dangerous." I take a bite of my chicken and after I swallow it, I explain. "She's the catalyst of Safe Spaces. Nonna didn't set out to save all the victims, she set out to save just one. She didn't succeed. Eventually, he killed her."

Rika placed her hand over mine. "How terrible."

I nod and swallow the sadness with a gulp of water. "She couldn't save her best friend, but she could save her daughter Sue."

"The Fishers adopted her?" Rika asks.

"Yes, and she went to a charter school that specialized in the arts, so I didn't see her often."

Rika nods and we eat in silence for a while.

I decide what I can safely discuss in the restaurant. Polishing off the last of my drink, I sigh.

"So, we already know Ashley Aniston is the reigning bitch supreme. Right?" Rika nods while chewing her food.

I swallow my forkful of salad and lift my eyes to her. "She apologized to Kateri and me." Rika's eyes bulge and I wait until she swallows before I snap her rubber band.

"Did you forgive her?"

I stop my fork midway to my mouth. "I didn't want to, but Kateri wanted her friend back. I followed her lead." Taking another bite, I shake my head. I still want to kick myself for not trusting my instincts.

"She told Kateri she hoped it was okay if they hang out at her house since seeing Morgan was still painful. She said she believed me when I explained there was nothing between Morgan and me. Little by little, she intertwined herself into our lives. She sat with us at lunch, she went to the mall with us, and she even set us up with her boyfriend's buddies. She was really nice, a good friend, and we went on group dates to the movies or the roller rink."

Rika speaks around a piece of steak. "Oh, that's good."

I thought so, too.

Rika swallows and tilts her head with curiosity. "How did the Fisher Men feel about you dating?"

I snort out a laugh. "Kateri, their baby sister, could date because she was one of the guys, but me…" I giggle. "They nearly lost their minds. Each in their own way. Morgan tried to lay down the law like a father."

I put my hands on my hips, draw in my eyebrows, and mock a stern manly voice. "If your bathing suit touches it, he shouldn't. You tell me, Sam, and I'll break his fingers."

We laugh at my lack of a manly voice.

"Connor, would sneak into my room and ask me a million questions during our postdate movie night." I shake my head. "My funny boy, Zack, would text me crazy memes. I mean obnoxiously. While I was out, my phone chimed every few minutes."

I sigh. "Xander, on the other hand, would make sure he was there when we met our dates. He would shake their hand a little too firm. Stand behind me, arms folded, and glare at my date. He would go so far as to kiss my head or cheek before leaving. Twice he managed to draw his name on me with a sharpie instead of the usual washable markers."

All the Fisher Men loved me. They all loved me differently.

CHAPTER 8

Closing the distance.

Sam's Diary Entry

My mom is stoked I have a boyfriend. She buys me cute outfits, offers to give us rides, and gives me money for the movies. I don't know how my dad would react to my having a boyfriend. I've opted to not bring it up.

The Fisher Men are all the "Dad" I need. Honestly, they are being ridiculous. Kateri is seeing Jason, and they don't bat an eye. I so much as think Kevin, and their jaws tick. I went from friend zone to honorary sister, to freaking daughter. One father is enough for a teenage girl. As if having the attention of the blog, Diary of a Casual Observer, isn't intrusive enough, four extra chastity guardians is too much.

Our eighth-grade graduation dance is this weekend. St. Mary's girl's school and Holy Cross boys' school converge for one night of ruler-measured romance. Eighth through twelfth grades are invited, and we get a special graduate sash like the seniors.

My mother is losing her mind. Her baby is going to a dance with a boy. She's dragged me from store to store dress shopping. Xander came with us. Every time I came out of a dressing room with a dress that didn't cover me from my neck to my knees, he shakes his head.

My mother told him he was being ridiculous. When she went to grab another rack of dresses for me to try on, he whispered in my ear. "I will tag every exposed piece of your skin with a sharpie in your sleep. You had better cover it up, Beautiful." I hate when he gets all possessive like that. Zack is almost as bad. Just because they can't have me, nobody else can either? I told him to go fuck himself, and he smiled.

I called him out. "Your girlfriend wears halter dresses, you don't seem to mind."

He shrugged and explained he doesn't look at her like a piece of meat. He appreciates her like artwork. He said Kevin doesn't look at me like that. So, he doesn't need to see me.

We compromised on a spaghetti strap dress. I also get a cover-up I have no intention of wearing. I like the dress, Xander likes the jacket, and my mom likes the price. Done!

Last night when the tap came on the window, I was surprised to see Xander. He looked sad. He apologized for how he behaved at the store. He wanted to explain.

He climbed up in my bed and held out his arms. Connor just lays next to me. I guess Xander likes to cuddle. I lay my head on his chest and he wrapped his arms around me. He told me that girlfriends, kissing, touching and the lot came too early for him. Having older brothers who paved the way made having a girlfriend and kissing her competitive.

He was curious, it seemed right, but if he could take it back and slow it down, he would. He couldn't see it, but I rolled my eyes. Boys don't think like that. I called bull. He strummed his fingers up and down my arm. He said he wants what his parents have one day. What special thing could he share with the woman he falls in love with if he wastes it on the girls he kind of likes. Sounds like Father Ken gave him the purity talk that Sister Mary Kate gives us.

I reassured him. I told him your heart, your mind, your soul, and your body are all the gifts you give when you love, not just your dick. Against his chest, my face rumbled with his chuckle it was the best feeling ever.

After a few silent minutes, he asked, "If I give my dick to one woman, and everything else to another, who has me?"

Easy answer.

"If you are doing that simultaneously it's cheating."

He took a deep breath and said I was right. He said Fisher Men don't cheat, and that I helped him make a really big decision. Then he warned me.

"I pay attention. I see things you don't. Jason doesn't love and respect my sister, and Kevin sure as hell doesn't love and respect you. Be careful. Take care of one another."

We are fourteen, of course, our dates don't love and respect us. They are just happy a girl wants to spend time with them. He said, "Kevin is lucky to have a date as exquisite as I am." Okay, I swooned. He said, "those boys have a reputation and we should be wary of them." Kateri has a reputation, too. It's mostly my fault, so I'm not about to judge them unfairly.

I asked what I should watch for, and he asked me, "have you ever been kissed?"

Connor kissed me while I was sitting in Xander's lap, and while I laugh about it, he still gets pissy at the mention of it.

He growled "Connor disrespected you. He caught hell for it when we left. That is not how Fisher Men were taught to kiss."

What girl wouldn't ask how Fisher Men were taught to kiss? He hesitated for a moment and ran his fingers through his hair. He said they were taught to get permission. I teasingly asked him if they needed a note or if they had pre-printed permission slips. I mean do they carry it in their wallet next to their condoms?

He wrapped his fingers in my hair and pulled me to his face. He held me in place, his lips a whisper from mine. I swear I thought I was about to get kissed. A real kiss. My first kiss. I was nervous and excited. He was so close I could feel his breath on my lips. He said, "this is as far as a real man takes the first kiss. We could be here for hours each time we meet. Until you close the distance, a real man won't kiss you."

I was tempted to close the distance. I should have. Instead, the stupidest thing I have ever said tumbled out of my mouth. "Oh, that's why Connor kisses like that!"

Xander sat up abruptly. He was pissed! He asked if Connor had kissed me. The question sounded more like an accusation. I tried to say no, but I barely shook my head when he grabbed my arms and pulled me up to look him in the face. He asked again in that accusatory way if the reason Connor and I hadn't kissed was because I didn't close the distance. I finally grabbed his face, pointed it to the spot and explained. I saw him. The only boy who has ever tried to kiss me was Colton, and we were ten.

His body relaxed and his eyes fell. He laid back down and pulled me back to his chest. "Please promise me you won't kiss any of my brothers."

I was confused. They were the ones with a pact, and just who did he think he was? He and Zack have girlfriends, although

Xander has been spending less and less time with his. Connor is always with someone. I have never dictated what they could or could not do with their girlfriends. Oh, but he can lecture me about my dress, scold me about how a real man kisses, warn me, and finally dictate who I can and cannot kiss? He can get bent and I pretty much told him so.

He let out a sigh. He told me he came for advice, and he thought he was helping me, too. He apologized and explained that if I kissed any of the Fisher Men, the others couldn't hang out anymore.

He said he likes me and didn't want to lose my friendship.

He likes me.

Xander Freaking Fisher likes me.

I like him, too. I like all of them. I don't want to lose what I have with any of them.

At some point, we drifted off to sleep. We were roused awake by the vibrating of his phone. He explained his family will be awake in an hour, and he had to sneak back in. He thanked me for listening and then he kissed me. Not on the cheek or head like usual, but on the lips. He kissed me like Colton or Connor did, except he did it slower. I liked it. I again gave him a hard time. He kissed me without permission. He smiled. He explained a real kiss requires permission, but that a peck goodbye was no big deal. I gave him an oh really look. I'm curious if he would still smile like that if I "pecked" one of his brothers a goodbye kiss.

CHAPTER 9

Things changed forever that night.

Sam

Sitting harshly on the bed I look up to Rika with tears in my eyes. "I've told this story only one other time. The coping mechanism I use is disassociation. I tell it like the stories I write. I will tell you the story oblivious to the fact you are here. You can't react. If you break my concentration I won't continue."

Rika sits at the desk in our hotel room with a notebook and a pen. "How about if you face away from me while you talk." I nod. Wrapping my arms around myself as tight as I can, I rock back and forth rhythmically. It takes a few deep breaths and a moment to collect myself. The Diary of a Casual Observer mentioned the long-awaited dance and the Safe Spaces benefit. I remember reading about it when Morgan and Chrissy picked me up. My mind falls into the front seat of his familiar pick-up truck.

The night that holds too much power.

Morgan looks over at me every now and then as he drives. I look at the hands in my lap and then return his smile looking up at him through my eyelashes.

"You look beautiful. Are you excited?"

I nod. Kateri and I are finally going to this dance we have been nonstop planning for. Kateri looks amazing, too. Her chest is so top heavy most people would never know how tiny the rest of her is. Her clothes usually hang straight down from her chest making her look big. My mom took in her dress, cinching everything below her chest. She looks amazing. She's floating on happiness.

I'm so glad everyone agreed to let Morgan drive us to the dance. Showing up with our parents is so not cool. Pulling up in front of the school, Kateri and I wait patiently for our dates while Morgan takes the obligatory pictures with my new camera. He does stand a little straighter and look a little meaner when Kevin and Jason join us for pictures.

Flowers.

He brought me flowers.

My insides warm and plummet as he stretches the elastic band over my wrist. I lift the corsage to my nose and breathe in the tiny sweetheart roses. "Thank you, Kevin, it's beautiful."

He is just about to kiss me when Morgan interrupts. "Sam, are you taking your camera with you or should I bring it home?"

I roll my eyes. "You can bring it home with you… Dad."

He pulls me into a hug and whispers in my ear, "Call me dad if you must, but if that piece of shit lays a finger on you, I'm going to break them." Pulling away from me, he plasters a fake smile across his face and shakes Kevin's hand just a bit too hard. While he hugs his sister and intimidates her date, I apologize for my caveman friend.

I danced, all night. There was not one point all evening in which Kevin and I were not on the floor. He can move. He wasn't afraid to dance. It's so stinking hot! Tonight has been magical and it isn't over yet. Ashley invited us to an after party at her house a few blocks away.

Leaving the dance arm and arm, I hold on tight so I won't float away. The cool air is a welcomed treat having sweated all evening. Goosebumps begin to rise up my arms. Kevin gave me his suit coat and wrapped his arms around me. A boy I didn't know approached us. "Hey Kevin, you guys going to the party?"

He started to lead me down the sidewalk. "Yeah man."

"Wait!" I started looking for Kateri. I hadn't paid attention to her all night. "I need to wait for Kateri. Have you seen her?"

Ashley Aniston rounds the corner and answers me. "She and Jason left an hour ago. She said she was coming to my party. You should come." She loops her arm through my unoccupied arm and together I was led off into the night.

That's really strange. I was not about to leave the dance without Kateri, but she left me without a word. Xander and Morgan were clear that we should watch out for one another. Is that the problem? Is she afraid I'll tell her brothers on her? I guess I can understand if that's what she's thinking. I may have been her friend first, but I'm closer to her brothers. Still, I would never do such a thing. Girl code.

Ashley's house already looks like something out of a teen movie. The trees are covered in toilet paper. The thumping music is making my insides jump to the beat. People are everywhere. It's madness.

"Ashley, aren't your neighbors going to call the police?"

She threw her head back laughing. "No! All my neighbors are at city hall for a fundraiser."

That's right! The reason Morgan drove us to the dance is that all of our parents are at a gala fundraiser for Mrs. Fisher's nonprofit Safe Spaces. In a playful creepy voice, the boy I don't know sneers, "No one will hear you scream!"

I roll my eyes.

Kateri and I are probably the only eighth graders here. Ashley hooked us up. We are going to enter our high school years as A-listers. It's a silly notion because it's the same school. Next year, we just move upstairs.

When we enter the party, everyone starts waving their phones at us, raising plastic cups, and even yelling congratulatory remarks to Kevin. He isn't graduating. Maybe he achieved some other honor I'm not aware of. "I need to find Kateri."

Kevin looks around for a second. "I think I saw her out there on the back porch."

Stepping out into the cool air is nice because it's quiet here. I look around but I don't see her. "Kateri isn't out here."

'She probably went back in to look for you. Rather than fighting through the crowd again, let's stay here. Let her find us." He smiles at me with his big brown puppy dog eyes. How could I say no? Slipping his hands around my back. He leans his forehead to mine and touches his nose to mine. "I've been looking forward to this night for weeks."

I lay my head on his chest. "Yes, it was a really amazing night."

"Oh, but it's not over yet." I giggle at his enthusiasm. I am mildly aware of more people coming outside. Again, they are waving their cell phones.

"What is everybody congratulating you for?" I ask.

"For not only getting the prettiest girl in all of St. Mary's to go to the dance with me." I swoon a little. "But also planning to get her best friend out of the way so I could fuck her." His hands dig into my back "They are all excited that you agreed to give the entire Holy Cross Football team a ride, too."

*** Trigger Warning

My eyes grew wide, his face grew sinister and suddenly I was being pulled and torn by what seemed like hundreds of hands. I screamed. I was begging for help, but everyone was pointing and laughing and oh my god streaming. The tears were stinging my eyes. I was fighting with everything in me, but they were stronger. There was more of them. My dress was gone. They could see me. All the noise disappeared the moment I realized this was going to happen and there was nothing I could do about it. I closed my eyes. I tried to go someplace else. Then everything did stop.

***

I opened my eyes. Kevin was perched between my legs already undressed from the waist down. Kateri was holding a large knife to his throat barking orders. Everyone backed away from me.

"Get up Sam. I called the police." She turned to the crowd of onlookers still filming. "We are walking out of here right now.

If anyone attempts to stop us, I'm slitting his throat first and then I will stab my fucking way out." I've never heard her cuss, but she looks and sounds fierce right now. Her face is bruised her lip is bleeding. She looks like she fought this whole crowd to save me, and she did.

We step into the front yard just as Morgan's truck comes to a screaming halt in front of the yard. All four brothers jump out with murderous looks and head straight for Kateri. She screams at them. "I'm not letting him go, don't ask. Don't touch me. Don't look at me." Four broken boys stared at their sister while she teetered on the brink of insanity. "Sam needs you. Take care of Sam." She barks.

I was naked. I wasn't hurt. Something terrible happened to Kateri. I didn't want help. I shook my head no. Xander took off his hoodie and handed it to me. He looked torn as to who he should be caring for.

"Kateri, you saved me. They didn't hurt me because you saved me. Who did that to you?" Now that everything has slowed down, I can see her dress is ripped. There is blood dripping down the inside of her leg. Her hair is wild and has grass clippings in it. Slowly I realize, I didn't save her. Tonight, nobody saved her.

The sirens and lights snap me back to the moment. The police are yelling for Kateri to put the knife down. First, she shoves Kevin to the ground at the feet of the police officers who have their weapons drawn. At their request, she lays down the knife and steps away from it. Her brothers try to get to her but are halted.

She yells out into the darkness with a clear, concise, and disconnected voice. "I have been sexually assaulted. I will go wherever you require willingly. Just, please don't touch me. I cannot bear for another person to put their hands on me tonight." She was sexually assaulted? The world went wonky in waves then black.

I woke up in an ambulance. Zack and Xander are with me. Xander is tracing swirls into my skin. They both look defeated, then excited by my fluttering eyelids.

"Kateri?" I ask.

They stammer excitedly in the unison only twins can manage. "She's ... Are you?"

Xander pushes my hair off my face. "Morgan and Connor are with her. They went to the police station my parents are meeting them there."

Zack took my hand, kissing my knuckles. "You whacked your head pretty good when you fainted. We need to have you checked out." I nod.

Zack sighs. "I'm just going to straight out ask you. Where you raped tonight, too?" *Too?*

"No." *He hurt Kateri.* Tears burn my face. "I think it would have happened had it not been for Kateri." The world went black again.

The emergency room visit is a blur. I faintly remember a CAT scan. I wake up and tick off a mental checklist. I'm in a hospital bed. The twins are still here. My parents are here now. They are keeping me for observation.

The police come and I recounted the entire evening with disassociated clarity. The words methodically come with an emotionless robotic tone. I finish and begin checking off my surroundings again.

I'm in the hospital.

My parents are here.

The twins are here.

I have a head injury.

I am safe.

Safe?

I am in the hospital.

My parents are here.

The twins are here.

Zack interrupts my checklist by giving his statement. "We were at home when Xander saw a Facebook post from Ashley Aniston." He showed the officer a screen shot. "She announced a post dance party at her house. She also announced front row seats to Samantha taking on the entire football team in an epic gang bang." He looks at me with regret and swallows. "Next pictures of her at the party surrounded by guys making lewd gestures behind her back started posting." He showed the officer. Morgan texted Kateri on the way to the car asking what the hell the girls were doing. When we arrived at Ashley's house, well, you saw what we saw."

Shortly after our statements are taken and the reports are signed, Morgan and Connor join us. My head is pounding and I am so tired, but I need to know that Kateri is okay. Morgan locks eyes with me. He knows me well enough to know what my questions are.

"Kateri is downstairs. She's having a rape kit done." The dam in my core broke and it isn't just my tears that spill out. My heart breaks and I sob for my friend. She is the kindest nicest person I know. How could anyone treat her like that? The Fisher brothers surround me with hugs and soft assurance.

"What happened? She left without telling me." I plead.

Connor sighs and scrubs his hand over his face. "She was dancing it got hot. They went to the drinking fountain to get a quick drink of water. Jason suggested they step outside for a minute to cool off. Kat went with him." All of us stiffen, we can just about figure out what happened from there. Nobody wants the details.

Morgan picks up where Connor left off. "Afterwards she went back in the school and locked herself in the girl's locker room. She was scared and broken. She called the Safe Space crisis line. When she got my text and saw what was happening on Facebook, she hung up called 911 and ran to Ashley's house. She grabbed the knife out of a knife block in the kitchen."

After everything that happened to her tonight, she came to my rescue. If she hadn't come, they would have taken turns. Oh my god, people would have pictures and videos of it.

Of them.

All. Of. Them.

Of me.

They would have videos of me losing my virginity over and over until there was nothing left of me. My heart sinks, that's what happened to her. I will never get over how much privacy and dignity she gave up for me tonight. How can things ever be better? There are naked pictures of me all over the internet. There are pictures of Kat in a ripped dress and a blood trail down her leg. He hurt her. He hurt my friend.

"Zack and Xander, you haven't seen her yet. You should go to her. Tell her I love her."

Zack hugs me and kisses my cheek. "We'll switch again soon."

Xander kisses my lips to the shock of everyone in the room. Then traces a heart on my arm. "We'll tell her you are thinking of her."

When they leave, their vacated seats are filled by Morgan and Connor.

"Sam." I'm stirred awake by Connor calling my name, his lips on my forehead. "Sam."

I moan a groggy, "yes?"

"Kat is finished downstairs. She wants to see you before she goes home. Are you up for a visit?"

I sit up and rub the sleep from my eyes. "Yes, please I need to see her." He nods.

When Zack, Xander, and Kateri come in, it takes all my resolve to not cry. She looks terrible. She locks her bruised blue eyes on mine and hugs her body. "Out." It's all she says, but her meaning is clear. Everyone files out of my room. Even my parents. When the door closes on us alone, she sits on my bed.

Staring in the distance, her voice just as far, she explains, "In my head, I'm hugging you, but I can't be touched right now."

"Kat, I..." She holds her hand up in a stop motion.

"We aren't going to talk about it. Not now, not ever. I am going to tell you this. Ashley Aniston set this up. She wanted me hurt to punish my brother, and she wanted you to be the slut she framed you as. In her mind, you stole Morgan and she wanted to make sure nobody would want you ever again." She locks her vacant eyes on me. "I don't want my brother to feel responsible for this."

"I don't want that either." I sigh.

"If we make a pact to not let that detail free, we save his soul but give her freedom. If we save Morgan, she gets away with this. Can we do that?" I stare at her for a long moment. This is a difficult decision.

Tapping my lips, I think out loud. "Everyone knows who set it up. She posted it all over Facebook, she made me a hashtag. Morgan will know it was her." I twist my lips and light up with an idea. "We just need to offer an alternative reason. Something so petty she will be famous for being that... extra." We sit silently thinking again.

Kateri slaps the bed. "What if we start the rumor that she set you up to be attacked and tried to ruin you because you wore the dress she wanted to wear."

"That's perfect. She will be the most hated girl in all of Champagne Falls. Morgan won't think he is responsible, and I'd be honored to take the attention off of what happened to you tonight."

A tear streaks down her swollen purple face. "You already did. The camera phones. They were everywhere. The pictures are everywhere. Nobody's talking about what happened to me, because the pictures and videos of you, are dominating the conversation."

I stare back and shrug. "It's time to change the conversation."

CHAPTER 10

The video.

Sam's Diary Entry:

From my hospital bed, we changed the conversation. Kateri, the Fisher Men and I took screen shots of every picture posted of me including the poster's name. Then from my hospital room, we made a video.

I told the world about how Ashley Aniston was so jealous that I bought my dress first, she arranged for me to be violated. A social media account with the handle TheCasualObserver forwarded us months of messages from Ashley Aniston trying to gossip about Kateri and me. She also forwarded us a picture of my shredded dress being collected as evidence. We peppered the photos, screen shots, and other messages into the video. I looked solemnly at the camera. "She won. I can never wear that dress again." I detailed the attack with flashes of pictures that others had taken of me. The only way to not be humiliated by this is to own it. I ended the video highlighting all the people there that could have done something but instead took pictures. I called each and every one of them out by profile name with their photo.

I posted it on every social media outlet I could find. The Diary of a Casual Observer re-blogged and shared it, too. It was

5:00 in the morning when it posted; everyone was sleeping. I tagged all the people involved and created the hashtag #extraAshleyAniston. By sunrise, I was trending and Ashley was the most hated girl in the world, not just Champagne Falls. She did a YouTube video claiming her innocence. TheCasualObserver commented with screenshots of her Facebook posts and months of messages. Soon, everyone turned against her.

She had witnesses of her dress jealousy come forward with detailed accounts of shopping with her. She finally came out and said she was just mad because I took her boyfriend, and she didn't think anyone would be assaulted, she thought we would be called out as prudes and become unlikeable. *Bullshit, she knew what was happening.*

That's when America really let loose on her. If she hadn't set me up to be publicly gang rapped and had my best friend tortured, I could feel sorry for her. As it was, she couldn't be convicted of any crime so the court of public opinion had to crucify her. It was justice.

Why did I feel so icky then? After a week of the drama, I felt sicker. I didn't really want any human to feel the way I was making her feel. I took it too far, so I took the video down. It's been three months and while nobody talks about it anymore. Everyone remembers.

I can't go in public anymore. The stares are as degrading as being naked on the internet. The whispers, the pointed fingers, and the cleared paths are gut wrenching.

When the criminal case for Kateri's sexual assault went to court the defense brought up her eating alone at lunch every day. They entered evidence of her seeking therapy as a child when her house burned down and a baby they were watching died. The even had a priest at Holy Cross High School call her a troubled girl and paint Jason as an all-American boy. They slapped him on the wrist and sent him back to practice. My parents and the Fishers agree, St. Mary's doesn't need our money anymore. We start at East Champagne Falls next week.

Kat pulled away from her brothers and me. She said she didn't want us to look at her like that anymore. She spends her days in the treehouse in her backyard. The Fisher brothers don't know how to help her, so they spend more and more time with me.

Great. A new school with no friends and a reputation. I would go live with my mom and start fresh if the Fisher men didn't need me as much as I need them.

Excerpt from Rika's Recorded Interview with Morgan Fisher:

"What changed after the incident?"

"Everything. Kat was clearly hurting, but she wouldn't let us come near her. By that I mean, not physically or emotionally. She shut us out and insisted she was dealing with it. Every time I managed to be in the same room with her, she yelled at me. She would say, 'Stop looking at me like that.' I don't know what she was talking about. Sam was different."

"How do you mean she was different?"

"Sam was hurting, too. She needed us. We took turns making sure someone was always with her. She cried a lot, she was scared, she developed anxiety, a weird skin condition, and paranoia. I had to build a new bed for her because she said she couldn't run away from an attacker with her bed so high. She was afraid to sleep. She needed us."

Excerpt from Rika's Recorded Interview with Zack Fisher:

"I hate what those fuckers did to her. When she stood in the front yard naked, I could see all the handprints on her skin as if the hands themselves were still there. I mean that literally. Her skin was flushed red and white fingers were all over her. I couldn't look at them. Xander tried to soothe them away by tracing swirls over them."

"The skin condition?"

"Yeah, before that night, Sam was a badass. She wasn't afraid of anything. She was my equal in every way; my soulmate. She hung out in a tattoo shop as a kid. She didn't squirm at the darkness I embrace. She found beauty in the dark. I love her strength, but they made her think she was weak. She's not. They made her afraid. They made her question every decision she made. They compromised her ability to love freely.

It took a lot of time and work to remind her of who she is. It took a lot of pushing her before she decided to take her life back. Morgan was the strong dad she needed. Her father was lost and painfully shy. I was the coach she needed. Connor was her new best girlfriend. You can tell him I said that. I never understood Xander's dynamic with her. He was just… there."

Excerpt from Rika's Recorded Interview with Connor Fisher:

"I wasn't her girlfriend. My brother is a Neanderthal. I was just her friend. We liked the same movies, read the same books, and shared a lot of common interests. I love her. I will always love her. We are going to raise the head on our double bed in a nursing home to watch Star Wars one day. I'll kiss her wrinkly hand and say, "That was lovely. Who are you again?""

"So, Morgan was her dad, Zack was her coach, you were her best friend, who was Xander?"

"I don't know, her savior maybe. He took care of her, but she didn't really need saving. I can't define their dynamic. I always teased she was my future wife, I kind of meant it. Sam was always meant to be a Fisher, but after that night I couldn't break the rules. She needed all of us."

Excerpt from Rika's Recorded Interview with Xander Fisher:

"I still want to rip apart every single person that had a hand in hurting her. She is the most brilliantly beautiful soul I have ever encountered and I resent that light is dimmed. I can't get over the fact that the piece of shit took the time to date her. He took two weeks to know her, he saw how stunning she was that night, and he still wanted to harm her? I have wanted to be with her from the moment I met her. I had every intention of breaking the rules. I wish I had done it before that night. She wouldn't have been there.

After the incident, I crawled into her bed every night to keep the demons at bay. I held her every time she fell apart. Soon, I handed her the pieces to put herself back together. For the rest of my high school years, I never dated another girl. I couldn't after the incident. She said that I should give the woman I love my heart, soul, mind, and body. She said dividing any of that was cheating. I couldn't cheat on her, she owned me.

"Wow!"

"I couldn't have her either, so there was that. The incident was when I discovered she has Dermographism. How ironic, a woman who was custom made in the cosmos, just for me, but I can't have her."

"Dermographism is the skin writing rash she gets? I saw the hives when she was sick once."

"When she's sick, stressed, too hot, too cold, her skin becomes charged you can write on it with just a fingertip. How sexy is that?"

Muffled laughter "Yeah, you might be in the minority on that one."

CHAPTER 11

Rika's interview with the Fisher Men.

Sam

Pacing Connor's living room, I wring my hands. "Okay, guys. I gave you permission to disclose anything Rika asks for in this interview. She's never going to publish it." I pace back and forth in front of my guys on the sofa. "She'll take you back to her room one by one. I have it on good authority that Connor won't complain at all if you drink his beer and jump on his bed while you wait."

We all chuckle as Connor protests loudly out of my phone's speaker.

"She needs to practice interviewing people." Holding up Rika's wrist I show them the rubber band. "Anytime she reacts emotionally, or if she rambles off topic. Snap this rubber band" I point again before dropping Rika's hand. "Now, I know this is difficult. I just want to say, I really appreciate you doing this for me."

Picking up my phone which holds Connor, he can't be here today, I sit on the coffee table knee to knee with Morgan. "Connor, do you want to go first or have Rika call you later?"

"I need to get back to work. Veronica, I'll text you when I'm back at my hotel." He disconnects abruptly.

Rika wrings her hands nervously. "I guess we'll begin with Morgan then?"

Standing up, her neck strains to look all the way up to his face. She swallows hard. "Right, follow me."

The two disappear into her bedroom. Zack leans forward and gives my knee a squeeze. "Hey girl, you okay?" I nod, but I'm not sure. This is difficult at best.

Interview with Morgan Fisher:

"You drove the girls to the dance that night?" Rika asks.

"I did." Every time I recall that night it is that point that haunts me. I knew it was all wrong. "Sam and my sister were so excited they squirmed in their seats and chatted in excited chirps like birds around a feeder." I feel my smile disappear the minute I remember them talking about their dresses.

I'm not sure I can do this. I scrub my hands down my face and sigh.

"It's okay, I know this is difficult." Rika's smile is warm. My sister used to smile like that. She lost something that day. Even now that she is happy and in love, she still doesn't smile like she used to.

"We arrived at the dance and we took pictures." Pulling out my wallet I retrieve the photo of Kat. It's my favorite picture. I know having my photos in a wallet is an old-fashioned thing our parents did, but my phone isn't where I keep what's close.

Handing the picture to Rika, she again smiles. Her smile is that of a woman who got to keep her innocence. She looks at the laminated picture of Kat in the dress Sam's mom altered to fit her perfectly.

In the photo, she's twirling like a little girl. Her shiny black shoes have the straps across the top as her little Kindergarten shoes did. Her toes are pointed like the Irish step dancer she was. The dress she's wearing flares like the good twirly dresses her younger self was drawn to, and her long blonde hair is splayed in the air. Her smile, that smile, that is the sister I will never forget. That asshole ended her on *the night with too much power*.

"She's beautiful isn't she," I ask, but don't wait for a response. "Sam's picture is on the other side."

Rika flips the picture over and smiles at the young girl with a hand on her hip, glare on her face, and attitude for days.

"The picture of your sister is a fun care-free candid shot. Why do you keep this less than sweet shot of Sam?" Rika asks.

Taking the picture from her I flip to the Kateri side and hold her up. "This is the last time my sister was happy, innocent, and free. This is the last time she smiled that smile and felt good about herself. She has never smiled like that again. Not even now. She's in love and happier than she has ever been, but she's still not her." I point to the picture again for her to see.

Flipping it to the Sam side, I continue explaining. "See that attitude, it comes from confidence, self-assurance, and a general feeling of invincibility." I smile at old Sam. "She never felt that way again." Rika gives my knee a squeeze for reassurance. "Sam was the best at everything she put her mind to; first chair, captain, company dancer, anything. She knew it was already hers. Zack calls her a badass. What she was, stemmed from confidence, being loved, and feeling safe. It took her a long time to recover some of that semblance. Have you noticed?"

"Noticed?" Her confusion is evident.

"She checks all the door locks twice, the shower curtain and closet doors have to be open, and she sleeps in a tiny ball at the foot of her bed if she has to sleep alone." Recognition sparks on Rika's face.

"She wasn't always like that. It's partly my fault."

"How so?"

"After these pictures were taken, their dates arrived." I put the photo back in my wallet and slide it into my back pocket,

"The boys were smarmy and smug and clearly not well-behaved gentleman. I was ready to knock them out. Neither deserved the privilege of the amazing ladies they accompanied."

Rika tilted her head, "aww." Her hand flies to her heart and she fans at the forming tears.

"Isn't that the reaction you're avoiding?" Her face goes white and she hands me her wrist.

I shake my head, "Sam knows better. Fisher men don't hurt women. You'll need to snap that band yourself." She smiles and does as directed.

"I had half a mind to keep my truck parked in front of the school and stalk them through the gym windows."

"Why didn't you?"

"Sam would have never forgiven me. In hindsight, I'd rather her hate me." I look down and breathe out the hurt building in me. "I tried intimidation instead. I squeezed their hands a little too hard, kissed the girl's heads possessively, and even told the girls loud enough for them to hear that I would break those boys' fingers."

"How did the boys react to that?"

"My sister's date stiffened up and was respectful, but his eyes never met mine. He was a pussy that preferred to overpower her alone when she was vulnerable. He acted like the coward he is. But Sam's date, motherfucker, I still want to kill that slimy prick." I slam my clenched fist on the surface of Rika's desk startling her.

"Sorry, but my blood still boils. He put his hand to the small of her back, guided her to the stairs and stopped with his back to me. He then said to her loud enough for me to hear, 'Don't worry about grandpa over there. He won't need to break anything. Then he dropped one hand on her ass scooching her forward, and the other hand flipped me the bird behind his back."

"What? What an asshole!"

"I wanted to rip him form limb to limb and feed him his own dick and balls. Don't forget to snap that rubber band by the way."

"Why didn't you?" She snaps the rubber band without breaking eye contact.

"Sam leaned into him and smiled at him. I thought about it. Maybe he was just a macho alpha asshole in his world. He wasn't her husband, and it would only be a matter of time before she put him in his place. Maybe she needed the opportunity to do so." I shrug. "I figured one of two things would happen, she would humiliate him for being an ass, or she would soften him like she did to Zack. I did not see door number three, and I regret it every day."

"How did things change after the incident?"

"Sam developed anxiety. She couldn't sleep without Xander or Connor. She would get so overwhelmed she would throw up. She was skinner than a rail, and my soup was the only thing she could tolerate sometimes for days at a time. She couldn't approach her front door let alone go outside of it. She would shake like a puppy when she heard the voices of teenagers outside."

"And Kateri?"

"She withdrew. She would avoid everyone at all costs. She was buried in her phone or computer. She would go out, and I would find her in secluded places to be alone. She would fly off the handle screaming at us. She punched my chest and screamed 'Stop looking at me like that.'" I shake out my hands to avoid the tears. Violence is so far out of the realm of what is normal for her. "It was painful for her to be around people. What choice did I have? I had to respect her request and go to the girl who needed me."

"Did time help any of them?"

"Kat went down a dark path, she would bite or pinch herself until she bled. When I discovered it, she was embarrassed and it stopped. Eventually, she threw herself into social events." I scratch the stubble on my chin in thought. "I think she felt like he won if she turned into Sam. She snarled a glare at how broken Sam was. She was not going to be broken. She threw herself into cheerleading, and popular friends, and her step dancing. She distanced herself from the heap of mess Sam had become. She wanted to make sure everyone knew he didn't break her, but he did. She just broke differently."

"When would you say she mostly healed?"

"It was the strangest thing, she went to Florida for a cheerleading competition, she came back with a new best friend in Texas. Slowly, this whole new Kat evolved. She was stronger, braver, and even silly again. She even embraced a new name. We call her Chrissy now. I think Kat was the girl who was hurt and broken, but Chrissy is who she is now. I find myself using the appropriate name when describing points in her past. It was like changing her name changed everything."

"How did the incident affect the way you feel about Sam?"

"I may have wanted to protect and take care of her, but I needed to be needed. I felt so helpless. I'm a fixer, and I needed to fix this. She taught me not everything can be fixed and sometimes the scars are part of the perfection. I love her, my life is incomplete without her. She is just as much mine as I am hers."

"A sister?" Rika asks.

"Different, more than a friend, not really a sister. She's… Sam." I shrug my shoulders. My relationship with Sam defies labels.

Rika

I pour myself an extra full glass of red wine and curl my legs under me on the sofa. What an absolutely draining day I've had. It's heart-wrenching enough to know what my best friend went through, but the front row seat to how it affected her and everyone else has taken a toll on my psyche.

I gulp an unladylike drink from my glass and rub my temples then my sore pink rubber banded wrist. It's not even over yet. I still have to interview Connor tonight. Hearing Dad-like Morgan break at the unfixable mess she was, Zack defeated by the loss of the badass that settled him, and Xander fall apart at the loss of the girl who taught him what love is, broke my heart. Not the traditional heartbreak either.

I interviewed a priest one time. He said that listening to confession all day at a grade school was like being stoned with cotton. They are still innocent enough to not have the heavy weight of adult sin, but you listen to their little hearts break with guilt. It's both over and underwhelming. Interviewing the Fisher men was like being stoned with needles. Each strike pierced uncomfortably until my heart shredded under the weight of tiny blows. It was overwhelming, all overwhelming.

I glance over to my phone vibrating on the coffee table. My heart sinks when I see it's Connor. I swipe to answer and my hand shakes as I raise it to my ear. Time to be a human pin cushion one more time. I place the call on speaker and pad off to my bedroom.

"Hang on a second, I have to set up the audio recording." I lay the phone down on my desk, plug the microphone into my computer, and launch my audio editing program.

"No, problem Roomie, everything okay?"

"Yes, it's really strange timing that we aren't going to meet any time soon." I hear a muffled sound of amusement.

"Sorry, I'm rarely home for long stints. I guess it makes me a great roommate though." We chuckle.

"Okay, everything is set. Let's begin." I ease him into the interview as I did with his brothers asking how they met, and amusing anecdotes about the early years of their friendship.

"You kissed her first?"

"I did, admittedly, it was a dick move." He chuckles. "My brothers and I are fiercely competitive. When I saw the twins trying to stake a claim, I had to throw my hat in the ring."

"Was that the initial appeal? She was coveted?"

"Maybe, but when she broke Ashley's nose defending the honor of my sister, I felt differently."

"How do you mean?" Since he isn't here, I plop on the bed with my pad and pen getting comfortable.

"She became a part of me. She loved my family, she's beautiful, smart, and funny. Our hearts and souls are two halves of a circle. I don't know where I end, where she begins, or when it began. It just… is."

"You like her because you have a lot in common?"

"No, I am very precise. I like everything in its place. I like to have a Plan A, B, and C. I need order and control, and I was suffocating with the need. She brought unwelcome chaos. I didn't live until her." He lets out a sigh.

"The kiss happened because I took control of the situation. They were playing tug of war, and I was going to end it. When my lips touched hers, her eyes got wide and she was surprised. I suddenly felt like as ass. I took control without permission. I thought I may have even hurt her." His voice cracks painfully and I'm hovered over the side of the bed hanging on every word. "At that moment, I was not the boy Nonna Fisher raised." He sounds so sad. My face drops, and I snap the rubber band. Fuck its really starting to hurt.

"I brag all the time about how I kissed Sam first, but deep down I violated her. I'm no better than the boys that night."

Unexplained anger wells in me. "Oh, c' mon. You touched your lips to her Spiderman style. You didn't cop a feel or make lewd comments. Hell, you didn't even use your tongue. You weren't on the same playing field as those assholes, let alone playing the same game."

"I think that requires more than one rubber band snap."

"Shit. My wrist is so pink and sore, but you're right. I shouldn't have been so emotional. I do, however, stand by what

I said and the snap will be worth it." I pull and snap the rubber band several times, and I think I hear him moan. *What the hell?*

"You okay."

"Yep, just stretching. It's been a long day."

"Tell me about it," I grumble.

"Sam was in eighth grade, barely fourteen, and as far as I knew at the time, that stolen kiss was her first. I stole a moment that should have been given. The gift was not intended for me."

I know it wasn't her first kiss, but that isn't my secret to tell. I hadn't considered a sweet teenage kiss could be looked at as amoral. These boys were raised differently, obviously, if he felt that guilty over a stolen kiss...

These Fisher Men are something else. How could one family hold so much perfection? I bet there is some dark twisted secret hidden under the surface of these impeccable people.

"When I climbed in her bed to watch Harry Potter, we compared it to the books and how we imagined things. We were sad the death day scenes didn't make the movie. We clicked. Our interests mirrored on everything. Our personalities, well, not so much. Her dirty clothes in a pile on the floor made my eye twitch so bad, I bought her a hamper. She refused to use it just to spite me."

That garners a chuckle from both of us. In context, it doesn't require a snap.

"When did you discover what was happening that night?"

"Xander ran downstairs red faced, followed by Zack and Morgan. They ran to the truck and I followed. I didn't even know why."

"You hadn't seen the posts?"

"My parents were gone for the night. What do you think four teenage boys were doing at home on a Saturday night unsupervised?"

"Ah, you had a girl."

"I was knuckles deep inside her and loving every minute of it, but the look on Xander's face made my blood run cold. The look on Zack's face made me think he might need bail money, and Morgan was pale on the verge of tears. No matter how fine the girl under me was, it was clear. My brothers needed me."

"They told you on the way?"

Zack and I were in the bed of the truck. He asked if I had thought to grab a bat. He couldn't even tell me. He gave me his phone. I started taking screen shots of everything. He wasn't thinking clearly. I knew we needed them."

"Why did you think they would be needed?"

"We knew she wasn't agreeing to a group gang bang. She was a virgin, and any of us would have relieved her of the v-card gladly if she felt it needed tossing. I suspected something nefarious not sinister though. In my heart of hearts, I did not believe anybody would hurt Sam. I thought their intentions might be to demean or humiliate her. I couldn't imagine a world where humans wanted to defile her. I took the screen shots in case Sam wanted them expelled. I didn't want to believe they would be needed for anything criminal."

"You pulled up on the house…"

"What I wasn't expecting to see was my sister. She had a knife to the fucker's throat. Her eyes were disconnected. Her hair was wild. I didn't notice the dress right away. I couldn't take my eyes off her bloody lip and bruised face. We tried to go to her, but she screamed at us to stop."

"When did you notice Sam?"

"Kat pointed to her. She was naked, her skin was flushed bright red, and you could see white handprints, like bruises but white, directly on her skin. It was alarming."

"Her skin condition?" All of the brothers describe the handprints. It was clearly a haunting vision.

"Rika, look at your pink wrist." I do.

"Yes?"

"That's what color her skin was. Now press your finger into the pink hard. That white imprint your finger left for two seconds, it was like that. Everywhere." A tear spills down my cheek and I snap the rubber band.

"What was that?" He asks his voice lower than our conversation a minute ago.

"My rubber band snap," I explain.

"It has a surprisingly erotic sound to it." He laughs.

"Oh, you're one of those," I chide the freak.

"One of those?" He asks.

"I get the pieces now, everything just so, everything your way, in control, picturing my pink skin, and now a slapping sound gets your motor running."

"Whoa, whoa! Easy there. I am not into BDSM. I can't hurt a woman. You're putting together pieces of the wrong puzzle. Snap your wrist and get back on task."

Oh my god, I could die. Did I seriously just go there? I clear my throat. "How was your relationship affected after the incident."

"I held her every Tuesday night. I made her watch romantic comedies because I wouldn't let her give up on love. I didn't want her to think what she had with him was love."

"Romantic comedies?"

"Yes, and the teen movies where the right guy gets the right girl. From Pretty in Pink to Ten Things I Hate About You. I did a really good job with her because she loves romantic comedies now, much to my dismay. These days we compromise, one rom-com for every two normal movies." We both laugh again. "I just needed her to believe a happily ever after was still possible for her."

"Why?"

"At first, I thought she might harm herself. The anxiety was debilitating for her. I also saw the situation as an opportunity to make things right for stealing a kiss." He lets out a sigh and I hear the phone shuffle. I bet he's running his fingers in his hair as his brothers do. "If I'm honest though, I always hoped her happily ever after would be with me."

Aww, poor Connor. He's a good man but is probably loving a girl that doesn't feel the same.

"Do you still feel that way?" I ask, hoping for a no.

"Now, I just hope I'm included." His answer is simple and heartbreaking.

CHAPTER 12

How do I explain that I am the one breaking The Fisher Men rules?

Sam

I didn't sleep well. Recalling all those ghosts made it impossible to rest. Washing my face in cool water, I look at my pale sunken face. My brown eyes are nearly black. It's obvious I spent the night crying. I try to look alive again with a little BB cream and Chapstick. Brushing my hair up into a ponytail, I secure it to the back of my head and put on Zack's old trucker hat. I've been wearing it since I was sixteen. Some people have security blankets, I have Zack's hat, Xander's hoodie, Morgan's first pick-up truck, and Connor's first metal sculpture, the one that went through my window.

"Good Morning Rika. You ready to get to Champagne Falls today?" I chirp.

She holds up one finger and takes a sip of coffee before she answers. "I am looking forward to meeting my new editor." She scrolls through her phone and looks at me curiously. "I got a text message from Connor. He said you have keys to his place."

I throw my dirty clothes in the plastic hotel appointed laundry bag and look up at her. "Yes, I do."

She raises an eyebrow. "He's on an assignment out of state and won't be back any time soon. I guess I won't have a roomie for a bit."

While Connor is a gifted artist, he is a structural engineer first. His sculptures are amazing, and he is locally famous. If he pursued his art, he would be wildly successful. Mrs. Fisher ordered all of her children to pursue a career with a steady paycheck before pursuing their passion. She wanted them to always have a plan B.

"Sometimes he gets called away like that. We keep in touch with a weekly skype and movie date. He didn't mention anything. It must be an actual emergency."

Once we finish getting ready and packing up, we do one last sweep of the room. Rika smiles brightly and claps her hands together. "That looks like everything."

Closing the door, we head down the hall to the elevator and Rika leans into me. "I'm sorry that happened to you."

I lean back against her. "It could have been worse."

We drop our keys off at the front desk and saunter into the day room for our complimentary breakfast. "Did you and Kateri ever repair your friendship?"

Taking a tray and adding my banana, cereal, and a muffin, I shake my head. "We never became what we were again." We find a seat in the corner and while we eat I explain.

"She came with me to cheer tryouts and decided to try. We both made the team. She immersed herself in the cheerleader lifestyle. She had a mean-girl clique with three girls named Heather. It wasn't like her. Then she went through this slut faze. It was like because she wasn't a virgin anymore, sex wasn't a big deal. She was with a new guy every other week or so and sleeping with all of them."

Rika pauses a spoonful of yogurt on its way to her mouth. "What did you do about it?"

I shrug. "What could I do. I let her know I would be here when this life implodes."

Cleaning up our breakfast mess, we grab a couple of pieces of fruit for the road and climb back into my pick-up truck. Backing out of our parking spot, I'm anxious to get on the road. I am a bit nervous, too. I hope it's not too late to pursue the Fisher Brother I've wanted since day one.

Once we are comfortably on the highway, I continue Kateri's story. "Our sophomore year of high school, our cheer squad was going to nationals at Disney World. The week before, Kateri twisted her ankle and wouldn't be able to compete. I knew she was faking it."

I grab one of the bananas from the center console and peel it.

"She still went with us, but she wasn't able to compete. Day two of our week-long trip, she announced she had a family emergency and had to leave. I was concerned. Her family was my whole life."

I take a bite of the banana and recall how scared I was. "She pulled me into my hotel room alone. She finally confided in me that since she was ten years old she has had a pen pal that she emails. She said he was the one that helped her through the incident. He bought her a cell phone. He has been taking care of her soul for years, and she was going to attend his Airforce graduation in Texas. He bought her airline tickets, a hotel room, and even gave her cash for food and transportation. She would fly right back to Orlando and come home with the rest of us, but she trusted me with this secret."

Taking my Dr. Pepper from the cup holder, I twist off the cap and I am grateful for the sugar and caffeine. It was a long night. "I made sure Kateri was safe. I was so happy she trusted me with this huge thing. I felt like I was getting my friend back. I gave her my camera so she could take pictures together, and then I let her go."

"It turns out, she had a crazy relationship with him. They both decided that they can say anything to a person they don't know. They worked out all the stuff they were going through together without ever sharing names, addresses, or other personally identifiable information. She was in love with him and never knew his name."

"That's crazy!" Rika yells.

I shrug, "They liked it like that. She went to the graduation ceremony without ever knowing which Airman hers was. I went through the camera memory when she was finished. I recognized one of those Airmen. Matt BaddStone, Colton's big brother. When she said they began communicating after he lost a sibling, I knew it had to be him, but I kept the secret."

"What a small world and an awesome story. I want to turn that into a movie. It would be like *You Got Mail* crossed with *Pretty in Pink*."

We laugh and come up with a dozen other Rom Com's that could be Matt and Kateri's story.

"Anyways, after her trip to Texas, she changed. She began to smile again. She was happy and the Kateri I remembered. She changed her name to Chrissy, and her dating habits. We became acquaintances."

"But not the friends you once were?" Rika asks.

"Well, she did come to me when she wanted her nipples pierced." I laugh; that's true love in my mind. "The girl at Stone tattoo pierced them. I was hoping Matt was there that day. That would have been awesome."

Rika taps her fingers on the console. "I'm glad she moved on. Now, about you, which Fisher Brother is your man?"

"Take a deep breath Rika, it's not Connor. I love him with everything in me. He was my best friend when I needed him. After I lost Kateri, he was there. He is still my best friend. He kisses me on the mouth every time he sees me, but it has all of the emotion of a kiss from grandma. We talk about everything. We openly discuss sex, love, and Star Wars. I have been his go-to for dating advice since I was fifteen. We may have started with the spark of attraction, but somewhere along the way we lost that spark, and we enjoy the comfort of being friends. You won't be awkwardly waiting for us to finish shower sex to pee at your place."

We laugh until we have tears. I had to pee in our kitchen sink once because Rika was being ridden by a loud asshole in our shower.

"I know you were nervous about me having a key, but I have a key to all four of their places. Nobody wanted me stranded without a place to go if I popped in for an impromptu visit."

"Did you ever do that? Fly home just to visit. You would sometimes disappear for the weekend."

I smile a mischievous smile. "No, I would get a hotel room in Times Square when the Fisher Men came to visit."

Rika looks at me like I just grew a second nose. "Why?"

"The Fisher Men are all drop dead gorgeous. They are muscle-y, panty melting, mouthwatering freaks of nature. I never bring them near female friends. They aren't players. They are good men, but they aren't exactly opposed to a one-night stand. With us not living in the same state, that's what it would have been. I preserved your heart."

She crosses her arms over her chest. "I could have said no."

I wink at her. "You could have tried."

We drive for a while in a comfortable silence when Rika blurts out, "It's not Morgan."

I glance at her and then back to the road. "What's not Morgan."

"You're not in love with Morgan. He was like a father to you. He was the caring protector. You even jokingly called him dad. I know there is this whole Daddy fetish, but you don't strike me as a girl that's looking for that."

I scrunch my nose. "Eew."

"So, it's not Morgan?"

"No. He is extremely attractive. The day he called me a twelve-year-old, all attraction for him was gone."

We laugh at my stubbornness. "I love Morgan, but our relationship revolved around him thinking he was protecting me, and me knowing it was him Kateri and I were protecting. You can't fall in love with someone with that kind of secret between you."

She taps her finger on her chin. "So, one of the twins."

I smile and nod. "My heart plummets and soars when I think of him. Even after all these years, he is still the one."

"I can see why the edgier darker side of Zack would appeal to you after the incident. He forced you to embrace the pain and conquer it. He made you see the scars as battle reminders, not pieces of you. He gave you strength when you needed it. It would have been easy to love someone who thought you were invincible."

He did do that. He made me feel strong. He screamed get up when I wanted to give up. He is responsible for the independent woman I am today.

"Xander was your protector, he held you through the storms rather than make you face them head on. He fought your demons for you, rather than handing you a sword. Your best friend Connor said you didn't need a savior."

"That's not accurate. He held me through the storms so I didn't have to face them alone. He fought the demons with me, not for me. Connor was right I didn't need a savior. I needed the twins."

I pull off the Highway and head down the familiar country roads that lead to Champagne Falls.

"When I was afraid to leave my house, four men brought me to school. They intimidated anyone that might have thought about hurting me. When I was afraid of people, four men brought me to the mall, school dances, the carnival, and parties. When I took drivers education, four men taught me to drive in this pick-up truck." I tap the dash lovingly. "Morgan and Connor took me to their proms. The twins took me to my junior prom."

I stop at the stop sign in front of East Champagne Falls High School. "Senior year, when I had no Fisher Men at school, they took me camping, to sporting events, and hung out most evenings in my kitchen. They handpicked my senior prom date and helped me find a dress. When I graduated, they handed me the keys to the pick-up truck where all our memories began."

A tear slides down Rika's face as we enter our hometown. I take and squeeze her hand. "I needed and loved all of them. I have been in love with one of them the entire time. I couldn't disrupt the dynamic. The rules are once I date one of them the rest of them would need to leave me alone. I couldn't do that to Morgan. He felt responsible for the incident. I couldn't do that to Connor. He's my best friend. I may only be in love with one twin, but I needed them both."

"Oh my god Sam, nothing has changed. What are you going to do?"

"I did what I had to do. I left. With time, distance, and maturity we can move forward. We don't need each other anymore. We choose each other now. We will always be special to one another. We will always be family. I'm hoping I'm not too late to claim my love. I'm ready to begin my happily ever after."

We roll to a stop in front of Xanack Ink. Zack and Xander own the tattoo and piercing shop here on Main Street. I can see them both inside. Neither is working on a client at the moment. This is my chance.

Stepping out of the truck, my smile spreads across my face. I cross the street, they stand when they notice me. They are so happy to see me. The bell rings as I open the door and I am met with open arms, kisses, and smiles.

Zack rolls a stool over to me. "Hey girl, you are a sight for hungry eyes. Have you been home yet?"

"No. My friend Rika is checking in with her boss at the Gazette across the street. I wasn't going to park here and not see my boys."

Xander rolls his stool over to me, yanks me up and drops me in his lap like always. "You can have your seat back Zack." He motions to the vacated seat with his chin. Xander squeezes me in his arms and whispers in my ear. "I missed you. You look good. Are you doing okay?" I nod.

"Of course, she's okay, She's a fucking beast! Aren't you babe!" Zack fist bumps me. "Nice hat." He winks. We slip right into our familiar banter. Chatting about everything, but mostly tattoos. Both boys are talented artists and have been practicing on one another since they were seventeen. I got some old tattoo guns from Mr. Stone. I offered to buy them, but to him, I will always carry a piece of his lost son. My money is no good with him.

Rika joins us, and I introduce her to my boys. She is all checked in and begins column work tomorrow.

We talk a bit more before I lock eyes on him. "Is it possible to get a moment alone? I need to talk to you." I ask nervously.

Everybody's eyes widen and Rika says, "I was going to go get some ice cream at Lickety Split. It's been ages." She smiles down at my beautiful friend. "Care to join me?" she asks.

As my friends leave, I turn to the man I love and lead him into one of the piercing rooms. "There is something I have to show you and a whole lot I need to tell you."

Now, how do I explain that I am the one breaking their rules?

CHAPTER 13

Rika's interview with the Fisher men

Interview with Zack Fisher

Rika's desk begins to shake with the bouncing of my leg.

"Zack, you don't have to sit if you don't want to."

That's all the permission I need. Standing up, I move the chair out of the way and drum my fingers on my thigh. It's a nervous habit, and anybody who doesn't like it can go fuck themselves.

I'm on edge, a live wire, a force of nature. I don't want to talk about this. "She's better now." I blurt out.

"She is." Rika smiles calmly at me.

"If you dredge this all up again she might not be better." The thought puts me in motion. Pacing is how I think.

"I've already interviewed Sam. She struggled for a little bit, but she's okay now."

Cold washes my skin and my feet plant facing Rika. "She's fine because I made her tough again. I made her embrace her darkness. I taught her scars are beautiful."

"She's your badass?" Rika questions.

"Damn straight, and I won't have you making her feel like anything less than fierce." I'm agitated, so I resume pacing drumming my hand on my thigh. "It took a long time of me yanking her back up before she stopped sitting out. I made her leave that goddamn house and face the public. I made her ignore the whispers and convinced her she shouldn't care."

"Why did you do that?"

"Because she needed me. The soup wasn't going to fix her, movies weren't going to fix her, and nightly cuddles sure as hell weren't going to fix her. Pushing her outside her comfort zone, tackling the bull by the horns, and finding peace in the chaos, that's what fixed her. She needed fixing, and I'm the asshole who pushed her. My brothers were the pussies who held her hand."

"How did you know what she needed?"

I plop down on the bed. My leg bouncing won't disturb her away from the desk. "She told me."

"She told you?"

I scrub my hand over my face. "Not in so many words, but yes." Standing up, I take to pacing again. "I never fit in with my family. If everyone was to pick a movie, mine would be a horror flick, and nobody else would pick that. I watched my sister get her ears pierced, and I wanted to feel it. I buried myself in dark music, and my thoughts often traveled to dark places."

"Why is that?"

I whip my head around to glare at her. "You don't need to know that. Instead, understand that when I felt out of place in my perfectly wholesome family, Sam got me. She told me my darkness is fascinating, and it was okay to be curious and stirred by it. It was okay to embrace my trauma and understand that it changed me."

"Before the incident, I'm guessing."

"Yes, she didn't think I was weird or bad. She didn't accept that ADHD made me stupid. She thought I was smart and caring, and she is the only person in my life who could get me to slow down. She got me to sit and watch sunsets. She made me appreciate that the absence of light isn't always dark. The sun being gone isn't scary or wrong. It's just another view."

I grab at my hair in frustration. "That motherfucker took that away from her. He made her afraid of the dark. He made her afraid of me."

Rika's face pales.

"She took me to the top of Dan King Hill. She put me on the handlebars of her bike and rode down as fast as she could peddle. The air was a rush, my heart flipped, adrenaline filled my body and when we reached the bottom, for the first time I felt peace. Peace in my mind, in my body, and in my soul."

"Wind therapy?"

"Yes. She studied ADHD medications and discovered they were stimulants. She had a theory that adrenaline would have the same effect. She taught me to thrill seek. Instead of changing who I am, she embraced me as I was. When those assholes broke her, she had nothing to embrace."

"You helped her live with the darkness?"

"Fuck no! I taught her to love the darkness. I taught her to fear nothing. I taught her that death is a great reward, not a punishment."

Rika gasps.

"I can't snap your rubber band. Fisher men don't hurt women," I wink, "unless they ask for it."

She laughs nervously at me, and I realize she might infer a different meaning. "I'm a tattoo artist and body piercer women ask me to introduce them to pain regularly."

She snaps her rubber band. "When did you discover that night went afoul?"

"I had my girlfriend Jill in my bed. It was almost my first time. Her back was arching off the bed when Xander barged in, grabbed me by my hair, and removed my mouth from my girlfriend's pink parts. Before I could murder him, he shoved his tablet in my face. It was a video of a guy air humping Sam behind her back and making blow job references. I stood up and said, 'Show Morgan. He's driving.'"

On my way down the stairs, I was checking out Ashley's social media accounts. She had a 'watch Sam get fucked' hashtag started. I searched the hashtag, and lava burned from my core to my skin. I couldn't look anymore. I gave my phone to Connor in the truck."

"When you arrived, what was the first thing you noticed?"

I drop my head and fight the emotion pooling behind my eyes. "Sam was naked. She looked like she had been painted."

"Painted?"

"Her derma-whatever. You know the stark contrast of removing your tank top from sunburnt skin?" She nods. "That is what Sam looked like. It looked like she fell asleep in the sun with ten sets of hands on her naked body." I grab a bottle of water off the desk. "The memory still churns my stomach."

"I've seen a flare before. When she had the flu. Her arms had the prints of her pillow. It's really strange looking."

"Her arms aren't as sensitive as her torso and thighs." I deadpan with a solemn frown.

"You noticed Sam before your sister?"

Morgan drove straight into the front yard. Xander and I were on the side of the truck with the best view of Sam, Connor and Morgan saw Kat first.

"When she fainted, she fell backward and smacked her head on the sidewalk with a sickening thud. Blood pooled. I thought she was dead."

"That must have been frightening."

"We didn't know what happened to her skin. We didn't know if it was okay to touch her. I thought she may have been doused by a chemical." I shrug. "We touched her anyway, but it left hand prints so we backed away. It was scary."

"How long was she unconscious?"

"The ambulance was close when she fell. Paramedics were assisting her quickly. She was awake and staring blankly in the ambulance. She was awake, but not really there."

"How did you decide who would go with Sam and who would go with Kateri?"

"Proximity maybe? I don't know. I just got in the ambulance and sat next to Xander. The paramedic told us the name of her skin condition, and I Googled it from my phone and read it aloud."

Sitting down on the bed, I finally shake the last of the jitters from my fingertips. I feel like a match after it's struck. A steady consistent flame. Not the on edge feeling of an impending strike, or the raging inferno I was, I feel like a single flame, and that's bearable.

"Are you in love with Sam?"

"It doesn't matter. She doesn't need a boyfriend, she needs a friend who will push her to be great, and we made a pact to be who she needs."

"So, you swallow your feelings; ignore any attraction?" Rika asks.

Is that what I do?

"I love Sam the way I can," I answer with a shrug.

Do you remember the first time you met her?

Interview with Xander Fisher:

Rika motions to a chair near the desk in her room, so I sit. I think my sister decorated this room before Rika added her touches to it. Connor likes everything pristinely white. Unlike the rest of his space though, it's soft and inviting in here. I feel immediately at home.

"You helped Sam pick out her dress for the dance?" Rika's voice startles me. I am so enthralled in my thoughts I'm thrown by the sudden interruption.

"Yes, I went shopping with Sam and her mother."

Rika crosses her legs and considers me for a moment. "Shopping isn't an activity typical teen boys volunteer for."

I chuckle and smooth my hands down my legs. "I always wanted to be where Sam was. I was interested in her dress because the guy she was going with buried the needle in my creep radar."

"What didn't you like about him?"

I blow out a breath and consider what it was that triggered the feeling. "When my brothers or I looked at Sam, it was with reverence. Other boys saw her with awe, but that dick looked at her like lunch. He didn't get lost in the depths of her curious eyes. He wasn't mesmerized by her smile, and he didn't see how amazing her skin was. He saw a sexual being."

In hindsight, she was a little girl. At the time, all I saw was innocence. He didn't see how amazing she was. "If he had seen her. If he had really seen her, he would have never been able to hurt her."

I drop my elbows to my knees. *I don't want to do this anymore.*

"When did you first realize her night took a bad turn?"

I look up at her and choke back the lump in my throat. "I was writing her a letter."

"A letter?"

"An email, actually. I wanted to break the rules. I typed up all the pros and cons. I even defended that she and I were tighter than her and Kat. Why couldn't it be me?"

"You wanted to date her?" Rika asks.

I snort out a disgusted laugh. "No Rika, I wanted to marry her. The fact I was only fifteen was irrelevant." I run my fingers through my hair. "I am not blameless in what happened to Sam."

"How so?" She scoots to the edge of her seat and leans in.

"If I had told her how I felt, if I had kissed her like I wanted, if I had asked her to be mine, she wouldn't have been there with him."

"Oh Xander, that's not your fault." She grasps her shirt over her heart and fights tears.

"You'll need to snap your own rubber band…"

"Fisher men don't hurt women." She finishes.

I thump my chest in solidarity while she snaps the rubber band on her wrist.

"So, you were typing an email?"

I'm sucked back into the despair immediately. "Yes, and my messenger started blowing up. My recently made ex-girlfriend saw what was happening on social media and began accusing me of dumping her for a whore. I was confused. I started following the trail and then I found the hashtag."

My stomach still turns with the memory.

"I nearly lost my mind. I was yanking on my hair. I cried, and then I watched closely. She didn't know, she didn't agree, and she most certainly didn't realize what she had stepped into. I ran into mine and Zack's bedroom white towel on the doorknob be damned and showed him. I left our room, threw my tablet at Morgan and then vomited in his garbage can. She didn't know what was about to happen to her."

"But you did?" Rika's eyebrow lifts with her question.

"I knew she wasn't leaving that party with her innocence."

"You arrived at the party. What was the first thing you noticed?"

A tear tracks down my cheek. "The handprints." I dry heave and feel sick. To this very day, I feel sick when I see handprints on skin. People ask me to tattoo baby handprints all the time and I'm pissy for the rest of the day.

"All of you were traumatized by the handprints."

"You could see where and how they held her down, you could see where and how they spread her legs, the evidence of their groping was visible on her breasts. She was mauled by animals."

"You gave her your hoodie?"

"I couldn't look at her, and I couldn't look away. My sister needed me, and the girl I loved need me. I was frozen until her head hit the pavement. Kat was still standing and in control. I ran to Sam, then I felt guilty for running from my sister. I was torn apart when I needed to hold it together." Rika hands me a bottle of water. It does little to soothe the burning in my throat.

"The police removed my hoodie. They photographed her in the ambulance and covered her for transport. I traced my finger over her skin. I wanted to turn all the angry marks into a beautiful pattern. Maybe, if the pain wasn't visible, she could heal."

I scrub my hand over my face again and snort a bitter laugh. "I love her dermographia. I have been drawing on her skin since the moment we met. In an odd way, I also felt that God showed me my soulmate by giving her a skin condition that allows me to turn her into artwork. I hate myself for feeling that way. It was stress from the incident that caused the first flare."

Rika nods. "Zack says the scars make her who she is just as much as the perfection. I think it's okay to appreciate all of her."

I give her a grateful look. He's right; she may not be her scars, but they are a part of her.

"You're in love with her, still?" Rika's question catches me off guard.

"I'm in love with her always, but I can't have her."

"Because of the pact with your brothers?" Rika asks, but I'm certain she knows.

"No, because I promised to always do what is best for Sam."

"Even if it hurts?" she asks.

"Especially if it hurts," I answer simply.

CHAPTER 14

For the first time, I closed the distance.

Sam

I step into him standing as close to him as I can. The familiar heat of his body surrounds me. "Do you remember when I gave you the tattoo guns from Mr. Stone?

"Heck yes! Crazy set of circumstances, but Mr. Stone is my sister's Father-in-law. He's getting ready to retire, and he is going to merge Stone tattoo with us."

"Wow, so Kateri finally realized that Matt BaddStone is her pen pal?"

He pulls back from me confused. "You knew?"

"Yes, it's a story for another time. The night before I got the tattoo equipment, I had a date. Do you remember?"

His teeth clench. "Yes."

"You took certain liberties to ensure he was not getting anywhere with me."

He smiles mischievously. "Fuck yes, I inked your tit. You would have had one hell of a time explaining that."

"Yes, he would not have been able to go to second base without an explanation."

We share a small laugh before I sigh. "Xander." I place my hand on his chest and look up through my eyelashes at him. "I loved you and I wanted to prove to you that it was always you. When I stood before you one day saying fuck you to the rules, I wanted you to know how long I waited for you. I went to Stone Tattoo to make it permanent."

"What?" He shakes his head, "we would have done it for you. I would have done it for you."

He doesn't understand yet.

"You did." I pull my shirt over my head and unclasp my bra. "I had your mark tattooed." His eyes grow wide as he traces the ink on my left breast. Goosebumps trail my skin. Heat floods his eyes.

"I tagged you first."

"Xander Oliver Fisher, you tagged me forever." He drew his tag on me like he often did that night. I loved this one because there was an "X" across my heart."

He scrubs a hand across the incredulous look on his face. "My brother in law inked my XOF on your tit?" He smirks and rolls his eyes. "I should have been the one to tag you."

"How do you know Matt did it?"

Tracing his mark again, he explains. "We recognize each other's work."

Grabbing his shirt and wrapping it into my fist, I pull him to me. "Am I too late?"

He lifts me onto a step stool in the room and puts his forehead to mine. "I can't lose you, Sam. I won't go down this road if you're leaving again."

I rub my nose to his. "If I'm not too late, If I'm still yours, I'm never leaving you again."

His arms tighten around my waist. "Then Baby, you are right on time." He puts his mouth a whisper away from mine and for the first time, I close the distance.

His fingers tangle in my hair, his mouth hungry on mine, my knees go weak. I have been waiting for this kiss for far too long. I'm about to be consumed by him when he abruptly pulls away.

"Wait!" He drops his hands to his knees and takes a few moments to breathe. "There are too many details to be worked out. My sister, my brothers, my girlfriend. We can't do this right now. Just. I…"

"Your girlfriend?" I ask slow and deliberately.

"Yes, I'll take care of it. Fisher Men don't cheat. We need…"

"Time." I interrupt. *Oh my god, I'm so stupid.*

"Yes, time. Can you give me that Sam?"

I am humiliated. I can't believe I didn't work into this. I fumble putting my bra back on flustered. I've completely embarrassed myself. I need to get out of here.

Fast.

Pulling my shirt down over my head, I focus on breathing not crying. Opening the door, I slip through, calling over my shoulder "You know where I'll be."

I practically run over Zack and Rika as I fling open the door to the tattoo shop and sprint to the truck. I can hear Xander calling my name. Tying my hair back up and putting on the trucker hat, I yell back, "We'll talk later." Rika runs to my truck and jumps in seconds before I put it in drive. She desperately tries to fasten her seat belt with ice cream dripping down the cone and on to her fingers.

"Jesus Sam, what the hell just happened?"

"I made a complete and utter ass of myself. I stripped from the waist up, kissed him, told him I'm in love with him, and he told me… He has a girlfriend… and needs time."

"Wow!"

"I'm such an idiot."

CHAPTER 15

I don't love her like that.

Xander

It's always been me? I sit on my stool scrubbing my hand over my face. It's always been her. Isabell and I just started seeing each other. It's a no brainer. I have to end things with her, today. My brothers are going to be the hard part.

All of us love Sam. Maybe for them, it was the fact she was forbidden, but I wanted her before she was forbidden. They are going to be pissed.

I have a few dilemmas. Each of my brothers thinks they know what is best for her. They are going to ride my ass and be over-involved in our relationship. By rights, per our rules, now that I've kissed her they are supposed to back off and not be in her life anymore. That is never going to happen. I can't ask them to give up Sam, any more than I can demand Sam give up her family. How can we achieve balance?

What if we don't work out. We can't move on. She will always be a part of my family.

"Dude, if you keep disinfecting that same spot it's going to disappear." I look down at the towel and spray bottle in my hand. I've been absently cleaning the same spot lost in my thoughts. I shake my head to clear the fog and look apologetically at my brother.

"Sorry. I've got a lot on my mind."

He tilts his head and stares at me. "Want to talk?"

Man, do I.

I shake my head. "I can't yet."

Setting down my towel and spray bottle, I pull my phone out of my pocket. This is going to suck. I've been dating Isabell for over a month. She's really nice and I'm going to hurt her. It has to be done. I text her to ask if she is available for dinner.

Zack interrupts my train of thought. "Is everything okay with Sam?"

Looking up from my phone, I jut my chin at Zack in acknowledgment. "I think so." I return my face to my phone. I can't look at him. I kissed Sam. He's going to be crushed. I think he thought if it was any of us, it would be him. I thought it would be Connor. The fact that it's me and it's always been me is still something I can't wrap my head around.

The thought of finally having her be mine as much as I am hers brings a goofy grin to my face. It's quickly replaced when I get Isabell's text confirming dinner plans tonight at Murphy's Bar and Grill. At least step one will be complete tonight.

I debated about the best way to do this. Murphy's is walking distance from Isabell's house. When we break up, I don't have to give her a ride home unless she wants one. I have to do it after we eat. The least I can do is feed the girl before I hurt her feelings. It isn't the first time I've broken up with someone, but it's the first time I can't point to something concrete and say this is why.

The reason we are done is that the woman I have silently loved since my sophomore year of high school just chose me. I can't tell her that. I don't know, maybe I should. If I was going to be dumped by a girl would I want to know it's because she is in love? I can ponder it no more. I've just arrived at her house.

I pull up to the curb and see she is outside waiting for me. She looks up from her phone smiling and waves while I step out of the car. Damn. She looks really happy to see me. She looks beautiful. I try my best to plaster a smile. Running down the stairs from her front porch, she throws her arms up to embrace me. Normally, I would hug and spin her and maybe give her a quick kiss. Doing that today wouldn't be right, but I have a plan. Instead, I give her a quick hug and lead her to the car with my hand at her back.

She didn't miss a beat. As soon as I slide into the driver's seat, she asks me what's wrong.

I let out a sigh. "I have a lot going on. We'll talk about it over dinner."

Once the car is parked, we walk through the parking lot, and she takes my hand. I feel skeevy holding her hand. I used to hold Sam's hand all the time when I had a girlfriend. In reverse, this feels so wrong.

I am relieved to let go of her and get the door.

Taking a seat across from her in a booth, I quickly grab a menu. I can't even look at her. This is going to be the longest meal ever.

"What's wrong? You are not at all yourself." I look over my menu at her concerned face. Shit. I'm going to have to do this before dinner.

"You know how I always talk about my buddy Sam in New York?"

She nods. "Yes, your best friend."

"I apologize, but I purposely never used pronouns when speaking of HER. Samantha has been my friend since freshman year. I was her date for every dance. We hung out every day. I used to sneak into her room and sleep with her. Literally, not … you know."

"Did you think I am insecure enough to be jealous of a woman you love like a sister?" I blow out a deep breath and scrub my hands over my face.

"That's not why." I can think of no way to say this without sounding like an ass. I fold my hands and look up for a moment before I crash my words on her. "I didn't tell you Sam was a woman because I don't love her like that. I mean I don't love her like a sister. I am in love with her and have been since we met. It is hurtful to say we are just friends out loud, so deception is the least hurtful lie." Her eyes drop to her lap.

"What am I supposed to do with this information?"

I take her hand across the table and wait until I have eye contact. "You should understand that there is nothing wrong with you. You're beautiful, kind, smart, and perfect. I just gave my heart to someone else a long time ago and you deserve someone willing to give you theirs."

"So, we're breaking up?"

"Yes, and any time we bump into each other, I'll be honestly happy to see you. If you still want to join me for dinner, I'd be happy to treat. If you want to walk away and never look back, a lie of omission is still a lie. I will understand."

She tilts her head curiously and thinks for a moment. "I suppose we could have dinner and part as friends. If you think about it, we haven't ever had sex."

The whole world disappears. Sam is here. She walks in with another girl and I can tell she's been crying. Why is she sad? In a Charlie Brown teacher voice, I think Isabel is saying something about a blow job. being as far as we've gotten. I motion for Sam. She hesitates, but with her head down she slowly makes her way to our table. She arrives just as, "What's a blow job between friends? We can totally be just friends." Tumbles out of Isabel's mouth.

I throw my head back against the booth as Sam takes off and flings herself out of the door. *Shit*. I know I can't chase her, not while she's like this. She is only reasonable after the initial blow up.

Holding up a finger to Isabel, I pull out my phone to shoot off a text.

Xander: It's not what you think. When you're done pouting, pull up your big girl britches and call me like a real woman.

My Girl: Sit and Spin X!

Xander: Only if you promise to watch, Baby. <Kissy face emoji>

She'll call or bang on my door to rip me a new one soon enough. I know better than to go after her.

CHAPTER 16

The moon over my Sammi.

Sam

Checking my phone, I roll my eyes. Just like him to try humoring me out of anger. How could it not be what I think? He breaks up with a woman by offering to be her friend with blow job benefits? Creepy asshole. I haven't been gone that long, how did he turn into a douche while I was away? I'm in love with Xander Freaking Fisher, not whoever that imposter is.

I text Rika explaining my hasty departure and my need to be alone right now. She was understanding as usual. Part of me thinks maybe I'm overreacting. Walking through the park on Main Street, I slow down and take in the gorgeous day. A group of familiar girls my age stare and whisper. All these years, and it still hurts. Taking a seat on a park bench, I let out a sigh. Maybe I shouldn't have come back.

A pair of black boots approach the bench. "Would you rather tell me what the fuck is going on, or come back to my place and drink shots until you don't care?" I smile.

I don't need to look up to know Zack Fisher has found me.

"I choose shots."

Stepping up behind me, Zack takes my face and tilts it back to see him. "Yeah, you do. That's my girl!"

He leans over and kisses me upside down with puckered lips and a loud mwah.

Once the bench is no longer between us he wraps me in a lifted hug.

"There's a moon over my Sammi?" It's a uniquely Zack way of asking what's wrong.

"Nothing I can't handle," I smirk. Wrapping his arm around my shoulder he leads me out of the park.

"Of course, you can handle it Battle Cat. Whose ass are we kicking?" Zack has always thought of me as invincible. I'm happy to have him in my life because I rarely feel invincible. Sometimes he makes me believe I am the warrior he thinks I am.

Pausing at his motorcycle, he hands me his spare helmet. I look up at him with a skeptical look and a tilted head. "How did you know where to find me?"

He gives me an apologetic look. "Xander called me. He said you're pissed about something happening in your mind and not reality, but it's too fresh to engage you. Since there isn't a shower to shove you in, he sent me."

A smile splits his gorgeous face while he bounces on the balls of his feet. He's always happy when I'm angry with one of his brothers. Now that were older, it hardly ever happens anymore. I shove his shoulder before putting the spare helmet on. He fastens the chin strap for me. "You know, he's probably nearby watching. You could just kiss me and then he'll have no choice but leave you alone." Zack has teased me like that a thousand times, all the Fisher Men have, but today it struck a different chord. I kissed Xander, by rules of the pact, Zack shouldn't be here.

I feel the color drain from my face. I'm suddenly very warm, and it's hard to breathe.

"Easy Sam, howl at the moon don't let it consume you." He quickly removes my helmet as I drop my hands to my knees. I look up at him with blurry burning eyes. He shakes his head. "Oh girl, if we kissed I would never keep my brothers away from you. Come back to me. Deep breaths."

"What if I kissed one of your brothers?" I blurt out between pants. "Would you still hold my hand and tell me I'm fierce?"

His jaw tenses, the fingers that were drumming his thigh still, and his face morphs to anger. "Did you kiss my brother?"

I hand him the helmet. "It doesn't matter. You already shut down at the thought. You only care for me if there is the possibility of having my heart. It's not real." I turn on my heel and stomp back through the park.

I don't even get a moment to mourn the loss of The Fisher Men when I hear his black boots marching right behind me.

"Bullshit! Whatever your deal is, deal with it. You don't get to tell me my feelings aren't real. You don't get to invalidate how much I care for you just because you're angry. I didn't hurt you, you are the one that cut me. Turn your tight ass around and dish it out, because I did nothing to earn that."

I freeze, turn around and glare at him. "Maybe you're right. Maybe I'm just a bitch." I'm going to lose them all, might as well go out with a bang. I turn back continuing my stomp to… I don't know where.

Zack walks around me bends his shoulder to my waist and picks me up and carries me off over his shoulder. *What the hell?* I bang my fists on his back and ass, which only hurts my hands.

I hear him using his cell phone. "Morgan, I haven't seen her like this since she was a kid. Sam needs a shower and I only have my bike." He pauses.

Xander used to throw me in the shower with all my clothes on when I was angry. This is their plan. I'm an adult, not a moody fucking teenager.

"On Main street, the park near Murphy's."

As we exit the park, Xander joins us. Asshole.

"Jesus Xander, what the fuck got her this riled up?"

"A misunderstanding." He answers solemnly. "Sam, are you going to chill the fuck out and talk about this?"

I spit on Xander's shoes. "Fuck you, Asshole!"

The red rage coursing through my body is turning white. Who do they think they are? Zack sets me down. I turn fully intending to run as fast and as far as I can. Instead, I land with my face on Morgan's hard chest.

He wraps his enormous arms around me and it feels like home. I break down. Sobbing into his chest, he whispers a quiet shush into my hair. Kissing the top of my head, he soothes me with his voice. "Hey Sweetheart, I missed you." He lifts my chin and thumbs away my tears. "It's okay, let's get you out of here and away from these assholes." He motions with his chin to the twins and then winks at me.

I'm going to miss him the most.

Opening the truck door for me, I take my usual passenger seat. I look out my window to the forlorn twins. I don't know who hurts more right now, them or me. The truck pulls away and we drive to my childhood home in silence.

From the Diary of a Casual Observer,

The object of the Fisher Men obsession may have made her choice. Witnesses say that she turned her back on the twins vying for her affection and left with Morgan Fisher. Are they still just friends? Time will tell and so will I.

CHAPTER 17

Choosing me means losing them.

Xander

It isn't the first time, I watched her leave with one of my brothers while pissed at me. Hell, we've all been the recipient of that scowl at one time or another. She's an Irish Italian Scorpio. She holds everything in all the time, then that one little thing overflows the cup, and she flies off the handle at something seemingly stupid.

I'm guessing being back here is stressful. Most of the town has pictures of her teenage self, naked. It must be difficult to see people from school and know that at one point, they were taking videos of her near sexual assault. She was so much happier in New York.

I suppose she is also upset by having to move back home. Nobody wants to admit defeat and crawl back to Daddy's house where your childhood bed awaits. On top of all of that, she heard Isabel say something about friends who give blow jobs. She either thought I was making that offer to Isabel, or that we were talking about Sam. She knows me better than that. It's everything else that's bothering her.

Zack and I head over to her house. I called Connor. He was at the airport ready to head west, but he has been bumped to the next flight all day long. The wildfires out west are interfering with travel. The timing is perfect. He's been delayed until tomorrow afternoon and is already ten minutes away, he'll meet us at Sam's house.

I know we have a pact. I know that now they are supposed to step away, but I can't ask any of them to do that. I'm not sure where that leaves Sam and me. I'm in love with her. I loved her before I was in love with her. I loved her as all my brothers love her. It changed for me, but I know how they feel and how much the loss of her would hurt.

She was at all our games in high school. She was at our high school and college graduations. She gave us dating advice, helped us with our homework, resumes, and even helped Zack and me begin our dream business. She is our family. I used to feel a twinge of jealousy when my brothers would hold or kiss her. It killed me to find Connor in her bed watching a movie. Now that she chose me, it doesn't faze me. I could be okay with them in her life. Could they stay in hers if she's mine?

If I'm honest, had she chosen one of them, I'd walk away. I couldn't bear to see her happy with any of them. That has to be heavy on her heart and mind, too. Choosing me means losing them. I push the thought away as I park in front of her house.

Climbing the porch steps, I realize I haven't knocked on her door since I was fifteen. I always just came in. Do I knock now? Scrubbing my hand down my face, I hate how it's different.

"Dude you really pissed her off if you're afraid to go in." Zack shoulders past me and opens the door.

I call after him as I walk in. "I didn't say or do anything to piss her off. She was already stressed, you are the one who pissed her off."

He turns around and flips his hand in the air. "I didn't say or do anything I haven't always said or done."

We continue making our way to the kitchen. "See, I told you she already had a bug up her ass."

"Fuck you, X! You became an ass while I was gone." She's leaning in Morgan's chest while he is propped against the counter. I glare at her and take the seat that's always been mine.

Zack assumes his usual seat, bouncing his leg one hundred miles an hour. "Hey girl, I'd be inclined to believe you about Xander if you didn't just rip my heart out of my chest and squeeze the life from it."

Sam buries herself deeper into Morgan. She has got to know she's being ridiculous. Damn her for being too stubborn to admit it.

The front door slams and Connor's voice rings out. "Hey now, where's my Sam I am?" Sam looks up from Morgan's chest with a face full of hope and runs out of the kitchen. We can hear her body crash into him in the hallway. He walks in carrying her. Her face is buried in his neck, her legs around his waist. He gives us a confused look and takes his seat. "The Diary of a Casual Observer has already posted that you breezed into town with a bang. What happened?"

Pulling her back to face him, he thumbs tears from her cheeks and asks her what's wrong again.

Zack drops his elbows on the table making it vibrate with the bouncing of his leg. His whole body is a live wire but his voice is steady, "I blame Xander. She's pissed at him about something." he offers.

We all watch her stiffen. Morgan gets her attention and she turns around to make eye contact with him, while he takes his seat next to me.

"Sweetheart, you always sit on Xander's lap. If you are in Connor's lap, you're clearly pissed. Tell us what he did so we can beat him up."

Her eyes lock with mine. I don't care if my brothers know. I want Sam, and I'm not about to lose her, but I had hoped it would come out more delicately. I think she can see the apprehension on my face. This is about to get ugly.

She clears her throat. "Rika and I went to Murphy's."

CHAPTER 18

They thump their chest in solidarity.

Sam

Xander looks like he may lose his lunch. He doesn't have the same feelings for me, but I kissed him. Kissing him means I've lost them all. I bury my face in Connor's chest taking in his comforting scent. I'm not ready to lose them yet. So, I shake out my hair and do something I have never done before. I flat out lie to the Fisher men.

"Xander was with a girl. He was leading her to believe that blow jobs are something female friends do. She was on board. I was not. I get enough shit for being friends with all of you. Everyone thinks I'm your fuck buddy. I sure as hell can't have one of you confirming it out loud."

Three blonde heads whip to Xander in disbelief.

Zack throws his hands out in disbelief, "Dude!"

"That is NOT what happened," Xander demands while he glares his way around the table. "You all know me better than that." He lowers and locks his eyes with me. "You know me better than that."

My face flushes. Deep down, I do. It's like I'm outside of my body watching myself go down a path to crazy town.

He folds his hands on the table and we meet glare for glare. I'm glaring because he's glaring, not because I'm angry. Well, maybe I'm angry? I'm something. Whatever the emotions are flashing through me, a glare seems appropriate.

He doesn't lose the glare but he engages me again. He may be talking to his brothers, but he doesn't take his eyes off of me.

"I was breaking up with Isabel. I explained to her that I have feelings for someone else, and Fisher Men don't cheat." Each of the brothers grunts in solidarity.

He was breaking up with her? My ass. He was trying to demote her from girlfriend to side piece.

"I told her that if I bump into her I'll be happy to see her. I even offered to treat the dinner she was meeting me for. I didn't want her to feel hurt or insecure. It had nothing to do with her. Fisher Men aren't jerks."

The brothers thump their chest in agreement. When they were small boys, they made a promise to Nonna that they would treat people like the gentleman she raised them to be. The little Fisher boys crossed their hearts. They often remind one another of the promise by thumping their heart with a closed fist.

Something dark happened in their family, and Nonna took measures to insure it will never happen again.

"She said we could have dinner and part as friends. Then she went on a signature Isabel million word a minute explanation." The other brothers nodded and chuckled probably because they found it to be a really annoying thing about her. "Her ramble included the idea that it would be easy to move on because we hadn't had sex."

They hadn't had sex yet?

That surprises me. If she was a girlfriend, they had to have more than three dates.

"Since as far as we had gotten is a blow job, she suggested it would be no big deal." He holds his fingers up in air quotes, "So, 'What's one little blow job between friends.' Didn't mean whatever you thought it meant."

Four sets of blue eyes bear down on me.

Shit, that's what was going on? He was breaking up with her to be with me. I fucked this up big time.

Zack leans back in his chair and kicks out his feet. "I've never had a friend offer me a blow job, but if any friends in this room were to make that offer, I sure as hell wouldn't say no."

Xander punches him in the arm. Connor pulls me into a tighter embrace. Morgan takes off his baseball cap and begins hitting him with it across the table. "What the fuck Zack, you can't talk to Sam like that."

Zack holds up his hands in defense and snatches Morgan's hat before he can be swatted again. "My point is, are you really begrudging him a no strings attached blow job? Sam, you're our friend. Don't be a cockblock."

I roll my eyes. "I'm sorry X. I belong to all of you and I come without," I make air quotes, "benefits." I sigh, "I thought you were looking for a different dynamic. One my heart can't do."

I hope he understands the meaning. It can't just be a kiss.

He stands up, pushes in his chair and fixes his wounded eyes on me. "You know me. You know me better than anyone. You know there is nothing casual about me. You said if you aren't giving your heart, soul, mind, and body to one woman, it's cheating. I'm not a cheater. You need to right yourself." He motions to Zack. "Climb on his motorcycle and get a little wind therapy." He motions to Morgan, "Curl up with his homemade chicken soup and have a good cry." He motions to Connor, "grab the popcorn and have an all-night movie marathon." He slides around the kitchen table yanks me out of Connors laps and holds me to him by my upper arms. "Baby, if you want time with me… you need to take care of your hang ups first." He releases my arms and calls out over his shoulder from the hallway. "You know where to find me. I won't wait forever."

The door slams and my heart fractures right along with it.

What choice did I have? I climbed on the back of Zacks motorcycle. After strategically slipping a Wonder Woman action figure in one of his saddle bags. Zack and I have had our own longstanding version of Elf on a Shelf. It started when I stuck Wonder Woman in his backpack one morning as we were heading off to school. The top half was sticking out of the pocket waving her hand up and it created quite a stir. He hid it in my bookbag, I hid it in his football duffle. Soon it escalated to lockers, cars, and one morning I woke up in New York with her on my pillow. He wasn't even in town. If the goal is to release stress, this is helping.

Wrapping my arms around his waist, I look at the beauty of the country that surrounds our city. Wind therapy, that's what Zack calls it, and it is an excellent way to clear the cob webs and soften the tension. We stop in a deserted place near the water.

This used to be a mining town. When the land was stripped of its resources, they imploded the mines and filled them with water. We have a large chain of lakes, ponds, rivers, and several small waterfalls. I bet it's prettier now than it was one hundred years ago.

Sitting on the grass next to the motorcycle, I lean my head on his shoulder. We watch the sun dip into the water while the sky turns the prettiest pinks, purples, and gold.

"What's going on with you, girl?"

I let out a breath and my lips flap together in frustration. "What's not going on?" I push the hair back from my face and try to explain. "You see that perfect sunset?" I motion across the lake. "My whole life I've gotten small glimpses of it but was too afraid to sit and absorb it. When it's gone, it's dark. There will be another sunset, but none as perfect as this one. I've only taken in small glimpses, so it will always be there. If I sit and absorb everything it has to offer, I could lose it forever." My shoulders fall. "I guess I'm trying to grasp sunlight without getting burned."

A small deep laugh rumbles in his chest. "I have no idea what that is supposed to mean, but if grasping sunlight completes you, if holding on makes you happy, you need to risk getting burned." He wouldn't feel that way if he knew what getting burned means.

While we were out, Morgan made his famous chicken noodle soup. It's actually his mother's famous chicken noodle soup, but I never call him out on it. Since high school, whenever I was sick or sad, he made me soup. It's not just comfort food. Every part of Morgan is my hearth. My dad came home, saw Fisher's in my house and soup on the stove. He took a bowl to his bedroom kissing me goodnight. He knows that if more than one man is in the house with a pot of soup it's nothing he wants to deal with. My dad is a smart man.

I curl up with Connor and Morgan eating soup and watching chick flicks until midnight. Morgan excuses himself, he has work in the morning. Connor takes me to bed and spoons me for an hour.

"I really have to go Sam I Am. I have a four-hour drive to the airport. I should have been sleeping."

"Do you need me to drive with you?"

He kisses my temple. "No, I just downloaded a new sci-fi book about a universe named Bob. I'll be okay. You get some sleep, and I'll see you on skype night." He kisses my temple again. "Love you, Sam."

When I hear the front door close, a tear slips down my cheek. I don't want to lose my weekly skype date. Part of my rational brain thinks I should just drop the pursuit of Xander. It's the rest of me that isn't so convinced.

My bedroom door opens, and I sit up when I see Xander. He holds up his hand in a stop motion. "I'm too old to climb a ladder with dry rot. I used the front door. I know my place in making you yourself. We aren't having this discussion tonight."

He reaches back for the neck of his shirt and pulls it off over his head. He climbs into my childhood bed like he's done a hundred times before, wrapping me in his strong inked arms, my cheek on his chest. Slowly, I drift off to sleep, as I've always done.

I wake up alone, and with a renewed sense of myself and what I need.

CHAPTER 19

Beautiful art that burns.

Xander

I didn't want to sneak out of her bed, but she was crying when I walked in. She isn't ready to face what comes next. Still, having her in my arms, her soft breath on my chest... Well, I could see us like that every night, forever.

Looking at the schedule I'm relieved to see a full line-up of clients today. Getting lost in art work is therapeutic for me.

Zack is here early. He's never here early. We have a drafting table in the back corner where we can sketch designs. He is so enthralled in his sketch he doesn't even notice me. He usually has ear buds in when he sketches, so he didn't hear the bell over the door ring. I walk closer until he looks up at me and pulls out his ear bud.

"Hey bro, new client?" I ask.

"No, I'm not sure who this is for. I had to get it out of my head and onto the paper. You know?" *I do.* Sometimes a design just speaks to me, too.

"May I see it?"

"It's not done yet." This is another way we differ. I can show him my work at any phase. Hell, he can even watch me draw. He doesn't like anybody to see his work until it's done. His favorite clients are the ones that close their eyes and go to sleep while he works. I like to engage my clients.

Disinfecting my work station, I throw on my beanie and adjust my mind set. Sam taught herself how to crochet watching You Tube videos. She hates how shabby her first piece of work turned out, but I love it. It holds my hair out of my face, and it was the first thing Sam ever made. I like to start my day thinking of her.

"Yo, Zack! What's for lunch?" I look over to him where he is painting with watercolors. That's new.

He looks up from the drafting table and shrugs. "It's up to you?"

Pulling up the menu on my phone from a restaurant named *It's Up to You*, I glance at Today's soup of the day. Making my decision I look up at Zack. "Your usual?"

He nods. "It's finished, do you want to see?"

Getting up from my workstation, I head to the back. Zack's artwork although usually very dark is intriguing. I love to see what he comes up with. He always has hidden meanings, secondary pictures, and obscure symbols. You can't glance at his artwork. You have to stop and really take it in to see it.

Today, however, is different. I'm not accustomed to seeing bold colors and peaceful imagery. "Dude, that's beautiful! What brought this out of you?"

Pride is evident in his smile. "Something Sam said."

I tilt my head to look at the sketch again. I can understand Sam being an inspiration for such beauty, but as I absorb the beautiful sunset, I see the water it dips in are actually hands.

The bright sunshine and setting colors are flames as it hits the hands. At a glance, it is a beautiful sun setting in a body of water, but at closer inspection, it's dark and haunting. Typical Zack, but how did Sam lead him here? "Walk me through it."

"We were watching the sunset at Lake Shirley and I asked her what was going on with her." I nod. "She said she was trying to keep this beautiful perfect sunset. She never stopped to admire it, because then it would set beyond the horizon and be gone. Now that she has decided to take it in, she's trying to figure out how to catch the sun without getting burned."

I may be able to paint a perfect picture, but Sam can paint with words.

Baby, I want the sun, too.

"That's really powerful."

Zack nods. "It is. I have no idea what she means, but she painted the imagery so clear in my head I can't think of anything else.

"When she was young, she was so high strung, we would throw her in water when her emotions got away with her. It was the only way to settle an impending panic attack. She learned to control them as she grew up. Well, mostly anyway." We both laugh. Sam feels everything with so much passion it seeps out of her sometimes. "It looks like you made her gloves of water. She would find them calming and protecting."

"I appreciate that you understand my art."

"I got ya, bro."

Walking back to my station I slide into my phone and place our lunch order. I take off my beanie and run my fingers through my hair. How do we fix this? How can I get the girl without losing my brothers? They're my brothers. They have to forgive me. That isn't really my concern. My worry is that she will resent me if she loses her best friends.

CHAPTER 20

Guy friends are guy friends until they have a girlfriend.

Sam

When she answers with a tired hello, I begin pacing and spilling the thoughts from head rapidly. "Rika, I'm okay now."

She giggles into the phone. "Hello to you, too." I'm too excited for telephone etiquette. Once I got out of my own head, I had an epiphany.

"I admit, sometimes I bottle everything up, and when I explode, I can't contain the fire."

Since the incident, My Fisher Men have all found a way to douse the flames. Last night was no different.

Leaning back on my bedroom wall, I white knuckle the phone. "The thing is, I managed for four years without them. I am stronger than I give myself credit for. I indulge in the solace of my boys because they're available."

She giggles again. "Well, that is an epiphany."

"That's not the epiphany." I shake my head even if she can't see me. "It's not always going to be like this."

"What do you mean?" she asks.

"Do you really think that when Morgan gets married and has a family, he's going to come to make me soup when I'm sick? Or Connor's wife will scooch over while we Skype our weekly movie date? I can't see what ever freaky goth girl Zack ends up with waving goodbye when I climb on the back of his motorcycle to go watch the sunset."

"I suppose not."

"Guy friends are guy friends until they have a girlfriend. I've always known that." I slide my back down the wall until I am sitting on the floor. "I've been patient this long, I can wait until they move on before I pursue Xander. Nobody has to get hurt."

"What if Xander moves on."

My fists clench. "Then what choice do I have. If Xander falls in love with someone else, I'll leave."

After I shower, dress, and eat I feel human again. Sliding into my phone, I send Xander a text. I've decided that he should know my plan. Choosing to wait should be his decision, but he should at least know my intentions.

Sam: I'm ready to talk now. Come by after work?

Xander: Sounds serious. How about my place.

Sam: Why?

Xander: I live alone. No need to disturb Dad.

Sam: Okay, what time?

Xander: I'll text you.

I know I'm going to Xander's house to explain that I want him, just not yet, but deep down, I think he may not feel the same. I don't want to be insecure. I don't want to second guess myself, but what woman doesn't? What person doesn't feel like they can't measure up?

My only defense is to look as good as I can. It's a fact. The better someone feels about themselves, the better everyone around them feels about them. So bring on the fake bravado and confidence, and let's rock this shit.

Confidence begins with the first layer. Scrubbing my skin with a sea salt scrub almost to the point of discomfort, shaving, and then soothing my skin in a hot oil bath ought to make my skin glow and hopefully not set off my Dermographism. I've learned a little vitamin E oil makes my inked chest shiny and new looking, so I slather a cotton ball in it and smear it into the tag over my heart. Stepping out of the bathroom, I feel radiant. My skin is soft and smooth. I can't help running my fingertips over it. Shit, I left marks.

Xander has always loved my skin flares. I, on the other hand, do not. Hopefully, it subsides. I hope polishing my skin until it is pretty will help me feel comfortable in it.

Next layer, my sexiest thong and matching bra. I know he won't be seeing this tonight, but when a woman looks sexy, she feels sexy even if nobody sees. Sliding the hot pink lace up my thighs, I love the contrast of it against my olive skin.

Wrapping myself in my ratty old robe, I take a seat at the vanity that once belonged to my mother and blow dry all the moisture from my heavy head. Sectioning off a lock of brunette silk, I flat iron my hair meticulously. My hair is so thick and long, it is easier to tie it up then to do this, but my hair is the thing I like the most about myself. I want it to be on display.

Drawing careful lines on my upper and lower lids has always been a challenge for me. With the help of You Tube and some nifty style guides, I have perfected the winged vintage look. I haven't seen Xander with a girl since the cute artist girl back in my spying days, but I think vintage is still his style. I know it's mine.

I tie my whole look together with a wrap dress. I found this amazing dress at a boutique on Long Island. I had to have it. It's black with pink polka dots. It closes with a wrap using large ribbons that make an adorable bow on my hip. Unlike a usual wrap dress, it has a big full skirt that comes mid-thigh on me. Pulling the bows as tight as I need on my waist, it fits me everywhere perfectly. I feel like I look like a million bucks covered in sex and ice cream.

Floating downstairs, I make a break for the kitchen. I'm a nervous eater, and nothing says tranquility like a big old can of Pringles. Popping the lid on my salvation, I'm pissed to find /Wonder Woman and a note. *I didn't eat your Pringles, Wonder Woman did! I bought you a new can and hid them on top of the refrigerator since you can't see up there it's a perfect hiding spot. Love Ya, Shorty!*

I smile and climb from the chair to the counter to get my chips. *Asshole!*

A surge of excitement ripples through my blood when he texts.

Xander: Leaving the shop now. See you soon.

I haphazardly slide into my pink Chucks. I'm aware strappy heels or Mary Janes would work better with this dress, but until Chucks come with a heel, it isn't happening.

I bounce like Tigger down my porch stairs and leap into my pick-up. I'm not thrilled about the conversation I'm about to have, but I'm so happy to be seeing Xander. I miss him. Zack may be my wings, and Connor may be my laugh, Morgan may be my hearth, but Xander is the missing piece of my soul.

I hit the puzzle piece hanging from my rearview mirror. It's from a puzzle I did in therapy. Dr. Sumner said that when I look at a puzzle with a missing piece all I'm seeing is the holes. I need to learn to look around them and see the picture forming and understand that like the puzzle, I haven't found all my pieces. I'm on my way to being whole again. I stole a piece and made it into a keychain because, after the incident, I felt like something would always be missing.

A gorgeous puzzle that is missing a piece is still beautiful, but the tiny missing piece is blaringly obvious. That's how I felt after the incident. I feel like everyone could see that something was missing. Xander held me every night and slowly he filled all the holes. He is intricately woven into the person I am.

With my mind wrapped up with thoughts of puzzles, sunsets, and Xander, I barely remember the drive. Dropping my speed, I keep my eye out for children while I turn into his neighborhood. He rents the first floor of a Brownstone in a nice neighborhood. Kateri's friend owns the building. On shaky legs, I pull myself together and knock. My resolve of a frank conversation, an unromantic evening, and the parting as friends a bit longer, melts when he beams that panty melting smile at me. Oh, my word, my ovaries are shooting eggs like basketballs and my uterus is the basket begging for Xander Freaking Fisher to shoot.

CHAPTER 21

I have a counter proposal.

Xander

Are you even shitting me right now? I open the door to find my best friend made up like every man's wet dream. I smile politely and think calming thoughts to stave off what will shortly be a raging hard on. She had better be here with a plan on how this will work because if she's here to say goodbye, I'm tying her to my fucking bed.

Shit!

That mental image did it.

Now I'm hard. I escort her into the kitchen careful to stay behind her. The swish of her dress atop her smooth shapely legs is mesmerizing. Fuck, fuck, fuck!

"I'm making burgers. Did you eat?"

She shakes her head and steals a piece of bacon before hopping up to sit on the counter. The skin of her legs looks smooth and tan. I so badly want to trail my fingers up them followed by my tongue. Fuck! This is Sam, this is Sam, this is Sam! I shake my head to clear the naughty thoughts pooling in my dirty mind.

"Do you want cheese on yours?"

She hops off the counter and sidles over to the refrigerator. "What kind of cheese?"

"You hate American cheese. Why would I keep such contraband in my home?"

She spins around holding the sharp cheddar in her hands. Sharp cheddar is her favorite. She's beaming a smile that takes my breath away.

"This. This is why I love you." She sets the cheese on the counter and wraps her arms around my waist.

Bending down, I kiss her lips slowly. "I love you more Sparkle Pants!" This exact exchange has happened a hundred times, but since she kissed me, everything feels more romantic. Even the nickname she garnered after being forced to wear sequined hot pants under her cheerleading uniform, seems intimate. Her wide eyes tell me she feels it, too.

Burgers. Get back to the burgers. Don't put your mouth on hers, don't pick her up and slam her to the nearest wall, don't take her to bed. Feed her a freaking hamburger.

Sitting at the counter with our burgers and chips we chat idly about her prospects for finding a job. Every now and then her arm brushes against my arm and a jolt of electricity shoots through me. I'm anxious to hear what she has to say, but we take our time getting there.

After we clean up dinner, I lead her to the couch and pull her into my lap. I've pulled her into my lap every time I see her for almost a decade, but now I wonder if I am supposed to.

"Okay Baby, let's hear what you got rattling around in that beautiful brain of yours."

She looks up at me with soulful eyes. "Do you have feelings other than friendship for me?"

Seriously? I'm in freaking love with her. Why are girls so blind? "Yes, I do."

She tries to conceal her smile. "Would you consider pursuing a relationship with me someday?"

Someday? How about right fucking now! "What's your plan?" I ask.

She takes a deep breath. "You know I love your brothers, and you guys have a pact to not pursue me."

I chuckle. "My brothers will forgive me. We're family."

The color drains from her face. "They may not forgive me so quickly, and our entire dynamic will change."

I shake my head. "So, you don't want to upset the dynamic?"

"No, but I want to see where this," she motions between us, "goes."

Again, I ask, "What's your plan?"

"It won't always be that way. One day they are going to meet women that knock their socks off, and those women won't allow them to have in bed movie dates, wind therapy, or chicken soup and cuddle nights with me."

I nod. Her point is valid.

She sighs. "We've waited a long time to admit feelings. I propose we wait until they have moved on before we pursue one another."

Fuck no! That is NOT happening!

I have waited long enough. She wants me. I have always wanted her. We're both single. I don't give a shit what my brothers think.

Calming myself, I clear my throat. "I have a counter proposal."

She shrugs. "Okay."

"The dynamic with my brothers is going to change someday anyway. I think our dynamic needs to change today. Let's see how this goes for ninety days."

She draws her eyebrows in, "Excuse me?"

"My sister had this dating rule. In order to sort attraction from substance, she wouldn't engage in any sexual contact for the first ninety days of a relationship. She required a weekly date and if one week was missed, the clock started over again. She never told her prospects about the rules. If they were generally interested they stuck it out. She could easily separate the players from the good men in ninety days." Sam nods her eyebrows still drawn in. I kiss her forehead and smile. "We already know that we love one another. We don't know if a relationship would work between us. If I understand you as well as we both know I do, that's your concern. What if you lose all the Fisher Men?" She seals her lips shut but doesn't say anything because I'm right.

"I suggest a secret romantic relationship for ninety days to see if we will work. If we do, time to break the news to my brothers. If we don't you changed the dynamic with only me. You still have your wind therapy, movie nights, and chicken soup. Eventually, you'd have me, too. I'll be wrecked for a while, but I could never hate you."

She reaches her hand up my shirt and runs her fingers up and down my chest. It's a thing she does. "By romantic relationship, you mean everything we have now, plus sex?"

"I place a strong need for love and commitment on sex, so, not at first, if at all in those ninety days."

Her face draws back in surprise. "What?"

"I mean it. I am not a man whore. I don't do casual."

She squints in disbelief. "So how many women have you been with?"

"Two."

She curls into my chest. "You've been in love twice?"

"No, girl number one was the reason for the rules. I didn't love her. We were together for a year, and I didn't look at her the way my dad looks at my mom. In truth, I wasn't capable yet. I just felt like something was wrong. It was all about mechanics and not about emotion. I want what my parents have, and I'm willing to wait and work for it."

She runs a thumb over my cheek and kisses me softly. "You have such a good heart. And girl number two?"

"A drunken weekend in Vegas that lead to bad decisions."

She chuckles. "I remember your trip to Vegas. That wasn't long ago."

We sit in comfortable silence her face snuggled into my chest. I could hold her here forever.

She sits up abruptly, "You do other things, right?"

I smirk an evil grin at her. "Deliciously."

Her cheeks pink and she fans herself. "Whew, is it getting warm in here?"

"Seriously Sam, what do you think about giving us a try?"

She shrugs. "I think it combines everything we want and need. I say we go for it."

I can feel the tips of my smile touch the tops of my ears. "Good, because I have one other proposal." I kiss her nose.

"What's that?" She asks coyly.

"Move in with me."

CHAPTER 22

The crowd goes wild or maybe it's just me. Yes, me. I go wild.

Sam

Surely, I didn't hear that right. "Huh?"

"Move in with me. As far as everyone is concerned, I have a spare room so you don't have to stay with your dad. We can be roommates. Nobody would question you being with me all the time. I say if ninety days is a test, lets up the difficulty level."

"Moving in together is a huge step, X. We kissed ONCE! Now you want to skip the toothbrush and a change of clothes phase and go straight for the unclogging my hair from the bathtub drain phase?"

"How is it any different from sleeping in your bed almost nightly in high school. Oh, and I've unclogged your bathtub drain before. I bought you the hair catcher thingies. As far as the toothbrush and a change of clothes, what do you think my trips to New York were like?" He cups my chin. "Sam, move in with me." He kisses me. "You know it isn't scary." He kisses me again. "You know you want to." This time when he kisses me, I submit. Resistance is futile. I want to move in. It's fear that made me hesitate. I open my mouth and as our tongues explore one another, the thought of suitcases and logistics melts away with the passion of the moment.

I can't tell you how much time has passed, but eventually, I untangle myself from Xander and stand up next to him. "Dude, if sex is off the table, we need to slow down."

I stumble to the bathroom on weak knees listening to his chuckle behind me. Looking into the mirror I'm excited and horrified by my appearance. My hair looks freshly fucked and my lips are swollen. While Xander's view on sex is admirable, it's going to be the death of me.

I want him… badly.

I finger comb my hair the best I can and dab a little cool water on my face before heading back into the living room. I find him in the kitchen, where he looks up at me with his brilliant smile.

"Hey, baby." He pauses putting ice in a pitcher to give me a kiss. "Do you want to go get your stuff tonight or tomorrow?"

"Part of me wants to just wait until tomorrow while you're at work, but I don't have a hair or toothbrush."

He nods. "Chrissy left some stuff under the bathroom counter, and I have extra toothbrushes. If you want to stay, stay."

I still can't get used to her being called Chrissy rather than Kateri. She's been Chrissy a long time, but my relationship was with Kat.

"What are you making?" I ask.

He turns off the burner and sets the pot to the side.

"Iced Tea." He adds a collection of tea bags and sugar before stirring. "I need to pour it in the pitcher of ice in a minute." His phone rings obnoxiously loud startling me.

Glancing at the display he informs me, "It's my mom. I'll be back in a minute." He swipes to answer and steps out of the kitchen area to take the call.

My postponed thoughts on luggage and logistics return to the forefront as I absentmindedly stir the boiling tea and sugar. I should just pour it over the ice before it goes bad. I peek around the corner and see Xander writing stuff on the dry erase calendar in his hallway still talking to his mom.

Watching the steam rise quietly from the pot, I consider buying Xander a teapot. This regular pot screams *I'm a bachelor without kitchen appliances*. Steeping the tea bags one last time I squeeze out the access tea and throw the used bags away. I'm debating the least messy way to pour the tea in the pitcher. The other downfall to not having a teapot is the mess this is going to make. I decide setting the pitcher in the sink is my best option.

Lifting the heavy pot with both hands I carry it slowly to the sink. Xander walks in scaring the life out of me. I jump, and the pot hits the edge of the counter, dumping boiling tea down the front me.

Fuck!

I untie the wrap dress and tear the scalding scraps from my body.

Xander picks me up and whisks me off to the bathroom quickly. He climbs into the shower with me and turns on the cool water. The water is almost painfully cool, but it feels nice.

He begins cupping the water and smoothing it down my skin. At first, it was out of necessity, but now his movements are losing the haste they began with. Slowly, his hands cup and pour water in gentle ripples over my breasts. Each wave of cool water and warm hands force my skin to goose-bump. His cooling touch gives way to smooth flat hands down my abdomen. His hot breath in the bend of my neck. I have only just become aware that I am standing under the water in my sexiest bra and panty set.

Tenderly, he kisses my shoulder "Are you okay, Baby?"

Turning to face him I look down to access damages. There is a strip of red skin across my waistline where the dress was cinched. "No more than a sunburn, I suppose. I think it startled me more than anything else."

He runs his fingertips across the pink swollen patch. "Just here, anywhere else?" His voice is husky, low, and oozes sex.

I swallow hard and shake my head. Dropping to his knees he wraps his large hands around my hips and pulls me to his face. He peppers soft kisses and light sucks across the damaged skin, licking the droplets of water sprinkling my abdomen. Holy fuck! My ovaries line up the shot, they shoot, they score! The crowd goes wild, or maybe it's just me. Yes, me. I go wild.

Fisting his wet t-shirt, I yank it over his head and bury my fingers in his hair. The low rumble of pleasure escapes my mouth unexpectedly forcing Xander's wet eyelashes steaming around fire filled eyes to burn holes into mine. Gradually, he rises dragging his fingertips up my sides. Standing, he traces my tattoo with the barest touch followed by his lips. I moan my approval and climb him like a tree, wrapping my legs around his hips. Tipping us slightly, he turns off the water and crashes his mouth to mine.

In a tangle of fingers, tongues, lips, and beads of water we tumble in a dizzied frenzy through the bathroom door and onto the bed. Pinning my arms down he continues to violate my senses. Every nerve in my body is heated. I know he said sex is off the table right now, but the erection grinding me through his basketball shorts has other ideas.

Taking his hands off my wrists he glides his fingertips down my shoulders taking my bra straps down with them. My breasts spill over the lace demi cup. He gazes at them appreciatively. Taking my nipple into his mouth, my back arches off the bed and I hiss. He moans against my skin. Slowly he trails his mouth down my abdomen, my fingers raking through his hair.

His mouth cups my pussy with only a thin layer of lace as a barrier. The heat of his breath on my sensitive bits makes my head spin and my skin flush.

"Baby, you are so wet." I arch my hips upward needing to feel more but a sound in the distance distracts me.

"What was that?" I ask.

He slides off the bed groaning and adjusting a seriously endowed package in his still shower wet shorts.

"It's the doorbell. It's Zack. He has a key, so I have to answer it. Put on my shorts and a t-shirt and come out." He motions to the dresser by the closet. "I'll cover for you. Follow my lead." I nod and scramble off the bed.

Reaching into Xander's drawer for shorts, I realize they are so long, they go past my knee. I look like a little girl playing dress up. Dropping the shorts takes no effort, so I put on a pair of his boxer briefs instead. They are so baggy they look like regular shorts. I tie up a corner of the Xanack Tattoo t-shirt and follow the sound of my boisterous boys out to the living room.

CHAPTER 23

I don't have my ducks in a row. I have squirrels... and they're having a rave.

Xander

I grab towels on my way to the door and set them on the kitchen counter. Opening the door with one hand I drag the other through my hair. I'm mussing my mane in full view so it looks like I did this to my hair.

"Hey Bro, come in. Sam spilled boiling tea on herself, I'm just cleaning up in the kitchen."

"Shit, is she okay?"

I shrug knowing she is way better than okay. She's a horny little minx, and she's mine. "I think so. I got her dress off her right away and dumped her in a cool shower. She's looking for clothes in my room."

Zack chuckles and grabs a towel to help me clean the mess. "Dude, no wonder you're so frazzled. You saw Sam naked!" He punches my arm.

Running the towel over the counter and now cool stovetop, I look over my shoulder at my twin and roll my eyes. "She has a bra and panties on. All her bathing suit parts were covered."

"The awkward moment a girl walks into a room where two hot men are cleaning and discussing her bathing suit parts." Our heads snap up to see Sam with her arms folded over her chest leaning in the entryway. Seeing her in my clothes is hot, but the fact that she is wearing my underwear stirs the cock I worked hard at placing in submission. I swallow hard. Zack throws his head back laughing.

"Hey girl, it's funny you think that's the only time we've ever discussed your bathing suit parts." He crosses the room and lifts her in a hug. Setting her down, he plants a kiss on her cheek. "Seriously, are you hurt?"

"No, thank goodness Xander reacted so quickly." She lifts her shirt exposing the pink flesh across her waist. It's just a little irritated.

Zack checks the burn then looks over to me. "Where is Zan's key? She probably has burn cream or a first aid kit." He looks back at Sam, while I get the key out of a magnetic box on the side of the refrigerator. "Zan is our sister's best friend. She has an apartment upstairs. She doesn't live in it anymore, but since she is studying to be a paramedic, she's probably prepared." He shrugs his shoulders and takes the key from me.

When the front door latches closed, I rush Sam kissing her like I may die if I don't. "That was too close, we can't move that fast. We haven't even had a first date yet." I pull her tighter against me. "Damn if it wasn't perfect though." I quirk my mouth in a smirk. "Baby, I bet you taste amazing." She smiles as her face flushes.

"You were expecting Zack?"

I drop my embrace. "Yes, we made plans to go to Murphy's for burgers and to shoot pool. He got an upsetting phone call on his Safe Spaces phone. I wanted to check on him. I completely forgot about it." I scoot all the wet towels and Sam's dress into a pile in the middle of the floor.

"Maybe I should go home, pack and put clothes on. You two can still go through with your plans."

I want Zack to go and Sam to stay. She's right though. I hug her again and whisper in her ear. "I'd rather pick up where I left off. I was just about to peel your panties off and plunge my tongue inside of you." She swallows hard and her muscles tense. "If you promise to sleep in my bed tonight, I'll let you go get clothes." She smiles sweetly and I break away from her to put the soiled towels and her dress into a garbage bag destined for the laundry room.

The sound of Zack's boots clopping down the stairs above us echoes in the kitchen before the door latch clicks. He begins speaking before he even closes the door.

"I called Zan while I was up there." Zack rounds the counter with a bottle of aloe-vera and a change of clothes. "She said you can have these." He pushes the clothes into Sam's chest while reading the bottle intently.

Taking Zan's gifts, Sam excuses herself to my bedroom. Stupid Zack, I fucking love her in my clothes. I don't want her to change.

I wet a sponge and wipe down the sticky counters. "Hey, I'll be ready to go in a minute. Let me just mop the sticky floor." Zack nods.

We both turn when the bedroom door opens. Sam looks uncomfortable.

"I am guessing Zan is a tiny woman?" she asks.

I hadn't considered that. She is crazy strong with muscles, toned and cut like a bodybuilder, but her frame is small. She's so skinny, she has to run around in the shower to get wet. Sam has a woman's curves. She has shapely legs, hips to hold on to, a round ass, and amazing tits. Amazing tits that are on full display in one of Zan's tiny, form fitting t-shirts. Her bra isn't dry yet, so looking at her presents us with an eyeful of sex perfection. I smack the back of Zack's head. He doesn't know he's ogling my woman. but he knows he shouldn't be staring at Sam like that.

"Sam, go get a hoodie." I point to my bedroom door trying desperately to avoid looking at her perfectly pebbled nipples. She looks down at her shirt and immediately crosses her arms.

She glares at Zack. "I'm a woman not a hunk of sirloin."

His guilty expression speaks volumes. She turns on her heel to stomp away, the too tight yoga pants clinging deliciously to her ass. Fuck me. I smack Zack again for good measure. He punches me back.

"Why is she here anyway? Did you invite her to join us?"

"No, her Dad is dating, she feels intrusive at home. I told her she can move into my spare room."

That's a lie and I hope it doesn't come up in conversation ever.

He quirks an eyebrow at me. "I have a spare room, too." He doesn't but it doesn't matter.

"I told her any of us would be happy to have her, but you can suck it because I asked her first."

Zack flips me the bird. "Fucker, she bakes brownies when she's stressed, and you get dibs."

"I'll bake a separate batch just for you." Sam walks into the kitchen wearing my hoodie and beaming a smile.

"Hey girl, speaking of stress, what are your career prospects here?"

Sam lets out a sigh and plops onto one of the seats at the counter. Her shoulders drop. She looks so defeated.

"I don't have my ducks in a row. I have squirrels… and they're having a rave." She drops her head into her folded arms on the counter.

Poor Sam.

Zack smooths her hair. "Why don't you come have a drink with us. Let's chase away the moon over my Sammy."

"No, I look indecent. I need to go home and pack, too." She slides off the stool and hugs each of us. "Have fun boys." She fixes a heated stare on me. "I'll see you later." *Yeah, she will.*

CHAPTER 24

He made my bones buzz. He wasn't just nice; he was soulful and deep.

Sam

Walking into the house, my dad peers around the corner from the kitchen. "Hey, Sweet Pea. Are you alone?" I smile at the endearment. My dad is not very social and painfully shy. Over the years, he's warmed up to the Fisher Brothers, but he really is most comfortable with our one-on-one moments.

Embracing him in a hug, I melt. I've missed my dad and haven't had a moment with him yet. "Hey, Daddy. Sorry. You know my routine. I come home get pissy with the Fishers, and they spend the night making me regret it."

Chuckling, he untangles from my arms. "They're good boys. I'm glad it's all worked out then. You never had siblings, so now you know what you're missing." He winks.

"Are you still seeing Rose?" I ask cautiously. Dating has never really been my dad's forte.

"Yes." He turns to stir the contents of a pot on the stove. "I really like her. She doesn't seem put off by my…" He waves the wooden spoon but promptly returns it to the pot with a sigh.

"Your intelligence, kindness, and your beautiful daughter?" I chide.

Glancing over his shoulder at me, he beams. "You are beautiful, but I mean my awkwardness."

I wrap my arms around his waist. "Not everyone wants or needs a man to be the center of attention. Some women appreciate a quiet gentleman. I'm happy you found someone who appreciates you." He pats my head resting on his shoulder.

"Thank you."

"I love you, Daddy." I return to my seat at the kitchen table. "I'm moving in with Xander." He puts down the spoon, turns off the burner, and faces me, wiping his hands on a towel.

"Are you moving in as his other little sister, or are you finally going to pursue the brother you leer at just a bit longer than the others?"

Shocked, I look up at him. Opening my mouth, I snap it shut again. I'm not sure how to respond.

A small laugh escapes his smile. "Yes, I know. I know about the pact, too. I know he and Connor shared your bed almost nightly and I knew you weren't being pursued romantically." He leans back against the counter. "You have always looked at him the way your Mama used to look at me. I remember the instant she stopped looking at me like that, too. Be careful, Sweet Pea. Somethings can't be undone."

My eyes drop to my lap. "I know, Daddy. I have to see where this goes. I don't want to live a life of what ifs." He crosses over to me and kisses the top of my head.

"I wouldn't have you any other way."

Packing my truck is pretty easy. I never really unpacked. After promises of visits and phone calls, my dad hugs me and sends me on my way.

Gripping the steering wheel, I stare out on to the parkway. I'm nervous about whatever is going to happen next. I'm excited, but what if... The thoughts trail off as I pull out of my parking spot. I decide a visit to Rika is in order.

Friends are good for forming plans and thinking out loud. Taking the elevator up to Connor's condo, I'm practically shaking with excitement. I can't wait to tell her all of my developments.

My fist barely left the door with my first knock when it flew open. "Samantha Reynolds you have some explaining to do."

I drop my hand still poised in a knock form and open my mouth. "Uh," *what am I supposed to be explaining?* Rika grabs my arm and yanks me into the apartment positioning me in front of the photo over the fireplace.

"You never, not once, showed me a picture of the Fisher Men. You had these," she motions to the photo of the four boys on a beach, "In your pocket all this time and never thought to share one?"

I shrug. "I told you they are freaks of nature. I took that picture. It's one of my favorites."

She rolls her eyes. "I met the twins. Which one is Connor?" I point out Connor and she drops her hands to her thighs and glares at me. "That's my new roomie? Heaven help me. I might die if I listen to him having shower sex with some tart."

That won't be a problem.

I smile warmly at the photo. It was my senior year. We went to Key West for my spring break. I was in a bikini for a solid week. Fruity alcohol drinks were a first, and so was getting drunk.

"You had your pick of all of them. What made you pick Xander?" she asks accusingly.

I drag my eyes back up to the portrait and wrap my arms around myself. "From the moment we met, he stirred me. He wasn't just mouth-droppingly gorgeous. He made my bones buzz. He wasn't just nice. He was soulful and deep. He wasn't just friendly. He placed value on the needs of others. I was always more drawn to him." Looking away from the portrait, I turn to Rika with an excited smile. "I'm moving in with him."

"You know what this means. Don't you?" After a few swipes on her phone, the Bluetooth speaker blares "So What" by P!nk. Rika is all about the impromptu dance party. Three years of dance parties while we cook flood my memories. We sing loud and dance like toddlers. Collapsing on the sofa when the song ends, I take a moment to catch my breath.

"Thanks, Rika. You rock."

"Heck yeah, I do." She punches my arm. "Now, tell me all the details. I'll make popcorn if I can find some." I explain to her where the popcorn is with a smile. She and Connor are going to get along great.

I glaze over the intimate details in favor of detailing our agreement. Rika needs to understand that nobody can know Xander and I have begun a relationship outside of the friend zone.

"Oh, Sam." She clasps her fist to her chest, "How romantic."

"You think this arrangement is romantic?" I ask, unable to hide doubt in my tone.

Rika rolls her eyes. "Well, it's better than your idea of waiting for who knows how long. Yes, I think a quiet exploration of your feelings is romantic. I'm happy for you." Reaching across the sofa she embraces me. Every girl needs a Rika in her life.

We are torn apart by the ringing of my phone. A video call? Looking at the beautiful face lighting up my screen, I whisper. "It's Xander." I slide into the video call.

"Hey X"

"Hey, Roomie. Did you change your mind?"

Zack's face smashes against Xander's on my screen. "Hey girl, my place is still open if you changed your mind." He looks closer at the screen. "Why are you at Connor's place?"

Taking Rika by the shoulders I pull her into the frame with me. "I came to visit Rika. I thought I'd give you some extra twin time."

Zack rolls his eyes. "We don't have vaginas, Sam. We don't need twin time. I see his mug every fucking day. Now, get your fine ass over here so I can help this douche," he nudges his brother, "with unloading your stuff."

Xander puts Zack in a headlock. "Dude, how many times do we have to tell you, you can't talk to Sam like that." Taking a pillow off the sofa he begins whacking Zack in the head Morgan style. The phone tumbles to the floor and the screen goes dark.

"I guess I better get going before my boys kill one another."

Rika stands, grabbing her purse. "If I go with you, do you think Zack would give me a ride back? I can help you unpack."

Yanking her to me, I bounce excitedly, "That's a great idea."

We lock up the condo and head to the elevator arm in arm. "I may use you as an excuse to get Zack to leave. He likes to hang out with me longer than necessary to irk his brothers."

Rika winks, "I got ya, girl."

Xander

I don't want Zack here. He's going to help me carry Sam's stuff up and then he's going to find a movie, a card game, or something that keeps him here and keeps Sam out of my bed. I finally get to kiss her, touch her, and I want him to get the fuck out and leave me to it. In the same mind, I recognize how much he misses his friend. I miss her, too.

Sam has always had a way of painting words that speak to my brother in a way nobody else can. He has relied on her to put words to pain, fear, and anger. He used to respond with fists and blow ups. My brother is a better man because of Sam. She taught him to channel his ambition, as well as his hurt, into something beautiful. Xanack Ink would not exist without Sam's encouragement. She found a place where our very different, creative brains could meld and be successful. She handpicked a mentor for us. She introduced us to our purpose, our happiness, and our bond.

I can't deny him a friend who is responsible for molding the greatest parts of himself. She saw us as Zack and Xander from day one. I don't think she has ever thought of us as *the twins*. She may call us the twins. but we have always been two individuals in her mind. Even when she couldn't tell us apart, she knew us separately. I have to accept that my woman will always have a separate relationship with my brother.

When her truck pulls up and Zack's face lights up, I know I can step aside and let them have a connection that won't always include me. He loves her, not the same way I do, but the dynamic doesn't have to change. If he can accept she's mine in a different way, they can still have their wind therapy and life affirming conversations. He bounds down the stairs like he's on a pogo stick. She can still be his sounding board on life and love.

"Hey girl!" Zack scoops Sam up in a hug as soon as he barrels out the front door. Quietly exiting the building in Zack's wake, I hug Rika and exchange pleasantries. The look she gives me tells me she knows. I'm guessing Rika is a girl you don't keep secrets from. We both seem resolved to not mention it.

Each of us takes a box from Sam's truck and head back to my apartment. I hate that we are putting her things in my guest room. I don't want her in there. While Zack and I unload the truck in a few more trips, Rika and Sam begin unpacking. I didn't expect to be so bothered by photos on the nightstand, paintings on the walls. It looks like Sam's room. I want to have our room.

Rika asks Zack to go with her for a once over in the truck. She explains they are checking under seats and such. I barely hear them as I stare at Sam putting clothes in the dresser. *Those should be in our room.*

Now that my brother is gone, I lay voice to my thoughts. "What are you putting in our room?" She looks surprised.

Tilting her head, she grins at me. "All of it in ninety days. Remember?"

Hands in my pockets I lean on the doorjamb "I don't like your room being separate from mine."

Putting her hand on her hip she quips, "If you aren't happy with our current arrangement, I can pack this all back up."

"No." I look up at her, my chin still lowered and my voice quiet. "I just..." I throw my head back. I want to demand she move her shit in my room, and I want her to comply. I take a moment to remember this is Sam and I need to treat her in a way I'd expect a boyfriend to treat her. So, I go for honest. "I'm afraid you'll change your mind if you have a backup plan."

She places her hand on my cheek and forces my eyes to lock with hers. "Life is filled with choices, and that's a good thing. Now quit giving me shit, and let me choose you."

She's right. I let her know with a smile and a stolen kiss. Rika is loud enough to cue us in on the impending arrival of my brother.

Sam has a way of making me understand. If she moved in with no options, then she didn't choose me. Knowing that she doesn't have to live with me but chooses to feels good. I focus on knowing she doesn't have to sleep in my bed, but she could choose to. Having choices is sexy. I think I might like this after all.

While unpacking the last box, Zack pulls out cards against humanity. "We haven't played this in ages!"

I hang my head. Zack stammers excitedly throwing the box from one hand to the other, "let's play for shots."

Sam pats his head motherly. "Have fun with that, I'm going to bed."

She pushes us all out of her room and closes the door. Zack waggles his eyebrows at Rika. "She'll join us if it sounds like were having fun. What do you say?"

Rika looks pointedly at me. "Are you in?"

"Fuck no. I have a two-hour appointment first thing in the morning. Shots are the last thing I need to be doing."

Rika was unsure how to shut down the party. I gave her leverage.

She put her arm around Zack, "I need a ride home. I have samples from the Kentucky Bourbon trail and a coconut cake for anyone offering me a ride."

Zack smiles down at her. "No wonder Sam likes you. Let's go!" When they get to the front door he looks over his shoulder at me, "Goodnight, pussy."

"Goodnight, Asshole!"

The door closes with a victory clank, and I sprint for the locks and chain. I hear Sam's door click shut. Leaning against the door in her tiny sleep shorts and a tank top, her eyes travel from the floor to mine. Fuck, she's beautiful. The doors are locked, the chain secured, and in three strides my lips are on hers. She wraps her legs around my waist, and I have her pressed against her bedroom door.

My fingers dig into her waist. her ass, her breast. Anywhere I can touch while holding her to the door. I kiss her like the hungry man I am. The heat between us ignites and consumes me. I have no end, she has no beginning and a credit card couldn't slip between us. I have waited for an eternity to kiss the girl that owns my heart. It's surreal. This moment, like the last, is a fantasy born reality. She's mine.

Breaking our kiss in a heavy pant, she puts her forehead to mine. "I haven't had sex in a year, I'm clean, and I'm on birth control. Waiting ninety days is your idea, not mine. Say the word and my answer is yes." *Fuck!*

"Sam, I have loved you from the beginning. I can't just fuck you. I am so in love with you, and sex means something to me. It's love for me, not sex. Do you understand that?"

She slides down my body with a scowl on her face. "Who knows you better than me X? I am in love with you. I have your tag tattooed on my body. I chose you. I didn't ask you to fuck me. I told you I'm ready for the next step when you are."

Taking her hand, I pull her to the sofa to sit. "I'm scared. My concern is you are rushing me to sex because you're insecure about us. I'm insecure about us. We have a lifetime of love, but this…" I motion between us, "Is new, exciting, and a little terrifying. You're not just some girl. I'm not just some guy." I sigh. "We have too much invested. I want to hear my name leave your lips on a moan. I want to feel your pussy clench on my cock. I want all the physical pleasure we denied ourselves all this time, but I don't want it built on insecurity. I want you to know I'm not going anywhere, I need to know that your head is in the same place as mine."

She nods, but I can see how wounded she is. I pull her head to my chest and sprawl out on the couch with her. "A year ago? Who was he?"

She looks up at me with disbelief, "You want to know?"

"We couldn't talk about this before because it hurt. You're mine now. I want to know everything."

She sighs in resignation and gets comfortable. "There were four. When I first got to college, I was the only virgin. I'm certain of it, I wanted to know what all the hype was about. I started dating a guy with a reputation for being good in bed. After a few weeks of dating, we had sex a few times. I never heard from him again.

"Asshole."

She chuckles, "Yes, but that's what I was looking for. I wasn't after love and happily ever after. For goodness sakes, I had your initials tattooed on me."

I hug her tightly. "How did you explain that?"

"Honestly. I told anyone that asked the truth. Xander Oliver Fisher is my best friend and second love."

I quirk an eyebrow. "Second love?"

"Your brother-in-law was my first."

Pushing back abruptly, I almost yell, "Matt?" Admittedly I'm pissed and she can probably hear it in my voice.

"No, his brother. Colton BaddStone. He was the first boy I ever kissed. We were ten. He died that summer." *Wait, what?* Talk about a small world.

"Colton was the twin?" I ask.

Sam looks up at me. "Yes, how did you know that?"

"The BaddStones are my in-laws now. Piper is Colton's twin. She is supposed to get married in New York next year. I have my plane tickets. When I booked them, I booked an extended weekend so I could visit you. I better change that."

She nods. "Oh, wow!"

I'm surprised she is going to marry him, He seems like a douche and he perked my gaydar. I wave my hand in an erasing the whiteboard motion. "Enough about that, who was next?"

"I dated a few guys here and there, but sex is a third date thing, and I have really high standards thanks to you and your brothers. A guy from my journalism program, we broke up after a year when I won an award he wanted and he was a baby about it. A guy from my English class, I saw him having coffee with another girl and blew up at him. Turns out, she was his sister, but all my ugly was out on the table so we were done." I can't help but laugh at that.

"Guy four was the best story of humiliation. Rika and I shared a bathroom. One day I had to pee so bad, my bladder was about to explode, but I can hear Rika being fucked rather righteously in the shower. No way was I going to interrupt a girl having multiples. I couldn't take it anymore, so I plopped my barc ass on the kitchen sink for what felt like a forty-minute pee. Rika and her date stumble out of the bathroom barely covered in towels and catch me peeing in the sink. It was then I realized, hey I know that guy."

I burst out laughing. "Did Rika know?" I ask between breath catching guffaws.

She rolls her eyes, "Of course not, but seeing as we had sex in my bed the previous week you would think he would have recognized the place."

I wipe my tears and continue laughing. "What did you do?"

"I finished peeing, wiped myself with a paper towel. When I turned to clean the sink, I shouted over my shoulder 'carry on, but hey Rob… We're finished. Obviously.'"

My laughter halted abruptly. "Multiple orgasms and mind-blowing sex in the shower." I poke her with my finger. "Was he good to you, too?"

"I guess man-whores have the experience to be good, or maybe they get so many women because they're good in bed, to begin with? I don't know, but yes, I enjoyed sex with the two-timing asshole." That punched me in the gut in an unexpected way.

Sam looks at me with surprise. "Oh my god!" She slaps my chest. "You're insecure about having sex with me because of your lack of experience."

Am I?

"I am not. Well, yes, I am insecure. I am confident I can please you, so that isn't what my insecurity is all about."

Laying her head back on my chest she murmurs. "Good, because you brought me pretty damn close without sex. It's only going to get better."

I squeeze her tighter and kiss her head. "Fuck yeah, it is."

We lay in comfortable silence until her breathing evens and the faintest hint of a snore escapes her lips. Carefully, I lift her and bring her to bed. She looks unbelievable in my bed. Lifting my shirt over my head, I strip down to my boxer briefs and curl my best friend into my arms.

Diary of a Casual Observer,

Rumor has it that Samantha Reynolds was spotted moving her belongings into Xander Fisher's Brownstone apartment. Previous stats had Connor in the lead. What say you now?

Morgan 6%
Connor 44%
Zack 18%
Xander 32%

CHAPTER 25

Return it, he did.

Sam

The blaring alarm shook me senseless, and it took a moment to get my bearings. Waking up in unfamiliar surroundings can be jarring, but the low husky voice of a sleepy Xander rouses my memories.

"Good Morning Beautiful."

Attention men of the world, that is the perfect way to wake a woman. "I'm headed to the gym, lunch, and then work. You can go back to sleep if you want."

I can hardly manage a grunt before pulling him tighter to me. He lets out a low chuckle that shakes his bare chest against my cheek.

"It's not that I don't appreciate your counter offer, but I meet Morgan at the gym every morning. I can't have him popping in to drag me out of bed, now can I?"

I concede with nothing more than a sigh and the minor release of the grip my arms and legs have taken on him.

Squirming out from under my octopus limbs, Xander stands up. His morning wood is gloriously standing at attention in his boxer briefs. The boy is hung and curiosity is freaking killing me. He leaves the bedroom door open, giving me the opportunity to watch him take a towel from the linen closet and hang it in the bathroom before heading to the kitchen. A short time later, I hear the blender whir.

Stretching, I climb out of bed and pad down the hallway. I halt at the sight of him. He is a beautiful man to watch. He notices me and smiles a sexy grin. The eggs in my ovaries are floating down to my uterus with heart shaped parachutes.

"Protein shake?" I ask, motioning to his blended concoction.

"Yes, you want to taste?"

Oh, I want to taste a protein shake and I want him to give it to me. I leave my thoughts in the gutter while plastering a smile on my face.

"Sure." I take a small sip. It tastes like powdery chocolate. "It's not bad, certainly not delicious." My crinkled nose probably says more than my words. Xander laughs before taking my chin and planting a sweet kiss on me.

"Morgan and I are going to lunch at 12:00. You're welcome to join us, otherwise, I'll be home around 7:00 tonight." He makes his way to the bathroom pausing in the hallway. "The Wi-Fi password is 'Sexy Samantha kissed me first.'" He winks before strutting to the shower.

I watch his ass all the way down the hall. Damn, I am one lucky girl.

I float into my room to pick out today's clothes. Stepping out of my pajamas, I slide into my silk robe and round up my shower caddy. Two girls with one bathroom made leaving bath and beauty products in the bathroom inefficient. We each had a caddy we carried back and forth. I don't foresee it being an issue with Xander.

I meander into Xander's room and set my caddy on the nightstand. Taking a seat on the bed, I look around the room.

On the dresser, three picture frames are displayed. The first is a portrait of the Fisher Family. On the opposite end is the picture I took of the four Fisher brothers on the beach in Key West. The photo in the middle is from the same trip. We are sitting around a table; my bikini clad self is curled in my usual seat in Xander's lap. We are all smiling and happy. I enjoyed my college years, but I sure missed my boys.

The bathroom door opens, and stepping out in a cloud of steam is a low hanging towel wrapped around perfection. Holy hotness! He runs his hands through his wet hair casting water down his shoulders and chest. I swallow hard looking for moisture in my suddenly dry mouth. Slowly I stand. I feel like metal dragged to his magnet. We are chin to chest without conscious thought.

My dry mouth makes my voice breathy. "My turn in the shower?"

Leisurely, he nods before hooking his finger under my chin and bringing his lips to mine. Heat ignites in my core. I hope he gets past his abstinence agenda sooner rather than later because our chemistry has always been off the charts.

The devious part of my mind driven by apparent need unleashes my inner stripper. Feeling all kinds of confidence and a desire to push the envelope, I drop my robe. In all my naked glory, I stand before a slack jawed Xander Fisher wearing nothing but my smile. I slink around him and strut to the bathroom. Leaving the door open, I bend slowly and start the water. I grin when I hear his groan. Mission accomplished.

I glance over my shoulder and wink before stepping in the tub and closing the shower curtain, catching the final glimpse of his ticking jaw. I suppress a giggle. I am quite an evil minx.

The shower curtain slides open abruptly startling me stiff. Xander stands with my shower caddy in his hand, a smile on his face, and absolutely nothing else. His cock is hard, long, and thick, and holy hell… pierced. It is just as beautiful as the rest of him.

He clears his throat. "You forgot this?" I nod. "I thought I'd …" he winks, "return it." Handing the caddy to me, he smirks an evil sexy grin before turning on his heel and sauntering out in a brilliant imitation of my cockiness.

Closing the shower curtain, I shake my head. Return it, he did.

Xander

I need to be at the gym. I have an awful lot of frustration to lift out. Damn that siren is going to be the death of me. I need to abandon my resolve and make love to her. We're not moving forward like this. This game of cat and mouse is so sexy, fun even. There is a tiny piece of me who wants to keep playing the game, but the desire to be inside her is way stronger.

Adding a few pounds to the bar, I lay down and push out my frustration while Morgan spots me. A plan begins forming in my head with each inhale, but my brother's voice interrupts my thoughts. "You're in beast mode today. What's going on with you?"

I blurt out the truth before I realize it's leaving my mouth. "I saw Sam naked."

Morgan laughs. "Feeling a little frustrated then?" I roll my eyes at him. He has no idea. "Too bad you broke up with that fast-talking girl. Looks like you could use a good romp."

I shake my head. "You know I don't work like that."

"Yeah." Morgan puts the weight back on the rack and leans on it. "But you could." He winks.

I've never seen the appeal in sleeping around. I mean I like sex. It was designed to feel good; otherwise, we would have died out as a species.

We finish up our workout, shower, change and walk down to Xanack Ink. Morgan takes a seat at Zack's station while I begin setting up mine.

"What is your hang-up with sex? Are you a virgin?"

I look up at Morgan, frozen with my ink in hand. I'm obviously taken aback by the question. "No." He gives me a skeptical look. "Bethanie was my first and then there was that chick at Zan's wedding."

"You've dated a lot more women than that, so why did they make the cut?" Damn, Morgan isn't holding back. There is no skirting my big brother. He won't let it go. I sigh in resignation. He's probably going to call me a pussy.

"It was a series of events. First, we were all raised in a Catholic church, but I was in the children's choir and an altar boy. You barely paid attention. I was taught that sex was this amazing gift I would give my wife one day in the hopes of procreation. You snickered. It was hammered into my brain that I would cheat my wife and myself if it was wasted on any night other than my wedding night. I believed it whole heartedly. Until you and Connor started buying condoms and talking about sex."

I take the sketches my client and I prepared and hang them on the clipboard. Strangely, it is a rosary around praying hands with ethereal back lighting. "I had considered becoming a priest."

Morgan nearly springs from his seat. "What, why didn't I know that?"

I shrug. "I didn't tell anyone. The prospect of a celibate life made me more curious about sex. There was also this whole competitive brother thing hard-coded in our DNA. If you and Connor were having sex, then I needed to also." We smile at each other. He knows exactly what I mean. "Fortunately, Bethanie was curious, too. The summer before high school, we had sex. I knew nothing about how things were supposed to work. I felt stupid and freaked by the spot of blood on her sheets." Morgan nods, I guess that wasn't much different from his experience.

"That Sunday, I felt like I was going to burst into flames when I walked into the church." Morgan guffaws a full-on body shaking laugh. I throw my hand towel at him. "Stop laughing, I was really scared."

He folds my hand towel and puts it back by my sink. He's still smirking, but I continue. "When I realized nothing bad was going to happen, and mom and dad couldn't tell by looking at me, I couldn't get enough of her. We were like bunnies in heat doing it everywhere we could, even in Chrissy's tree house."

"I'm pretty sure all of us had a go in Chrissy's tree house." Morgan chides.

"Poor Chrissy." I shake my head. "Anyway, after nearly a year of a hormonally charged hump-a-thon, we had a scare. The condom broke, it was prime timing for her to have gotten pregnant, and we could do nothing but wait."

"Fuck, had you even started high school yet?"

"Barely; we were freshmen. While we were waiting to find out if we were also parents, there was a chlamydia outbreak on the football team. One of the cheerleaders tested positive, and it turns out she was popular for a few reasons."

Morgan begins emphatically pointing at me. "Dude! I remember that."

"This was when Sam became more prevalent in our lives. I began hanging out with her, I thought she was really cute, and I started to look at her a little differently. I thought giving me Sam was God's way of punishing me. Letting me know I picked the wrong girl too soon." Morgan puts his hand over his mouth casually but I know it's to cover a grin. "Fucker, stop laughing at me. I was only fourteen."

"I'm not laughing." *He is laughing.*

"I finally asked Sam what she thought. I asked if I was wasting something special on a girl I probably won't marry."

"Before or after the incident." I look at him incredulously. *Like I would ask such a thing after the incident.*

"Before. She said I would give my heart, soul, mind, and body to my wife one day and my wife will be grateful. She also said that if I am dividing those things between girls, it's cheating."

Morgan thumps his chest. "Fisher Men don't cheat." I thump my chest in agreement then drop my head.

"Her words haunted me. If I am having sex with a girl and my heart or my thoughts are with another, it's cheating. That's what my hang up is all about. I won't have sex with someone while my heart belongs to someone else."

"What about the girl in Vegas?"

"I scrub my hand over my face. "Well, that was something altogether different. It started with Zan's bridesmaid, Megan, passing out shots on the plane and talking about sex. I think she wanted Zack and me together." We both shudder. "Neither of us would touch her with a ten-foot pole because she's Chrissy's friend."

"Damn Skippy! Our sister's friends are off limits." We thump our chest.

"From the airport, we went to the bar, more drinks were had, and then I met Jane. I doubt that was even her real name. My inhibitions were low, she offered to walk me to my room. I remember being on the elevator with my cock in her mouth, and a few hours later she asked if I was a better lay when I'm sober." Morgan abruptly turns away from me. I know he's fucking laughing at me. His shoulders are shaking. "Stop laughing, ass wipe."

"Sorry, but Dude!" I glare at him. "C' mon Xander, I said sorry, but I have to know how you answered."

"The truth." I throw my hands up exasperated. "I've only had sex with one other person and we were virgins, and I don't actually remember having sex with Jane. She decided to use our extended weekend as a sex education lesson. She taught me positions, spots, answered awkward questions and taught me a few things I thought I knew. I suggested she make a living out of sex ed. Oh, and I also thanked her for having the good sense to put a condom on me when I was in no position to do so."

"Xander, think about that. If the roles were reversed you could have been charged with rape. What she did to you was kinda sick."

"Fuck, I hadn't thought about that."

He's right. If Sam had just told me that same story I would be hunting for blood. I can feel the color drain from my face.

Our conversation is abruptly interrupted when Zack barges in he looks off. "Hey Morgan, good to see you, bro, now get the fuck out of my chair." His tone is flat. He is not himself. Something is wrong.

Zack eyes me curiously. "You look like you just saw a ghost. What's up?"

"I didn't see a ghost, just a memory from another angle." I'm about to ask him what's wrong but my client walks in on Zack's heels and I plaster my professional mask securely in place.

CHAPTER 26

Lara Croft is a useful friend to have.

Sam

Twenty minutes after Xander leaves there is a knock on the door. "Who is it?" I ask.

"It's Zack. I need your help."

I open the door and find Zack standing with a young girl mid-teens maybe. Her eyes are cast down, the grain of the wood floor reflected in her glasses. I step aside letting them both in. Zack cups the girl's face and meets her eyes gently. He's cautious with her. "It's okay, you're safe here." She steps back away from his touch her blue eyes wide and darting around the room.

I step toward her and extend a hand. "Hello, I'm Sam. What's your name?"

She takes my hand in a whisper of a touch. Her voice is nervous and unsteady. "Becca."

I nod. "Becca are you hungry?" She shakes her head and backs up again. I take in her appearance. She's wearing black patent leather shoes, like a little girl. Her dress is white, mid-calf, and A-line. She looks like an old-fashioned American Girl doll like she grew up in a different century. Her long straight red hair stretches past her waist and the bangs are pulled back in a barrette. Like the young girls in a Nick At Night 1960's sitcom. I tilt my head in thought. She is a red-headed Jan Brady dressed in Laura Ingalls clothes.

"How old are you Becca?"

She looks down at her toes and whispers, "Almost seventeen." I look at Zack confused. She's a minor. What the hell? "Sweetheart, what do you like to do when you feel overwhelmed? Zack likes to draw, I bake. Anything you like to do to that makes you feel better?"

She casts her eyes down. "I build houses with sticks." *I can work with that.* Heading into my bedroom, I grab my Legos. I used them for a class project and kept them on hand for when I would babysit for extra cash.

"Do you like Legos?"

She eyes the box curiously. "I-I don't know ma'am." *Ma'am?*

My eyebrows knit together. She called me ma'am. "You don't know what Legos are?" I ask. She shakes her head.

I spread the tiny plastic pieces on the counter and show her the basics of how they work. "Here, build some houses while I step out in the hallway and talk to Zack." She nods and dutifully does as I instruct.

Grabbing Zack by his t-shirt, I drag him out into the hallway. "What the hell Zack? Is she a runaway?"

He rubs the back of his neck. "Sort of." I glare at him. He sits on the stairs that lead to Zan's apartment. "I have a call into my mom to get her some help. She's not Amish, but some sort of other religious sect. I overheard her essentially being sold to a husband she just met." I gasp. "Sam, he was old and creepy looking. They just met and were supposed to be married this afternoon. Her father was offering a money back guarantee that she's a virgin." He runs his fingers through his hair. "It was sickening. She went to use the restroom, and I followed her in. I offered to take her away if she didn't want to marry the old man."

Taking a seat next to him, I rub his back. "You're a good person. I understand why you stepped in, but she's a minor. You could be charged with kidnapping."

He scrubs his hands over his face. "I know, but I had to do something. Mom is making sure everything is on the up and up. There are organizations that specifically help girls escape forcibly arranged marriages. She is exploring her contacts and will come to get her this afternoon. Will you please keep her hidden here until then?"

I nod.

When we enter the apartment, Becca looks up at us visibly more relaxed. She has several small houses built with the meager number of Legos I own. I know some religions don't allow caffeine, so I pull a bottle of water out of the refrigerator and set it in front of her. "For you." She nods but continues silently building.

Taking a seat next to her, I set my chin on my hands and watch her. She curls in her bottom lip when concentrating. She's so young. I know age-wise she is only a few years younger than me, but her innocence is apparent. "Becca." She looks at me with her enormous blue eyes. "Would you like to watch a movie?"

Her spine stiffens. Zack looks up from his phone where he is furiously texting. We all stare at each other cautiously before Becca clears her throat. "I um...I am only allowed to watch pre-approved movies." She nervously disassembles her Lego house and assembles it again.

Crossing the living room, I turn on the television and head to children and family movies on Netflix. "Do you like Disney movies?"

Turning in her barstool she nods and her face lights up in a smile. "Finding Nemo. I like that movie."

"Okay, I can work with that. What else? Little Mermaid?"

She shakes her head. "No, ma'am. Mermaids are sea demons, and we mustn't exalt them." *What the actual fuck?*

"How about Cinderella?" I ask.

She shakes her head again. "No magic. Magic is the devil's tool."

Okay?

"Yes, of course, it is." I drop the remote to my side. This poor girl she never grew up and was about to be sold into a marriage. "Now that I understand your parameters: no supernatural, magical, or adult themed movies, may I make a suggestion?" She bites her lip.

"When my husband was chosen, Papa made me watch adult movies so I would understand."

"Romantic movies?" I ask.

She shrugs. "I already changed enough diapers to know boys and girls were different, but they were graphically educational for my night…" Her voice trails off and her cheeks pink.

"He showed you movies with naked people?" She covers her face with both hands and nods. "They were engaged in sex?" I ask. Her face pales and she turns her gaze away from me. I shake my head. "So, if I understand you correctly, we can't watch Disney movies because magic is evil, but you can watch pornography to learn about adult relationships?" Zack storms angrily into the bathroom slamming the door behind him. I don't blame him. I feel sick, too. "Oh, Becca, the mechanics of sex… the whole what goes where…is not what it's all about." I stroke the top of her head reassuringly.

"Have you ever met someone that makes your insides flutter? Someone that makes your heart squeeze and your skin prickle?" Heat creeps into her face and she nods. "That's where it starts. The tiniest spark of attraction, touching, comes next."

I ramble quickly, hoping I can make her see. "When you hate being apart when you want to always be close, when you feel their absence, that's when sex becomes prevalent. The closest you can be to another person is inside them, and have them inside of you." I take her hands and fix her stare; willing her to understand. "First you share a mind, then a heart, then a soul, then you share a body. That, Rebecca, is love. What you saw in those movies was sex not love." A tear runs down her face and I swipe it with my thumb.

Taking her hands, I hold them out and take in her clothes. "You look very pretty. Is this your wedding dress?"

"Yes, Ma'am."

"Would you like to change into some more comfortable clothes and hang up your dress?" I don't think she wants to, but she hesitantly nods. I lead her into my bedroom and pull out a pair of yoga pants and a sweatshirt.

"Will this work?"

She shakes her head.

"It's a sin for a woman to dress like a man. I am only permitted to wear skirts or dresses."

I would have never considered yoga pants to be men's wear, but I don't argue. I pull out a Navy skort; it's the kind where the skirt goes all the way around and the shorts are built in. I pair it with a yellow t-shirt.

Again, I ask, "Will this work?" She nods, so I leave her in my room to change. "Come out when you are dressed."

Stepping back into the kitchen, I find Zack leaning on the counter chewing on the side of his thumb. "How do you fix someone that broken? How do you make her understand her value and worth, if she was taught her value and worth in dollar, cents, and hymen?" His eyes glisten. He won't cry, but I understand the want. I want to shed tears for her, too.

I curl into his arms and place my hand on his chest. "I was broken, too. I was scared of everything, the anxiety, the depression, the pain. You remember it." He kisses my hair. "She can reassemble her pieces, too. It may take her a bit longer to find them, but she can do it." He wraps his arms tighter, hugging me for me, but more for him, I think.

Becca was silent, I didn't hear her exit the bedroom, I didn't hear her glide into the kitchen, but we hear her gasp. Turning out of Zack's grasp I see her shock, fear maybe, evident in her posture and face. "What's wrong?" I ask.

She folds her hands in front of her and looks down at her fiddling fingers. "I-um… It's nothing I just didn't understand."

Taking a slow step toward her I ask quietly. "What didn't you understand, Becca?"

She looks around the room wildly stammering. "No, it's nothing. I just… I misunderstood. I thought I belong to Zack. I didn't realize you are his." Her face takes on a green hue with a sudden understanding. "Wait, do we." She motions between us. "Are we both to…"

"Share?" I asked unable to hide my alarm.

Zack has had enough of this. He nearly shoves me out of his way in his angry stomp to Becca. She takes a step back and braces herself for impact. That causes him to freeze. His shoulders drop and he gently takes her hands. "Becca, girl… people are not property. You belong to you. I am unmarried and without commitment, just as my best friend Sam is." *That's not entirely true, but I don't need to interject.* "I hug her, I kiss her head or cheeks sometimes, and I love her. I do not love her like a husband loves a wife, I love her like a brother loves a sister."

He takes a sharp intake of air and shakes his head. "Dear God, I hope brothers and sisters love each other the same in your world as they do in mine."

He shakes his head again and forces eye contact with her. "I didn't take you away to keep you. It was to save you. I took you so you can live the life you choose. If you choose to marry the man you've been promised, fine, if you marry another man, become a sister wife, or choose to never marry at all, that is okay, too. The point is, from this day forward, you choose. This is your life, and you choose how to live it. Not me, not your Papa. You." Tears stream down her face. And Zack wraps her stiff body into a hug. Eventually, she softens. Her hands still at her sides.

"I have to go to work." He pulls back from their embrace and bends to look her in the face. "You're going to stay with Sam today. Don't go outside. I'm sure people are looking for you." Her head drops and he hooks a finger under her chin. "It will be okay. I have another friend coming to stay with you." He looks over his shoulder at me. "My sister's best friend, Zan, is coming over. She will probably just sleep. She worked last night, but I'll feel better if she is here to protect you."

I scrunch my nose. "Protect us?"

"She is a bad-ass. She could go pro MMA if she wanted to." Zack leans his huge muscular frame my direction and stage whispers. "Don't tell her, and I'll never admit it again, but she could probably whoop me." That makes me laugh. Zack sighs. "Here's the thing about Zan, she's a tough, freaky smart, like Rain-Man smart girl, but she is the most socially inept woman I have ever met. Every thought that enters her head tumbles right out her mouth. Maybe you shouldn't discuss Becca's upbringing in front of her." He winks.

Kissing me on the cheek, he whispers in my ear. "Thanks, Sam."

Like I had any choice in the matter.

I smile anyway and see him out. Leaning on the door after I close it, a weight drops off my chest. That is the first time Zack has ever explained out loud that I am like his sister. It was the first time he ever insisted he doesn't love me like that. It was everything I needed to hear today. I'm sorry for everything Becca has gone through, and I don't wish the navigation of this new world on her, but for me, today is a win.

I'm still leaning on the door watching as Becca meticulously builds and unbuilds Lego houses when a knock vibrates my back through the door. A woman's voice rings out. "It's Zan. Zack sent me here."

Opening the door, a petite woman only a bit shorter than me enters. She has long brunette hair pulled into a ponytail that swings shoulder to shoulder when she walks. She strides straight into the middle of the living room checking out the surroundings. "You must be Sam. She extends her hand to me. I'm Zan, and I am tired as fuck. Do you have any caffeine?"

"Hello, Zan," I answer as she walks to the refrigerator and swings open the door like she owns the place. Well, technically she does own the place. It's hard to accept the cute, tiny girl is the landlord here.

Slamming the refrigerator shut she grunts. "I need a Cherry Coke."

"I could go to the store." I offer.

She twists her lips. "No, Zack was pretty adamant I keep you here. Don't tell me why. I need plausible deniability." She darts past me. "I'm going to see if I left any upstairs." As swiftly as she entered, she was gone. What a strange woman.

Becca and I each look at each other with bewildered looks. When she knocks on the door again, it's an insistent banging. Maybe her hands are full. I hurry to the door wondering why she would knock at all. I mean if she is comfortable enough to help herself to a drink, why not come in?

I open the door and am surprised to find a man instead of the cute woman in search of a Cherry Coke.

"Can I help you?"

He looks over my shoulder and catches sight of Becca. His brows draw together with anger and his demeanor rings a sinister vibe. Becca looking like a lost doe. She lets out a muffled sob. "No!"

Shit!

I try to slam the door, but he pushes back on it knocking me out of the way. His hand connects with my face and the sting of pain sends me to the floor. Becca screams when he comes after me again, and I instinctively curl up protecting my face with my arms. The blow doesn't come. Instead, I hear the thud of his body as he crashes to the floor. I look up to see Zan with a Cherry coke in one hand, and an exploded can in the other.

"For the love of Joe! Geeze Sam, I leave you for thirty seconds, and you let a fucking stranger in?" She holds the leaky can away from her body and hurriedly walks it to the kitchen sink dumping it inside. "Stupid fucking waste of a perfectly good Cherry Coke," she mutters.

Taking out the kitchen towels from a drawer, she begins mopping up the mess. "Well…" She looks at me, waiting. I bend to help her but she rolls her eyes. "No, Sam. Call 911."

"Yes, of course." I don't understand how she has her wits about her with everything going on. I'm freaking the hell out. I can't think. I'm staring at my phone trying to remember the phone number for 911. She must understand I'm frozen, but she lets a giggle escape while gently removing my phone from the death grip I have on it. I'm bleeding my eye is swollen shut. There is a man on the floor also bleeding, and she's giggling.

Well, Zack, she's the most socially inept person I've ever met, too. She's also my new best friend.

She swipes into my phone when it is abruptly knocked from her hands. The stranger lunges at her knocking her to the floor his hands around her throat. I begin hitting and pulling the man trying to get him off Zan, she's laying perfectly still. Oh my god did he kill her? No effort I put into shoving him moves him. Becca tries helping me, but he's too big. Too strong. In a strangled voice, Zan yells, "Sam, go!"

I can't leave her here to be killed. I tell Becca to lock herself in my room when I catch sight of the knife block in the kitchen. I'm about to grab one and help Zan, just like Chrissy helped me that night when the man again hits the floor with a thud. I run to Zan.

Oh my god, oh-my-god, omigod please be okay. "Zan, are you?"

She pushes me off of her, spits some blood on the floor, and glares. "I'm fine. He didn't hurt me. The mother fucker just pissed me off. Don't let me kill him Sam. My husband is just getting to know me, and so far, he wants to keep me."

She smiles, but I have no idea if she is serious or not. I mean who jokes under these circumstances?

The man stirs again and this time he pulls out a long hunting knife. Zan's eyes grow wild. She sees Xander's pocket knife on the media tower and grabs it. She tries to open it and tries again, muttering curses. The man's lips snarl into a smile as he heads slowly to us. Zan finally shrugs her shoulders at the unopenable knife and throws it at the guy. It clocks him in the face, but it buys her enough time to run to the knife block in the kitchen.

He stares from her in the kitchen to me in the living room, and even I can see who the easier target is. He snarls that sickening smile again as he advances toward me. Zan's eyes grow wide. She removes a knife and hurls it catching him in the arm. She pulls out another knife and glares at him as he is clutching his arm.

"I have excellent aim. If you touch her, it will be with the last breath in your body." Zan holds a knife in a position that would lead anyone to believe she is a circus knife thrower. He takes a step away from me, and I let out the breath I've been holding. The man hurries out the door, leaving a trail of blood as he runs.

Zack is right. Zan could whoop him. Laura Croft is a convenient friend to have. I collapse to the floor with heavy breaths. Zan assures Becca he's gone, calls 911, and even makes us tea. She may be studying to be a paramedic, but I think that's to hide her superhero identity.

Becca's tears soak her face. "Maybe I should go. He won't give up until I'm married to the preacher. I get brought back every time I run." She buries her face in her hands.

"Fuck that, little girl!" Zan sounds fierce. "You are not cattle up for barter. Your body belongs to you. I know you're scared, but don't let fear end you." She pries Becca's hands from her face and stares into her eyes. "You are worth more than your body. You are a possibility. You might be destined for great things. Until you take ownership of yourself and be the person you want to be, you'll never know what you are capable of. Nonna was once like you. When you meet her, you'll see everything life can offer you. You just need to step up and take on the challenges."

I have been an unofficial member of the Fisher family since I was thirteen, but I never considered Nonna's upbringing. I know she and Mr. Fisher have no living relatives. I assumed that life was simple and beautiful for them because they are a simple beautiful couple. What does Zan know, that I do not?

Our moment is interrupted by the arrival of paramedics and police. All the first responders know Zan. The banter between them is so vulgar I worry about little Becca's psyche.

I feel disconnected from the scene. Everything moves in slow motion. Someone is tending to my eye, pictures of blood trails snap. Xander's pocket knife is placed in a plastic bag. The sound is muffled like the swishing noise made when under water. My phone vibrates in my hand. Xander's blood speckled face lights up the screen. I stare at his beautiful eyes until the screen goes black. I register his call after it has ended. I should call him.

Through the fog, I hear "What happened here?" I look at the small white circles on my skin. Without letting go of my phone,

I use my finger to write *it's okay* in my flared skin. I drop my arm. My hand vibrates again. Slowly I turn over my phone to the brilliantly blue eyes of my Love. I slide a trail of blood to the green phone icon and instinctively raise my phone to my ear.

I'm supposed to say something. I can't remember the words. I stare blankly. Zan snaps her fingers in front of my face and I hand her my phone.

Nonna and Mr. Fisher enter the apartment and her soft eyes immediately put me at ease. Becca looks up at the couple with recognition. Have they met? Becca throws herself into Nonna's arms and they collide with one another in a tearful embrace. What am I missing?

It takes a few minutes or a few hours, I can't be sure before I return to being aware. My head returns to the apartment with a vacuum suction noise.

"Oh, there yer are pretty girl." Nonna rubs a hand over my face. "The police are going to talk to yer, and then Morgan will be takin' yer to Xanack Ink. I'm afraid me sons might birth a heifer if they don't see yer mighty soon." She giggles a soft laugh and kisses my head before disappearing out the door.

It takes a moment for her words to sink in. Ha! Don't have a cow, boys. I clutch my sides in a wildly inappropriate fit of laughter. The stress of the situation melts out of me in wave after wave of laughter. It wasn't even that funny, but I can't control the laugh. I cackle so hard tears pool in the corners of my eyes, and then they fall and all my laughing turns to much needed sobbing.

I didn't see or hear Morgan enter, but he scoops me up like a baby, kisses my head and whispers, "Let it all out, baby. You cry until you have no more tears, and then we will laugh some more." He pulls me tighter to his chest. My hearth, my home, my sweet Morgan. "Take me to Xanack." I plead.

He stands up with me still in his arms and carries me to his truck.

CHAPTER 27

Maybe you should work on being my last.

Xander

I slap my towel down on my station and hang up the phone. "What?" I look at the black screen on my phone as if it has an answer. "That was Zan, Do you know why the fire department and police are at my house?" Zack's face pales.

Standing to pace, absolutely fuming, I ask slow and pointedly "Why are the police and paramedics at my house. What the fuck did you do, Zack?"

His head lowers, and his shoulders drop. "I didn't think she was in danger, but just in case, I had Zan go stay with them."

Yanking at my hair, I snap at him. "Obviously you felt she might be in danger if you sent Zan to protect her. What the fuck did you do?" I stop my pacing and glare at him. My words pool like venom around him. "Our job is to keep Sam safe."

Sliding into his phone, he begins furiously texting. I see Zan's name on his screen. I clench and unclench my fists. They only reason my brother is still breathing is that I still need answers.

Pocketing his phone he meets my eyes briefly before looking down. "Everyone is okay."

"I'll decide that. What. The. Fuck. Happened?" I leave no room for second guessing just how angry I am.

Dropping his face in his hands Zack stammers. "I-didn't… How could I…" His words trail off; all of his muscles tense.

The bell on the front door rings and Mama strides in with purpose. "You'll stop giving him grief now, you will." The door closes on her. She doesn't break her stride inside and right into my chest for a hug and kiss. "Xander luv, he did a good and right thing. I'll not have you making him feel wrong or responsible." She pulls from my arms and embraces Zack. "I'm so very proud of you for standin' up for da girl when nobody else would. Samantha knows exactly how the girl feels."

She rubs Zack's head and kisses the top, "of course she wanted to help. Neither of you could know." She waggles her finger between us before kissing Zack's head again. Setting her purse down on his client chair, she removes her sweater and drapes it over her purse. "Morgan is bringin' de girls here, and we'll be figuring this all out."

"Yes, Mama." We answer in unison. We both know there is no arguing with Nonna Fisher. Arguing with each other won't bode well for us either. Our age is of no consequence. That kind, tiny woman raised four headstrong boys. No matter how old I am, she won't hesitate to send my ass to the corner with a bar of soap in my mouth.

Zack and Mama tell me the story of what happened this morning. Sue, my adopted sister, who lives in Las Vegas, has been in contact with a sister organization that helps girls and women escaping Fundamentalist polyamorous religious sects. Nonna insists the girl is not a part of any religion we recognize. Whatever she is, it's clear, Zack helped her escape the clutches of a creep.

At Mama's insistence, Zack and I call all our appointments for tomorrow and Wednesday to reschedule. We aren't super busy on Sunday anyway and Monday and Tuesday we are closed. Fucking Zack. I had planned on taking Sam away on our days off. I want her so bad, I ache, and now it appears we'll be spending time as a family. Brilliant.

I halt my pacing abruptly when I see Morgan's truck out of the storefront windows. I didn't know my chest was tight until all the muscles unravel at the sight of her long brunette hair tumbling down her back when she steps out of the truck. She's safe. That's what is important. The stress melting from my body and pouring out my fingertips returns abruptly at the sight of her bruised face. She's hurt.

Heat ignites my body; my jaw tenses. I slap the door forcefully removing it from my way. My feet hit the pavement with angry purposeful strides until I have her face in my hands. One of her beautiful Amber eyes is swollen. Angry reds, blues, and purples mar one side of her face, and my heart breaks. Her eyes fill with tears. I gently trace the markings with my fingertips testing what is swollen getting angrier by the moment.

My words are harsh and as unyielding as the fury bubbling in my core. "Who did this?" I will rip him limb from limb and watch him burn for hurting her.

She doesn't answer, but her watery eyes finally spill down her cheeks. I gently swipe them with the pads of my thumbs. Folding her into my arms, I hold her while she loses the strength she's been holding in. As she shakes in my arms, I soothe her with a quiet shush.

Gliding my hand down her hair and holding her to my chest, I finally see the wide blue eyes of a red-headed little girl. Guilt washes her face. She doesn't look sixteen. She looks like she's in junior high.

Zan offers a little wave. Morgan steps up and places his hand on Sam's back. I know he wants to take over comforting her but I'm not ready to let go yet. I turn her away from him. Threading my fingers through her hair, I lift her face to mine and kiss her softly on her bloodied lip.

Placing my forehead on hers I whisper, "I love you, sweetheart. You're safe now."

The little red headed girl looks wounded. I don't mean to make her feel bad. It isn't exactly her fault they were in danger. Without letting go of Sam, I pull Zan into a one-armed hug and kiss the top of her short head. "Thanks for taking care of my girl."

She smiles and pats my back. "Dude. I need a fucking Cherry Coke before I can be pleasant." She steps around me. "I have had no sleep and entirely too much peopling today."

I laugh and shake my head. "Mini-fridge at my work station."

"Thank fuck!" She bristles around us headed for the shop muttering, "I was just supposed to hang out, sleep a little, no big deal, but nooooo. My life isn't complete without abusive pricks trying to stab me." I hear the bell on the door chime as she flings it open her tirade trailing off.

I know by the protocol we've always had, I should step back so Morgan can see she's okay. Mama would be pissed at my lack of manners since I didn't introduce myself to the little girl. I just… can't. I turn Sam toward the shop, drop my hand to the small of her back, leading her inside.

Zan is sprawled out on my client chair with a Cherry Coke in her hand. I've inked Zan before, so she is comfortable in my space. She smiles and pulls sunglasses down over her eyes. Taking a seat on my stool, I pull Sam into my lap and bury my face in her neck. The chatter becomes animated and abruptly stops when the bell chimes. All eyes are on the little girl being ushered in by Morgan. She freezes, looking terrified. The Fisher clan can be a lot to take in, I suppose. She's looking back and forth between Zack and me. We're used to that.

Zan lets a laugh escape her. She apparently noticed it, too. "Freaky isn't it. I'm not sure how anyone could tell them apart before they had tattoos." She lowers her sunglasses from her forehead over her eyes again.

The little girl's eyes trace the art on my arm and then on Zacks before offering him a sheepish smile. I get it. We are identical, but Zack and I are so different. It's alarming how many people can't tell us apart. We wore tuxes at Zan's wedding. Without visible tattoos, everyone was lost. Sam has always been able to tell us apart, but she doesn't see the world as most people do.

Mama claps her hands together. "Well aren't we are in a sticky pickle, Luvs?" All eyes turn to the woman who needs no help taking charge of a room. "Sue found a program for sweet Rebecca, she's flyin' out soon to get her. In the meantime, we need to keep one another safe." She takes the little girl by the hand. "I'm Zack's mother. Please call me Nonna."

Becca gives her a slow and deliberate nod.

What's that all about? Nonna already met her at the apartment.

She puts her arms around Rebecca's shoulders and addresses the rest of us. "Clearly Xander and Sam can't go back to their apartment. It'll be a wee cramped, but we can all go home." By home, she means our family home. Having Sam in my childhood bed where I fantasized about her is more exciting than it should be, but hell no. Not with everyone there. I shared a room with Zack for fuck's sake!

Zan interrupts. "I have a better idea. Jacob and I have a series of cabins in Edenridge. It's quiet, secluded, and in the middle of nowhere. There is plenty of room to accommodate everyone. If you're going to hideout for a few days, you may as well make it a getaway."

In the middle of nowhere sounds like a place where I can get some alone time with Sam. Mama nods her head, and a million sexy thoughts dance in my head.

Sam

Zan starts programming coordinates in everyone's phone. She warns us to stay in convoy because the cell signal is gone as you get closer. Her husband is leaving work to drive because, Zan hasn't slept and will need to be back at work tomorrow. Nonna is on the phone and preparations buzz all around us. I'm not caught up in any of the excitement or movements because Xander still has me wrapped in his arms.

Hanging up the phone, Nonna cradles it to her chest. "Oh, good! Connor is coming. He landed a little bit ago and will meet us there."

That reminds me... Rika hasn't met her roommate yet. I should invite her.

Pulling my phone out of my bra, I do just that, Xander brushes his lips to my ear speaking in an audible-to-only-me whisper. "I don't intend to stay jealous of that phone much longer. I want to lick, suck, and kiss every inch of you, including that cell phone warmed tit. It is taking all of my resolve not to drag your fine ass back to the piercing room and take you until you are screaming my name."

Holy hell, I want that. I swallow hard, increasingly aware of the hard-on growing against my ass. "Promise me, no matter the arrangements, you'll find a way to be alone with me tonight."

I nod, "Promise."

Like I wouldn't promise.

His grin is wicked and I squirm in my wet panties.

Swiping into my phone, I call Rika and smile when her picture lights up the screen. It's a New Year's picture of the two of us in paper hats and plastic lays.

"Hey, Sam."

"Hey. Rika, what are you doing?"

"I'm driving." Her voice is chipper. "I just passed a billboard that read 'Abraham Lincoln never slept here, but you should.'" She giggles more exuberantly than the joke demands.

"Where are you?" I ask.

"Kentucky. I'm on my way to Nashville and then probably a small Tennessee, North Carolina border town in the Appalachian Mountains. I'm hunting down a lead."

I laugh into the phone. "Connor just landed and is heading back."

"What?" Her laugh sounds maniacal. "Well, of course, he is. Sadly, I expect to be gone at least two weeks." It is kind of funny. They may be roommates for a month or two before they ever meet.

"Drive safely, and good luck, Rika."

"I will. Love ya, Sam. Bye."

Sliding my phone back through my bra strap my cheeks heat. Xander is staring, and his sexy words replay in my mind.

Zack steals my attention when he kneels down in front of me and takes my hands. "You're okay, right?"

I know he feels guilty; he shouldn't. I flash him a crooked smile. "Oh, honey, you know I'm tougher than that."

Relief softens his face. "Damn right girl! Who's my little badass?"

He offers his fist for me to bump before kissing my head. Xander's arms tighten around me. Is that jealousy? If jealousy enters our dynamic, how will it work? If I'm honest with myself, another woman referring to Xander as her anything would piss me off. Doesn't he have a right to be possessive when his brother calls me HIS badass?

I can't change that I am Zack's badass, Connor's Sam I Am, and Morgan's sweetheart. Parts of me are incomplete without my best friends, but Xander has always owned my heart. If that isn't enough for him, how will this work?

I'm jostled from my insecurity by the arrival of Mr. Fisher and Zan's husband. I'm dazed during introductions, and I mentally kick myself for not catching his name. In my haze, decisions are made, plans are forged, and we head down Main Street in a ridiculous convoy.

Zan and Mr. Zan, as I will call him until someone names him again, are in front. Behind their Prius, is Mr. and Mrs. Fisher in their Safe Spaces passenger van. Zack is on his motorcycle with Becca on the back. I'm surprised she agreed to that. Although, Zack could talk the moon into shinning brighter than the sun if he desired it. I wonder if he desired it. She's too young. Morgan's pickup is behind Zack and we are holding up the rear in Xander's Jeep. We would have all fit in the Fisher's van. What an extraordinary waste of resources.

Wasteful, maybe. Convenient, definitely. Once we are out of town and cruising the country roads, I bring up the elephant in the forefront of my mind. "What made you squeeze me tighter when Zack called me his badass and fist bumped me?"

He glances at me quizzically. "I know you felt bad because he felt guilty, I was giving you an 'it's okay' squeeze."

"It felt like you might be a little jealous." I slump down in my seat with the exertion of that particularly uncomfortable moment of honesty.

He glances a smile at me before returning his eyes to the roadway. "I will admit my heart used to pang when my brothers would pull you from my arms, or kiss and hug on you. I always thought if we were all permitted to touch you, then nothing was special about my affection for you."

I cross my arms over my chest. "And now?"

He shrugs. "You chose me. They are your friends and their affections are friendly as are yours, but mine and ours mean something else. It doesn't bother me anymore."

I place my hand on his thigh. "I'm really relieved you feel that way. I don't want to end my friendship in any way with them to pursue a relationship with you. I'm worried that due to the Fisher brother rules, I can't be the same friend I've always been."

"That's a valid concern," he shrugs. "But if I am okay with movie nights, and chicken soup and motorcycle rides to see the sunset, maybe they won't feel a need to step back. You were their friend before my girlfriend."

I am blushing like a seventh grader. He called me his girlfriend. My inner voice is jumping up and down and twirling with that girly squee junior high girls have perfected. Xander

Freaking Fisher called me his girlfriend. "I'm your girlfriend?" I ask way more nonchalantly than the cartwheels in my brain.

"Aren't you?" His knuckles go white on the steering wheel.

"Well, yes. It's the first time you called me that."

He laughs, light heartedly. "It's the first time I said it to you. I have claimed you several times over the years."

I quirk an eyebrow. "You have?"

"I have. Anytime I saw a douche ogling you, I would ask why they are ogling my girlfriend. I'd cross my arms flexing a little and lean in slightly when I looked down at them."

"No fucking wonder I had to go to college to get a boyfriend. That was a shitty thing to do to me. You sent me to the wolves with no experience, no way to identify creeps and players."

"I didn't do that to every guy that looked at you with interest, only the oglers. You're right, too. I never expected you to leave me."

I scrub my hand over my face, my previous scowl softening. "I didn't want to leave. I had to leave. I needed to put time and space between us so that your brothers could fall in love. I am not the little Sam that left. I'm a woman in pursuit of my second love."

"Colton BaddStone doesn't count you were ten!" He demands.

He looks angry. "C' mon Xander, I clearly didn't love Colton the way I love you, but I honor his memory by saving the spot in my heart where he used to be. It isn't a competition."

"But," His knuckles whiten again. He blows out a breath and shakes his head. "Nevermind."

"No, tell me." I give his thigh a gentle squeeze.

"I'm an asshole if I say it out loud."

I shrug. "So, be an asshole."

"Colton was your first love, Morgan met you first, Connor kissed you first, I know it's selfish, but I want something that is mine."

I level him with my words. "Maybe you should work harder on being my last."

He places his hand over mine on his lap and pulls my hand to his lips. "You're right, again. I'm sorry. I love you."

"I love you, too."

Quiet fills the Jeep, and there is one thought that has been circling in my mind since this morning. I end the silence with a raised eyebrow. "So, is that a Prince Albert?" I ask motioning to his cock.

He looks down, then at me. "You noticed?"

"Yes, I noticed," I smirk.

"Do you like it?" he asks with a sexy undertone.

"I don't know. What made you do that?"

His face flushes. "I'm not supposed to talk about it. Fisher men rules."

"What's another broken rule?" I ask coyly.

He lets out a loud sigh. "Fine, but it's a secret." I thump my chest Fisher man oath style. He takes a hand off the steering wheel and puts my hand back on his thigh. "When Zack and I were learning to pierce, we practiced on a slew of realistic dildos, but we thought we should do the real thing before we got our hands on a stranger's manhood." He cringes and I laugh.

"So, you pierced each other?"

He nods, "and…" He shakes his head. "Our brothers." I look at him confused. "I don't know who kept their piercings, but all the Fisher men at one time had a Prince Albert piercing. I did Connor's and Zack's"

I slap his thigh, "Shut up!"

He crinkles his nose. "We made a pact to never speak of it again."

"When you boys say you'll do anything for one another, you're freaking serious, aren't you?" I can't help but laugh hysterically for a good long while.

Ah, my Fisher Men. Never a dull moment.

CHAPTER 28

That was a short ninety days.

Xander

We watch the pinks, blues, and oranges of a fiery sunset descend on the prairies, cornfields, and lakes. We had to pull over for thirty minutes along the way so Connor could catch up before our cell service dropped. Nobody complains because watching the sunset is worth the wait. Arriving just after dark at the compound, that Zan and Jacob call their "cabins," we take in the vast surroundings. If I overheard correctly, they own seven square miles of land. We follow the convoy down a dark dirt path. At one point we enter what appears to be a tunnel of trees, but when they open to a clearing, a cabin with large illuminated windows appears in view facing a small lake with a pier lit by several lanterns.

"I can't imagine they leave the lights on. Is someone here?" I'm mostly musing to myself, but Sam shrugs her response. When everyone steps out of their vehicles we begin to stretch and look around.

Jacob and Zan walk back from the head of the convoy, and Jacob begins explaining our course of action. Sam and I agreed that our relationship is a secret, but I confided in Zan. I asked her to make sure Sam and I are alone. She agreed to help me.

Jacob points over his shoulder. "The main cabin belongs to Zan and me. There is a larger lodge where all but one of you will stay. I have a small one-bedroom cabin at the front of the property that has security camera screens. Alarms chime if a visitor is approaching. Xander, you have that one?" I nod. So far me on one side of the compound while Sam and everybody else is on the other side doesn't sound like anything I fucking want. A sleepy Zan grabs Sam's hand. "You come stay with Jacob and me, you can have our guest room." Taking Sam's bag, she drags her off to the cabin, but not before turning back to wink at me. I don't know what she has planned, but I'm glad she's planning. Jacob finishes discussing plans with the rest of my family.

Mama is glowing. "It's pretty here," she beams. As dark as it is, it's still evident. Watching her lean into my dad, I realize they have never gone anywhere without us. No romantic weekends, or overnight retreats. They spent every penny they had on raising us. We should send them somewhere beautiful. Maybe for their anniversary?

Everybody meanders their way back to their cars, it was a long drive. Nobody is anxious to sit again. The night rumbles with the sound of Zack's motorcycle, and one by one, everyone moves their vehicles in line to follow Jacob to the lodge. When the last of the brake lights disappear in the tree line, Zan and Sam come back outside.

Sam wraps her arms around my neck and kisses me despite Zan's groans of protest. "You'll have plenty of time for that. Follow me." She juts her chin to a shed behind the cabin. "Sam,

I'll show you how to use the four-wheeler to get from our cabin to Xander's and back without anyone seeing." She nods.

"Okay Xander, follow that dirt road to your cabin, and we will meet you there."

Zan puts her helmet on and assists Sam with hers.

"It's really dark, so I hope I don't get lost."

"It's easy," Zan says as she fastens Sam's chin strap and leads her to one of the two quads. After a quick introduction to start, reverse, gears and such, the girls take off out a garage-like overhead door on the back of the shed

Zan leads Sam to an undetectable path to reach my cabin.

I arrive first and I wait in my Jeep. The tiny cabin is completely surrounded by dense trees. Sam and I will be alone. After a few minutes, Zan and Sam round the edge of the cabin with helmets under their arm in an animated conversation that has them both laughing. I love her laugh.

Entering the cabin, Zan flips on the lights, Sam and I follow closely behind her. Opening a wood panel revealing a wall of monitors, she explains the surveillance system and flips through all the camera views. We can see all the cars at the lodge as well as Jacob returning to the main cabin in his Prius.

"We get alerts on our phones if the visitor sensors are tripped and we can see the feed. Nobody actually ever comes here to monitor it anymore. This is the refurbished security cabin from back when the mines were here." Zan explains.

Zan shows me how to operate all the different gates and cameras. She makes me take note of where the un-renovated cabins are, and she even discloses the Wi-Fi password before wishing us a goodnight. We watch her head out and wait to see her arrive safely at her cabin on the monitor before we peel our eyes from the screens.

Resting my hands below Sam's waist, I pull her hips into me. Her face flushes and the heat from her body can be felt through our clothes. I lower my voice to a whispered rumble, "I finally have you all to myself."

Running my fingertips gently over the bruises on her face, my wolfish grin falls. I pause my desire and replace it with concern. "Are you hurt?"

She leans into my fingertips, "It doesn't hurt unless I bump it or something." I'm sure my face gives away my anger because she comforts me with a hand over mine. "I'm okay. Zan is a small but mighty woman. I guarantee the other guy is in more pain."

"Too bad she didn't kill him." I scoff.

Sam wraps me in a reassuring embrace. "We wouldn't be in this secluded cabin in the middle of nowhere if she had."

Talk about looking on the bright side. My cock stands at attention at the mention of seclusion. Pressing my lips to Sam's, I devour her. I let all the worry I felt pour out of me in waves of passion. My hands exploring her body, as I deepen the kiss. Her hands slide up the inside of my shirt tracing the ridges of my stomach and chest, driving me mad.

I break our kiss suddenly. Grabbing the hem of her shirt, I lift it over her head.

"My Love," I can't help but smirk at her, "we are wearing entirely too many clothes."

She looks up at me with hooded eyes and licks her lips. "Have you got a plan?" Her play of innocence is masked by sexy lips and words that drip with desire.

Leading her backwards to the bedroom, I nod slowly. "It's been going pretty well so far." Grabbing the hem of my shirt I help her remove it. I stop when the backs of her knees hit a king size bed, then I kick the door closed behind me.

Pulling her yoga pants and underwear off in one pass, I place a kiss on her perfectly pretty pussy before I lift and throw her on the middle of the bed. I'm naked and climbing my way up from her feet a moment later. I suck and kiss my way from her knees to her pearled clit and back to her opening. Thrusting my tongue inside, I taste her, and I am not sure who is dizzier with desire.

Threading her fingers into my hair, she pants my name, and I moan against her skin. Drawing out her wetness with feverish strokes and flicks, I drag my tongue up and around her clit. Licking it with long slow deliberate licks; like she's ice cream melting on a hot day. I insert a finger and explore her, while my tongue shifts to quick hard strikes. Her shoulders press down harder into the mattress.

She's so beautiful.

I add another finger and massage the spot that has her moaning my name in succession and her back arching off the mattress. Her breathing becomes ragged. Her thighs clench the sides of my face. Her fingers dig painfully into my scalp and the soft pants of my name become a screaming plea. Every muscle in her body tightens and shakes with the intensity. I dive in with more fervor pushing her through her release. Then softly, I suckle and lap up the gift of her pleasure.

Her fingers soften in my hair and fall to the bed. Her knees once gripping my head relax and fall open. Her hooded eyes lock on mine.

God, I love her.

Kissing and nipping at her flushed skin, I circle her belly button with my tongue and cup the undersides of her breasts before finding her nipples. Pausing to worship them for a moment, her breath hitches and her thighs clench. She is so fucking sexy.

I trail my affection along her collarbone, up her neck, and back to her mouth. Kissing her long and ravenous, I position myself between her legs, and with little warning, I push my cock into her pussy. I'm a little jarred. I haven't had comdomless sex since getting pierced. I wasn't expecting the sensation of it moving. Her wide eyes flash to mine just as surprised, but all I can do is groan at the delectable feel of my woman.

She feels so good, it is going to take a Herculean effort to last. "You said you were clean and protected whenever I'm ready. I've been fucking ready forever. Is this okay?" She bites the corner of her bottom lip nodding.

"You feel so fucking good," I moan. Slowly, I continue sliding all the way in and all the way out savoring every stroke, kissing her with years of pent up passion. Her legs wrap around my waist and the position drives me deeper.

I want more.

Her fingers in my hair, her tongue in my mouth, my cock wrapped in her tight pussy, and I want more. I pull her legs up on my shoulders and the position puts me deeper. Her kiss is ragged with pleasure. She pulls back from my mouth digging her head and shoulders into the mattress, her skin flushing. her pussy rippling.

"Oh Xander, I'm going to come."

I smirk, oh yeah she is. "That's right, Baby, come for me."

I'm so close myself, but ladies first. It's a Fisher Men rule of engagement. I pinch her nipple, stretching it between my fingers harshly. Leaning back on my knees, I use my opposite hand and press my thumb into her clit. I feel her grip on my cock as her walls spasm in pleasure. Before she can come down from the orgasm that is tearing her apart, I join her, releasing everything I have into her beautiful body. Watching the sweat glisten on her gorgeous skin, I allow my eyes to take in every inch of her. As if she wasn't perfect enough, as if this moment wasn't already everything I had hoped for, the intense emotions filling her body activate her dermographia.

Collapsing on the bed next to her, I pull her into my arms and use my finger to write the word, "mine," into her skin.

"So much for no sex for ninety days." She giggles like she won a bet.

As far as I'm concerned, I'm the winner here.

Sam

We are roused awake by the obnoxious ring on my phone. The internet-based phone call doesn't utilize my usually subdued ringtone. I swipe to answer and grumble an exhausted, "Hello?"

"Hey sleepyhead," Zan's voice calls through my phone's speaker, "Nonna called to invite us to breakfast, although it didn't really sound like a choice." She laughs. "They are sending Connor over to pick up Xander so you better get your pretty ass in gear and get over here."

"Thank you, Zan, I'll head over." I slide my thumb over my phone to end the call and jump out of bed nearly falling on my spent ass. Xander and I only fell asleep about an hour ago. After eight hours of sexcapades, I can hardly walk. Clutching the bed for stability, I give Xander a shake. "X, wake up. Wake up." He groans and throws his arm over his face. "Connor is on his way and it smells like sex in here." He peeks at me from under his arm and smirks a smile that makes me look for yellow canary feathers at the corner of his lips.

"Fuck yeah, it does."

I smack his leg. "Xander!"

He rolls away from my assault, laughing. "Give me a kiss before you go, and I'll get rid of Connor so you can come back."

"No dice, X, he's picking you up for breakfast."

Xander sits up abruptly. "Shit, it's Sunday."

I slide into my yoga pants, picking up all traces of me.

"Better be your last cuss word, mister," I wag my finger imitating Nonna's unique accent. "Nonna 'ill be having none of tha' now."

She doesn't talk about it, and I've never asked, where her accent comes from. Leaning down, I kiss Xander. He winks and smacks my ass when I retreat.

Closing the bedroom door, I hear him call out. "I love you, Samantha!"

My heart melts. It's always been him. I love him so much, I ache.

Checking the cameras, I see Connor leaving the lodge. I squeeze the strap of my messenger bag and pull myself from the moment. Back to reality. I close the door and hop on the four-wheeler tearing out of here like it's on fire.

The ride is fun, and just like Zan showed me, pulling into the back of the shed made me invisible to Connor.

Zan is waiting for me on the front porch with a Cherry Coke in hand. "Good Morning. You look freshly fucked and glowing happily."

"Shut up." I shoulder past her to clean up and get dressed for one of my favorite family traditions. The Fishers have brunch together every Sunday. I better wash the smell of sex, sweat, and Xander off of me before I head over.

The guest bathroom is huge. Everything about this cabin screams luxury, but the stark white walls, floors, and tub give the space an open large feel. The shower stall is bigger than my whole bathroom and has three spray heads. That makes getting clean quickly an efficient task.

The towels are thick and soft. The whole experience is spa like. I wish I paid better attention to our own cabin. I was so lost in Xander, I didn't notice any of the surroundings. I need to snap out of my Xander fog before breakfast.

The tradition is usually held at the Fisher house on the screened in back porch. Looking in the mirror, I run my hairbrush through my hair and reminisce about my first Fisher family breakfast. The children were encouraged to bring home "strays." Anybody who needs a meal, company, or a family, is affectionately called a stray. We sit at the table as a stray, but we leave the table a friend with a devoted family in our corner. My eyes fill with tears. My chest tightens when I think about how much love this family has given me.

I step out of the bathroom only twenty minutes after I entered it. I find Zan and her husband Jacob sitting on barstools at the island. They are newlyweds, and the way she's sidled up next to him is adorable. He looks at her like she is the sole reason the world turns. I feel intrusive stepping into the kitchen, but at least now I know Zan will be eager to shove me off to Xander's tonight.

"Wet hair; don't care?" Zan asks with a quirked eyebrow. The way she asks isn't snarky so, I shrug and smile.

"I'm eager to fill up on Nonna Fisher's cooking." I laugh. "Anybody who has ever tasted Mrs. Fisher's cooking would understand, completely."

Jacob pops a piece of pineapple into Zan's mouth kissing her just as her lips wrap around the piece. While she is distracted by the sweet kiss, he slides a set of keys off the counter and takes off running out the door laughing maniacally as he goes. Zan looks amused, but I'm confused. "What was all that about?" I ask with a thumb over my shoulder in Jacob's direction.

"We fight over who gets to drive. It's an ongoing competition." She rolls her eyes. "He thinks that just because he stole the keys and got to the car first he gets to drive."

"Doesn't he?" I'm unclear on the rules of the competition.

She digs in her pocket and holds up a key fob with a wink. "If he had stolen the correct keys, he might have a chance. As it stands, the keys to my car won't make his car go."

I laugh, Zan is a trip. I check to make sure Jacob is gone, and I hold out my hand. "He'll try to steal it, give it to me. He won't expect it and until I get in the car it won't start."

She nods emphatically. "I like the way you think." She hands me the fob and I slide it into my bra opposite my phone.

"You know, some girls carry a purse in lieu of boob compartments." Zan snarks.

I laugh, I've heard it all before. "I doubt your husband will try fishing the key out of my cleavage."

Zan shrugs. "I wouldn't blame him if he tried, you have fantastic boobs." She cups them appreciatively before she hops off the counter stool and struts to the front door, her long brown ponytail swaying from shoulder to shoulder.

I have never had a woman other than Rika do that to me. She did it so nonchalantly. Given her personality, I'm not even taken aback.

Maybe I shouldn't meddle in the wars of others, but I can't wait to see who the victor is. I run after her slamming the door when I reach the porch.

Jacob is in the front seat and Zan is standing in the car doorway ordering him out. He yanks her into the car and attempts to start it. She laughs and taunts him, "No fob in the car until I'm in the driver's seat."

He smirks back at her, "I'm not moving, Sweetheart." I feel like I'm watching a tennis match, only more entertaining. Zan reaches behind her back and pulls out a water pistol from her waistband and begins to drench her husband. He takes a flying lunge out of the car bringing her to the ground. They begin rolling in the dirt fighting over the pistol soaking them both. They are fighting like five-year-old siblings, not like husband and wife.

I use the struggle to enter the game and take control. I jump into the car, close all the doors and start it. They both look up to the car jaws agape. Rolling down the window, I lean out. "Looks like I win. Get in, or I'm leaving without you."

Zan yells at me with a crooked smile. "Well, look who's living a thug life."

"Thug-lite," Jacob retorts.

Standing up, Jacob helps his wife up, and the two of them tumble into the backseat a tangle of arms, legs, and passionate kissing. Jacob breaks from his wife's mouth and looks at me in the rearview mirror. "I found a benefit to being chauffer driven." He shifts and Zan whimpers a little. "Just follow the gravel road it leads to the lodge." He disappears below the backseat and I'm a little unnerved. They wouldn't have sex with me in the front seat, would they? Eew.

My eyes pop when I get my first glimpse of the lodge. It's huge! The security camera view didn't do it justice. I have stayed in hotels smaller than this place.

"Jacob, tell me about this lodge," I ask.

"This used to be a mining community. The mines ran dry, and my grandmother began buying the land up at fair value so the displaced miners and their families could have enough money to successfully relocate. There isn't anything left here to sustain people without independent finances. The lodge was a strip mall of sorts that contained Village Hall, the town doctor, and a grocery store. We gutted everything and built it out. My Grandmother had hoped to run a bed and breakfast here in her retirement, but then her cancer returned. The Fishers are the first guests to stay here.

"I'm sorry about your grandmother. She sounds like a wonderful woman."

"She was. It's been five years, I still miss her every day."

The air feels somber. Grief can make the air feel as dense as soup sometimes. Pulling into the adjacent parking lot, I see Matt's truck. At least it looks like the truck he had. "Is that Matt BaddStone's truck?"

Zan perks right up. "Yep, yep, yep! Chrissy and he got here early this morning. I haven't seen her in almost four days." She sighs, "I miss her face." A full-on Fisher family Sunday breakfast strays and all? I haven't done this in years.

We open the door to the lodge. It's a beautiful building with large windows, vaulted ceilings, and exposed wood beams. A dining hall is to the left. It has a huge stone fireplace and a banquet table vast enough to accommodate everyone.

"Oh Samantha, Luv, dare you are. Did-ya sleep well now." Nonna embraces me as I walk in. She is just as much my mother as the woman who gave birth to me.

"I did Nonna, thank you for asking." I'm a dirty little liar, I barely slept, but I otherwise have no complaints.

Nonna slips from our embrace to hug and dote on Zan and her husband. "Zan and Jacob, thank yer much for this lil get-way. It's been lovely."

"I'm happy to have you. Did you find all the food you need? I had my cook stock the refrigerators for you."

"Tis right, we did. Yer cook Miss Patty even came this morning to help. She'll be joining us today. I gave her the day off. She'll be getting' on as our stray." Only Nonna Fisher could tell Jacob his employee will be getting the day off with a heartwarming smile. God, I love that woman. "Connor and Sue ought to be back with Xander soon, then we can sit down to eat."

My heart twists when she says Xander's name. Wait a minute did she say… "Sue's here?" I ask.

"Oh yes luv, Matt and Kateri picked her up from the airport in the wee hours." I guess like me, Nonna hasn't jumped on the Chrissy train. I can't blame her. She named her daughter Kateri, no need to call her Chrissy just because the cool kids do it.

The front door flings open and Connor runs at me with outstretched arms. "Sam I Am!" He wraps me in a big hug and spins me around. "You look so much happier than the last time I saw you."

"I bottled it all in until I blew up. I'm better now."

Setting me on my feet he kisses my forehead. "You need to stop with that nonsense. Stop worrying about everyone else's feelings before your own."

It's a nice sentiment, but I don't think that is my issue. I overanalyze and obsess over my own feelings and reach anxiety and panic attack levels when I try to balance my internal hurricanes with the feelings of others. In short, I am too much of everything and I never feel like I'm enough.

I'm getting better.

How did I skip the Zen calm my mother has, and the crisp, precise, albeit detached nature of my father? I'm like this whole other neurotic breed of human.

Xander wraps his arms around me from behind and walks me toward the dining room. He pulls out a chair with one arm while keeping me locked in the other. As he has always done, he pulls me into his lap. "Good morning beautiful. Did you sleep well?" He sneaks a conspiratorial wink and ass grab as he asks.

"I did, thank you for asking."

Nonna flashes him the mom look with one hand on her hip. "Boy, we discuss this too much. Sam is a big girl now, let her at her own seat."

He slides me off his lap and into the chair next to him. "Yes, Mama."

As soon as her attention is diverted, he grabs the seat of my chair and yanks me closer so our chairs touch and then lazily drapes his arm across the back of my chair.

"I see my brothers are still competing for your time?" I turn to see Kateri, or Chrissy as she prefers now. I really miss her. Standing up, I embrace her in a tight hug.

"I'm so happy to see you. I really missed you." I look up to her dark and broody husband. I can't help but wonder how much Colton would look like him if he had gotten to grow up. "Hey, Matt! So, you two finally met your pen pals, eh?"

"What?" They ask in unison.

"When you went to Texas for his Airforce graduation, I saw a picture of Matt and figured it all out. It wasn't my secret to tell, but I tried." I lean in and whisper, "I took her to Stone Tattoo to get pierced, hoping you two would meet. Some girl was in your room instead." They both nod and chuckle. They must have discussed this already.

Taking a seat across from us, Matt pulls out the chair for his wife. He's like six feet four inches of piercings and tattooed muscle, but also the gentleman she deserves. It warms my heart to see my childhood friends so happy.

"You can be, too." My spine goes ram-rod straight. Sue smells like lilacs and sunshine. Her caramel skin may make her light eyes pop with warmth, and she may be a kind sweet person, but her intuition is creepy as hell. She could make those Hollywood mediums and psychics look like circus freaks. I swear she can read thoughts and see the future. "I can't read your mind, but I can see what is happening and the best way to proceed is by ripping the Band Aid off."

I turn to look at her. My voice is shaky. "I don't know what you're talking about."

"Mm-hmm." She looks around the table and lowers her voice. "You're afraid to lose them. It's a valid concern, but if it is inevitable, why wait?"

I feel the air being pushed out of my lungs. "What if I lose all of them?" I glance over my shoulder at Xander.

Sue wraps me in a hug. "You won't. The longer you wait though, the more resentment they will need to get over. Rip off the Band Aid, Sam."

She kisses my head before taking a seat next to Becca further down the table.

Sue's mother was a Safe Space client. Her mother's crazy abusive husband kept finding her no matter which safe house she was moved to. Finally, she and her two daughters moved in with the Fishers.

Sue says that she isn't psychic, just perceptive because of her childhood. She had to be consistently aware of her surroundings. She has an eidetic memory, and she had to gage honesty and deception in strangers. The combination gives her an insight most don't have.

She is a great person to go to for advice, but taking this advice requires a dose of bravery I just don't have yet. After all, as perceptive as she is, her father still found her family. He blew up the Fisher family home while Chrissy was there alone with Sue's baby sister. As in tune as she is to her environment, she took the poison her mother offered her after the death of her baby sister. It's only a small miracle that Sue is alive, her mother is not. Maybe she is missing something this time, too. I'm not ready for that risk.

Morgan slides into my chair and pulls me down to his lap. "Hey Sam, I haven't seen you. Everything going well?" I nod and he kisses my cheek.

Zack takes my hand yanking me up and twirling me like a ballerina. "Fuck yeah, she is. She's a bad ass. Aren't you Sam?" There is a collective gasp when he dips me. His eyes widen and defeat washes his face. He stands holding a finger up. "Let me kiss the girl first." He pecks my lips with his then releases me to open his mouth.

Nonna slides a bar of Ivory Soap between his lips. "Yer know better, Son."

Matt guffaws and slaps the table "For once it isn't me! Zack said 'fuck' and 'ass!'" His laughing is abruptly halted by the second bar of Ivory in his own mouth.

Nonna slaps a jar in the middle of the table. "Delightin' in the misery o' others will cost you, son." He grumbles around his soap bar and digs a five-dollar bill out of his pocket to deposit in the jar.

I love the way my Fisher men were raised. They don't have a swear jar; you get a soaped mouth for that. They have a lack of kindness jar. Each week you must deposit a dollar in the jar for each moment when you chose something other than kindness. If you walked past a homeless person, didn't intervene when someone was bullying, avoided giving a compliment when it was due, you must pay. The money is donated to people who need kindness. When Zack helped Becca, it was because he was raised to make a difference. He was taught to leave the world better than he found it.

They are a part of my life because they were taught to care.

CHAPTER 29

"May you have the hindsight to know where you've been, the foresight to know where you are going, and the insight to know you've gone too far."

Xander

It's official. This will work. Zack kissed Sam on the mouth and it didn't bother me. It always bothers me, but there is something to be said about love and security. I know she loves me differently than my brother. I'm good with that. I also trust that my brother wouldn't push boundaries with my woman. He just doesn't know she's mine. Yet.

Connor slaps Zack's shoulder. "She needed to hear it, Bro. I'm guessing the soap is worth it."

He nods and mumbles around the bar between his lips. Connor wraps his arms around Sam's waist and yells "Sam around the rosy!" I can't help but laugh; she hates that.

We all form a circle and wrap her in a big hug and shower her with kisses, raspberries, and tickles until she threatens to pee her pants. Today is no different, we delight in her squirms and protests.

Dad emerges from the kitchen wiping his hand on a towel. "Breakfast is ready. Let go of the poor girl already."

We release her and begin heading to the kitchen. I wait for Matt and Jacob as they make their way around the table. Becca attempts to stand, but Mama stops her.

"The gentlemen serve breakfast, Luv, you just stay right here."

Becca looks downright distraught. "But the bible says a wife should…"

Dad cuts her off as he lays down a tray of French toast. "A man should honor his wife in all ways. It is his job to love, protect, and care for her. My wife just cooked a meal big enough to feed a small village. I thank and honor her by taking care of the serving and clean-up. Surely God doesn't have a problem with loving one another."

She opens then closes her mouth a few times but doesn't retort. I take a tray of bacon and a tray of eggs to the table. My dad bends to kiss Sam's hair. "I haven't seen you long enough to welcome you home, Sweetheart." She smiles at him before he retreats to the kitchen for more plates.

I want to have a marriage like my parents have. Both work at making one another happy. My father is a quiet, reserved man. My mother is outgoing. My father is patient and methodic, my mother is a pinball who always has one hundred things on her to-do list. As opposite as they are, they are both kind. They strive to leave the world better than they found it and are committed to making life better for the other. They are truly partners. Love is evident when they look at one another. I hope Sam still looks at me the way my Mama looks at my dad when we've raised a family to adulthood.

Once all the food is laid on the table, we start with the kindness casualty jar which got an early lead today. Most families have swear jars. In my family, you drop money in the jar for being unkind. Zack began with his usual $20. It's his penance for being a prick to me at work often. We're brothers, it's a normal relationship.

Zan dropped in $40. "I work with people for a living, and my ability to make the truth sound pleasant is broken." She shrugs.

I really like Zan, but she is absolutely correct. Every thought that enters her head vomits out her mouth with unrefined precision. I heard her suggest to a woman holding her newborn that some babies aren't born cute they become cute with time and the development of a personality and smile. She thought she was being gentle because the woman had an ugly baby.

All of my brothers paid penance. Chrissy dropped in $5. She hardly ever has to pay. She was blessed with my parent's automatic kindness. She is becoming bolder now that she is with Matt. This particular bit of money is because she told her husband what he could do with himself while angry. Heck, even Mama does that sometimes.

I put in my penance because of a misunderstanding that hurt Sam's feelings. In actuality, my penance is for the hurt I am causing my brothers. They don't know I've wronged them yet, but that doesn't mean claiming Sam is a kind thing to do to the three men I made a pact with. Sam dropped cash, too. I'm not the only one that knows what is about to happen.

Once the cash packed jar made its way back to Mama, she announces cheerily, "Sue got to findin' a bed for our Rebecca here in a lovely program in Nevada. The two of 'em will fly out Tuesday night." Mama's face lights up and she beams, "All the money collected today will be donated to supply Rebecca with the incidentals and clothes she'll be needin' in her new home." Becca's face reddened and her eyes cast down. I wonder if she has changed her mind about leaving. There is something to be said about the evil that you know versus the evil that you don't.

Mama takes my dad's hands, and with the twinkle in her eye she has just for him, she says, "May you see your children's children, be rich in blessings, and poor in misfortune." Dad kisses her gently and turns to face Zack.

"May the grass grow long on the way to hell causing a lack of use. May your heart always win and your choices for love never lose."

Zack smiles and blesses Becca. "May your Love respect you, troubles neglect you, angels protect you, and after a long-lived life, heaven except you."

Our family stopped going to church after the way they treated Sam and Chrissy. My parents stopped praying, but never stopped believing. The blessing replaced a dinner prayer. It travels around the table from one person to the next. I got to bless Sam. In all our years, I've never gotten to bless her. She always blesses me. "May your long life be filled with love and laughter, I'll be true as long as you, but not a moment after." Squeezing her hands, I wink and she giggles.

She turns to Connor, and the ass wipe kisses her lips, surprising her. "He may have given you a blessing for lovers, but let us all remember who kissed you first." He winks.

I want to knock the smirk off his face, but Sam handles my brothers better than I could. I'm almost giddy to see her bring him down.

"May you have the hindsight to know where you've been, the foresight to know where you are going, and the insight to know you've gone too far."

Damn!

The collective sigh and sharp intakes of air around the table confirm she just burned him with a sticky sweet smile. He sheepishly blesses Jacob's employee and todays stray, who blesses Morgan and so on, until we all finally dig into our breakfast.

Our Sunday brunches aren't usually this big, the table seems to stretch on and on. We can't have a collective conversation, so the buzz of many conversations hang in the air. Leaning back into my chair, I take in the atmosphere. Even nervous Becca is smiling. I have a really fantastic family. Placing my hand on Sam's knee, I give it a little squeeze. I can picture our baby being passed from one arm to the next during Sunday brunch. She needs to get reacquainted with Chrissy and befriend Zan. She should also meet Matt's sister, Piper, and our friend Megan. She's going to need some girlfriends to team up with all these Fisher Men when she walks down the aisle. Otherwise, my brothers will have to be her bridesmaids. The thought makes me laugh out loud. Fortunately, the conversation doesn't find it inappropriate. I wonder if Sam would be alarmed to know that while I absently trace pictures into her inner thigh, I'm planning our wedding and kids.

She finishes her last bite of food and I pull her into my lap. If she is alarmed, she better get over it. Fuck the ninety days we agreed to. I'm not ever letting her go. I would rather lose every person at this table then to lose her. Well, Mama and my dad would never give me up, so I wouldn't lose them. I'm pretty sure my brothers would get over it eventually. We'll find out.

I'm ready to tell them right now. I just need to get Sam to agree. I think asking her on the verge of an orgasm will get me anything I want. I can't wait to get her back to my cabin.

CHAPTER 30

When the chips fall, I hope they still like me.

Sam

The front porch of the lodge is a huge wrap around with tons of rocking chairs. I snuggle into Xander's lap feeling rather fat and happy. All the Fisher's and guests lounge lazily. After an amazing meal, the ladies and I retreated while the men cleaned up, and now that the day is ready to be had, we are too full to have it.

Zan has to work this afternoon, so she and Chrissy are leaving. Jacob has offered to stay at the security cabin since he is without his "hot wife." Xander will stay with me at the Chance cabin, and nobody needs to know that.

The plan for today is to pack a lunch and go hiking. There is a waterfall we're going to explore.

Tomorrow night, the Fisher Men and I are going camping on an upper bluff. Tuesday we will all head back when Sue and Becca leave for the airport. While we lounge lazily discussing the plans, all I am looking for are holes in the schedule.

I can't wait to be alone with Xander again. I have wanted to kiss, touch, and taste him for almost eight years. Now that our passion is uncorked, I'm exploding with sexual energy and desire.

It is also satisfying to tell him I love him and have him know how I mean it. He will always be my friend, but now he knows how much more he means to me.

Morgan, ever the leader, stands clearing his throat, "Anybody wanting to hike should shower, change, pack a back pack, and meet back here in two hours."

Woo Hoo! Two hours of sexy exploration and a shower. Xander stands, picking me up wedding style from his lap and carrying me down the stairs to Jacob's Prius.

Approaching the car, as soon as we are out of earshot of the family Xander growls, "I can't wait to get you naked."

Whew is it getting warm? Without the slightest effort, Xander opens the passenger door and places me on the back-passenger seat. Sneaking a quick feel up out of view. His touch sets me on fire. I can't wait for him to get me naked either.

Xander buckles into the driver-side back seat and we wait for Zan and Jacob. I use the opportunity to reach over and give Xander's hard cock a squeeze. It stiffness under my touch and the look he flashes me is pure sex.

He groans a sexy growl. "Keep that up and I will take you right now, no matter who is watching." I flash a wicked smile knowing full well sex in front of Nonna will never happen, so I stroke him and wink. He groans and takes my jaw in his hand.

"So, this is it? This is how we are going to tell my brothers? By having them look over and watch me pawing you like an animal, while I taste every moment of your kiss?"

Shit! That can't happen, but oh how my body reacts to his threat.

"Sam, I am willing to work at their forgiveness, I want you out loud." I retreat my hand just as Jacob and Zan open their car doors.

Zan and Jacob use the drive to work out logistics. Xander and I are comfortably quiet and exchanging wonton stares. The sexual tension is palpable, and it isn't lost on anyone, least of all Zan. "Jacob, My Love, perhaps you should depress the accelerator a bit harder. The heat emanating from the back seat is giving me hot flashes, and I have no desire to see them naked."

"Zan!" We collectively yell at her audacity.

"You're welcome." She beams.

The ride is less tense after her outburst of honesty, or maybe it's that Xander planted his mouth on mine, and as long as our clothes stay on, we don't need to hide anymore.

Arriving at the Chance cabin, Xander carries me piggy back and Jacob has Zan on his back, too. At my signal, the guys take off running. Jacob may have won the race, but the excitement of being this close to naked is an awesome consolation prize.

Zan and I drop to our feet in the foyer and I don't bother with the four-wheeler. Wrapping my fist in Xander's shirt I yank him along to my room. He doesn't protest. Closing and locking the bedroom door, I turn around slowly and find Xander stepping out of his pants and underwear. Reaching behind his head, he grabs the neck of his t-shirt and pulls it off over his head. I love how he does that. Crossing my arms, I grip the hem of my shirt to follow suit, but he pulls my arms away. "I'll be the one getting you naked today, Future Mrs. Fisher."

My gaping jaw is momentarily shielded by my shirt as he pulls it over my head. "Future Mrs. Fisher?"

Xander unhooks my bra and trails kisses down my neck and collarbone inching the straps down as he goes.

"I've loved you from day one. I have fantasized about our future since we were too young to think about the future. I have every intention of being your forever." His hands unbutton my jeans and he kisses his way down my cleavage and abdomen. He drops to his knees sliding my pants slowly over my hips. "I'd marry you tomorrow, Samantha if you were ready."

"I'm not ready?" I suck in a sharp breath as his mouth heats the lace of my panties before hooking his thumbs in them.

"You need to make peace with my brothers before I assume this position with a ring in my hand." My legs give out, but Xander catches me before I fall. He stands up, lifts, and crawls me to the center of the bed. Kissing a trail from my lips, all the way down to my clit, before licking his way up and down my pussy. I moan with the relief. My lady bits ached for this attention. He gently places my thighs over his shoulders preparing for what is sure to make me ache and quake in all the best ways.

His tongue takes a lazy path from my opening to my clit. He circles it a few times before dragging it back again. When I feel like I may very well burst into flames, he gently sucks my clit with careful lips and tense pressure. I grab his hair and arch into his face seeking more heat, tongue, just… more. Recognizing my need, he responds with two fingers inside strumming that spot that makes me see stars and fireworks.

The sounds coming from me are foreign, even to me. My hips gyrate without my will. "That's right, Baby, show me how you like it. Fuck my mouth, ride my fingers." His words vibrate against my skin and my mind goes foggy as I lose myself in the sensations.

Heaven help me, but I shamelessly do as he commands, grinding myself on his tongue, riding out wave after wave of pleasure. My pants and pleas turn into a guttural animalistic sound when every muscle in my body tightens, releases, and tightens again.

My orgasm slams me so hard, I can't lift my head, and tears spring from my eyes. My fingers thread through Xander's hair while I hold on for dear life. I feel like I could shatter in a million tiny floating pieces. When the last wave settles, Xander lifts his chin kissing my thighs, hips, and belly button. I feel a sudden void at our lost connection. As his lips reach my neck, the void is filled slowly by Xander's cock. He whispers in my ear. "I love you, Samantha Nikkole Reynolds, and I'm ready to begin forever as soon as you are."

His push and pull is slow, his kiss passionate, and the pulse thumping between our bodies, the energy where our skin touches is so heady. I've had sex before, heck, we've had sex, but I have never felt this. The sensations and feelings are overwhelming. I could savor this moment forever.

"I love you, too. It's always been you, Xander. It will always be you."

We are lost in kisses, nibbles, and touches. Our rhythm picks up as our desire to please one another increases. Leaning back on his heels he drags me up against his thighs for a deeper angle and every nerve in my body tingles when his Prince Albert hits *the* spot. He rolls my nipple between his thumb and finger, and when I begin edging another explosion, he pulls me up on his lap driving into me while his blue eyes locked on mine.

The expression in his eyes isn't just heat and sex, it's adoration. I feel precious, beautiful, loved, and powerful. The warmth consumes me and together we let go riding out the climax.

Recovering in his arms, I feel safe.

It takes several minutes before we can move. Shower, dressing, and preparing to hike up a waterfall, was more difficult than I had anticipated. I'd rather stay in for round two through five, but my thighs are weak and a girl's gotta walk.

We head downstairs and we are met with Jacob's brilliant smile in the kitchen. "I packed your backpacks, I assumed you were busy." He winks.

My face flushes and Xander wraps me in a hug, kissing the top of my head. "Thank you, Jacob" I squeak.

"Yeah, no worries." He answers. "I packed some protein bars, bottled water, and fruit. You may want to throw a hoodie in the bag. It gets cold when the sun goes down."

I nod.

"I'll grab them at my cabin. I need to get there before someone comes to pick me up." Xander laughs.

"No, go get your stuff on the quad, and meet back here. We are leaving from here." Jacob explains.

Taking one of the backpacks, Xander hurries out the back door and I hear the quad noise taper off as it disappears in the tree line.

I plop my fat butt on the counter stool and rest my chin on my folded hands. "Jacob, what am I going to do?"

"About what?"

"The Fisher Men are my best friends. I love and need all of them, but it's against their rules to date me. When they find out about Xander and me, it's going to get ugly."

Taking a sip from his water bottle he studies me. "The Fisher Men are pretty adamant about their rules."

"I know." I blow a stray hair from my eyes. "I can't bear to come between them, but I won't survive losing them."

"Don't you think maybe they feel the same?" Jacob asks pinning me with his soulful blue eyes. He has a way about him. I feel like he looks straight through me and can see all my insecurity. No wonder he and Zan are so blissfully in love. She lacks insecurity. All she sees is the old soul and wisdom he exudes. I, on the other hand, feel uncomfortable holding eye contact.

"I hope they feel the same. I hope they can be happy for me. I'll lose all of them if they can't."

"Not Xander though."

I shake my head. "I won't be the object of resentment. How could he not resent the girl that drove a wedge between him and his brothers?"

Jacob scratches the stubble on his chin in thought. "It sounds like you need to rip the band-aid off."

I roll my eyes. "So I've heard."

"I'm a nurse." He flashes a brilliantly white teeth smile at me. "What if I can find a way to soften the pull?"

I hear the obnoxious whoops of the Fisher Men and the slamming of car doors.

"It's best to stay back, avoid the shrapnel."

The stomping of feet on the porch signals the end of our discussion.

Xander

If I thought being respectable while hiking up a waterfall behind Sam was difficult, the idea of camping with her and my brothers tonight is torture. When the idea of a Fisher Man camp out came up, I inwardly groaned. Not that I am opposed to snuggling around a campfire or heating up a sleeping bag, but I definitely had other plans. Yes. Plans.

Shit.

Sam was courteous enough to not send me out with a loaded gun. After our waterfall hike, I hiked her up against the steamy shower wall. Jacob had gone to the other cabin when our shower was done, so we spent the rest of the night exploring one another. I wish I could just get her to agree to let the cat out of the bag. Until she does, the secretive sneaky bullshit must go on.

Instead of a third night of adoration, exploration, and explosion, Jacob helps me load my jeep with equipment, overnight bags, and tents. Sam packed a picnic basket full of food, and my brothers will be here soon. The upper bluff isn't accessible by car. My Jeep will make the trek, but everyone else needs to take the four wheelers. I'm surprised to see Becca arrive with everyone. She must be warming up if she's comfortable enough to camp with us. Sam and I figure out an extra seat in the packed Jeep to accommodate her, but Morgan takes the vacated seat instead.

Jacob and Connor straddle one quad while Zack and Becca follow on the other. Sam shifts under her seat belt to face Morgan in the backseat.

"So, what's with that?" She motions to Becca who is trying to straddle the quad and Zack in a skirt-wearing, lady-like way.

Morgan shrugs, "She wanted to come. I told her it was a Fisher brothers thing. and she pointed out that you were invited." He holds out his hands, "What can I say? She has a point."

"Sam is a Fisher Man without the name or cock." I snap at him.

I catch a glimpse of his quirked eyebrow in the rearview mirror. "Who is to say Becca doesn't need us as much as Sam did once? Who's to say, she couldn't be a cockless Fisher man, too?"

Sam crosses her arms in a huff, "You make it sound like I was so needy."

He grabs her shoulder and softens his tone. "Sweetheart, you know we needed you as much as you needed us." He leans forward and kisses her cheek. "What I'm saying is, we don't need each other like that anymore. We love and care for you. You love and care for us. We will always have one another, but want is not need. What Becca has, Baby Girl is need."

Sam's scowl fades, but she doesn't smile. I see this as an opportunity.

"Hey Morgan, you know, if Sam falls in love and wants to marry and have children, she won't need us anymore." Sam smacks my arm.

Morgan shrugs, "She doesn't need us now." He laughs, "I feel sorry for the man that tries to love her though. He has to put up with us." Sam and Morgan laugh louder, but I don't laugh at all.

I try to steer the conversation back to suit my purposes again. "He would have to be somebody we can hang out with, like Matt or Jacob."

Morgan nods. "Yeah, but those two are already taken. You got somebody in mind?"

I give Sam a glance and wink with the eye Morgan can't see. "I might."

Sam punches me again. "When choosing my husband, will you be discussing my dowry? Will I meet him on my wedding night like poor Becca almost did?"

Morgan's face goes white. "Sweetheart, wanting to see you happy and with a man we know will treat you better than we do is not like what Becca escaped. You don't really believe that is what we were doing, do you?"

Sam reaches back squeezing Morgan's knee. "No, of course not, but even you have to admit, at best, that is an odd conversation to have in front of me. At worst, it's a little demeaning."

He leans forward grabbing the back of Sam's head and pulls her to his face he brushes his lips to hers and rests his forehead to hers. "Xander and I would never, ever disrespect you. I'm sorry you felt that way."

She nods bobbing their heads together. Morgan has never put his lips on hers. Connor, all the fucking time. Bastard. But Morgan, his role in her life has never been one that would require that level of intimacy. Has something changed?

"You never kiss Sam on the mouth." It comes out more accusatory than I mean it to sound.

He looks at me in the rearview mirror. "No, but you do, and you're driving. Since I do it better, you'll need to step up your game, or leave the kisses to me, Baby Brother." He smacks the back of my head playfully.

"Asshole, I can't kiss Sam because I'm driving, but you can hit me?"

Morgan leans back draping his arm across the back seat. "Suck it up buttercup." Just like that, we are back to normal. I feel satisfied getting Morgan to consider Sam could be happy with someone the Fisher men like. When the chips fall, I hope they still like me. They have to love me, I'm their brother, but nobody can insist they like me.

The view from the upper bluff is amazing. The sun is setting on the lake in the distance. It reminds me of Zack's painting. Catching the sun without getting burned.

I'm trying, Sam.

We have the sun; now we work on not getting burned.

Gathering firewood from a nearby stack, I get to work while Becca and Sam comb the surrounding woods for twigs and fallen branches for kindling.

We assemble our tents, and Sam begins working on the comfort of ours. She starts blowing up a queen-sized air mattress. I'm curious about its durability. Maybe if I cover her mouth, I can have Sam tonight after all.

"Am I sleeping with you, Sam?" Becca's little girl voice freezes all of us in our places. *Shit,* we didn't think about Becca. We've gone camping and on vacations several times. Sam always sleeps with me or Connor. The Fisher Men converge at the campfire.

Connor rubs the back of his neck. "We didn't discuss sleeping arrangements before grabbing tents." I think Connor was planning to sleep with Sam tonight. He would have been disappointed anyway.

Zack takes Becca's hand and pulls her to our circle. "Sam usually sleeps with Xander." He motions to me. Connor glares at him. "Or, occasionally," he nods to Connor "She sleeps with Connor. We will rearrange if you want, but if it's okay, the tent I grabbed has two rooms, you can have your own space. I'll be on the other side of the zipper if you need me."

She bites her lip and nods. "I think I might like that best."

She's too young, but she clearly has a crush on Zack. She isn't his type at all. He likes girls who embrace their dark side, girls who make him work for it. Becca is entirely to demure and innocent.

Now that the sleeping arrangements have been dealt with, I take a seat on a log by the fire. Just as I'm about to yank Sam into my lap, Connor grabs her by the elbow. "Before you climb into his lap for the rest of the night. Can we roast marshmallows, talk, eat, and you know, camp?" He looks me in the face. "In other words, before you hog her like usual, maybe remember I've only seen her once since she's been back."

I nod. He's right, I get to sleep with her. I guess I can let her sit with him. "Sorry Con-man, I do get stingy with my Sam time." I hook her chin and kiss her lips. "I'm sharing like a good boy." Her cheeks pink and I take my seat again on the log, without Sam this time.

Sam makes a s'more for me. She knows just how I like it. She makes another for herself and sits next to Connor. The conversation runs easily.

Connor learns that he still won't be meeting his new roommate, Veronica. It's funny, Zack and I have met her, but he still hasn't. "Dude, she's really pretty, and since Sam likes her, you know she's cool," I reassure him. Even though Rika is exactly his type, she has that sexy librarian look that makes him weak, he is very weird about his personal space.

As many times as Sam and he had curled in bed to watch a movie, it has never, not once, ever been in his bed. He's never even had sex in his bed. His apartment is not just clean, it's freaking sterile. I'm shocked that he loosened his control freakiness to do this solid for Sam. I'm willing to bet Sam asked him specifically in a match making attempt.

If Connor falls for Rika, coming out of the Xander/Sam closet will be easier. She isn't dark and broody enough for Zack, and there have never been sparks between her and Morgan, so getting them to accept me as the man in her life would be easier if Connor had someone.

Good luck with that, though.

Connor cycles through women like the spokes of a bike on Tour de France. He isn't bad or a player. Let's just say his apartment isn't the only thing pristine. He can't handle chaos or the messiness that a relationship would garner. Rika may be the specimen of a woman he would pursue, but if she didn't flip out like a mad woman when Sam peed in their kitchen sink, she's probably not the girl for Connor.

The last rays of the sun have long since dipped behind the lake while we are still deep in conversations of "would you rather" and relationship horror stories when Sam yawns and climbs into my lap.

Morgan takes a sip of his beer and points the long neck in a sweeping motion to us. "So, Xander asked what I would do if Sam fell in love and got married." He takes another sip as everyone looks at him wide-eyed. "I'm curious what you all think of that."

We all shift uncomfortably. Nobody wants to think of that right now. As her future fiancée, even I am reluctant to discuss this now, after everyone has had a few drinks.

Zack finally lets out a Pssht noise. "Sam is never going to get married, no guy is going to take us as a package deal."

Morgan nods pointing his long neck again. "That's what Xander said. He said it would have to be someone we like and could hang with, like Matt."

Jacob shrugs, "You do have a cool brother in law, but what if she married one of you?"

Zack waves a dismissive hand. "Can't happen. We have rules. You are aware of the Chrissy's friends rule?"

Jacob nods. "Yes, Chrissy's friends are off limits to Fisher Men. None of you ever laid a finger on my wife because she was Chrissy's friend."

Connor smirks. "Damn straight. I for one was disappointed Chrissy met her first." He winks but Jacob laughs.

"Dude, I love my wife. Zan is the nicest, hottest woman on the planet, but she leaves her dirty clothes on the floor, dishes in the sink, and have you smelled her damn car? You would have run screaming awfully fast, and since Fisher Men don't share, nobody else would have had a chance." To that, we all burst out laughing. He's right.

Jacob leans forward his elbows on his knees. "None of you will deem anyone worthy enough for Sam. Her only options are to marry one of you or lose all of you. If she chooses someone else, you'll lose her friendship because she has to choose her husband over you. She has to stop sleeping with Connor and Xander, no more kisses, no more sitting on laps, no more motorcycle rides, or Fisher-Men-plus-Sam vacations." He shrugs, "So, would you rather let Sam go, or watch her marry your brother?"

Morgan flips his hand in the air. "Damn Jacob, you don't play when it comes to would you rather." He scrapes his fingers across his jaw a minute or two and answers, "I'd rather she marry my brother. Sam is already a Fisher."

Zack blows out a long steady breath. "I'm not sure any of you would be cool with sleep overs, motorcycle rides, or kisses. I would not be okay with my wife sitting in Xander's lap, and

Xander would not be cool with Connor sleeping over on movie nights." He shrugs in defeat, "I think we'd lose her anyway. If she chooses someone else at least we won't have bad blood between us." He motions to his brothers. "I say if she marries an ass, we have no recourse."

Connor shakes his head, "I don't know man, we are okay with Sam's affections now, why would we need to change? I say I'd rather have her marry any brother but Zack because he'd kick me out on movie night."

"I guess it's my turn." I choose my words carefully. "I think that if she married my brother, I'd stop sleeping with her. I mean dude, respect. I'd step away a little while because I'm in love with her and I'd need to get over that." She stiffens in my arms. And looks at me with a wide eyed cautious look. "I love her too much to walk away forever though. I'd have to stick around to make sure the lucky asshole is treating my girl better than I would."

Morgan stands up abruptly. "What the fuck Xander, you're in love with Sam? We have rules, asshole."

He isn't wrong, but I'm not going to lie. I shrug. "Sorry to put you on the spot, Sam." I look back at Morgan with a new sense of calm, the kind that comes with respect and honesty. "I loved her before the pact. I can't turn it off. What I'm saying is I love her enough to do what is best for Sam. The pact was best for Sam, but if you guys start falling for other girls, I'm pursuing her."

"Even at the cost of losing me?" she asks with an even tone reminding me of the consequences. I don't care. She needs to hear it as much as they do.

"Bet, I am going to try before I let some other asshole marry you."

If looks could kill, Zack would be convicted of murder. "So, what? Fair notice? You're going to break the rules?"

I glare right back. "We committed to doing what is best for Sam, and if she agrees one of us is good for her, we need to accept that."

Zack smirks at me in challenge. "So, if she chooses me. You're cool with the rules being broken?"

"Rule number three. If Sam chooses you, you are still my brother."

Becca's voice timidly speaks just barely audible over our argument. "What are the Fisher Men rules exactly?"

Morgan begins, "Rule number one, our sister's friends are off limits. We've had girls use her to get close to us. Sam was Chrissy's friend first."

Connor holds up two fingers, "Rule number two, first one to kiss a girl, gets the girl, and once one of us kisses her, nobody else may pursue her, ever. We dust our lips on Sam from time to time, that isn't a real kiss. If it were, she'd be mine." *Asshole!*

Zack leans toward Becca, "Rule number three, treat women with the same respect our dad gives our mom. Don't do or say anything that would make our Mama ashamed." All the Fisher Men thump our chest in solidarity. "So, Xander is saying that if Sam married me, he would respect my wife and her decision."

Becca nods curtly.

I hop right on number four hoping to break the tension. "Number four, Fisher men don't eat pussy with their ass in the air."

We finish in unison. "We lay down, like a sniper."

Becca looks alarmed. "You eat cats?"

The laughter is deafening. I feel sorry for her and I don't want to keep laughing at her confused face, but tears spring from my eyes.

Zack puts his arm around Becca's shoulders and rubs her arm. "How old are you kid?"

"Sixteen." She answers.

He musses her hair. "I'll explain in two years."

Sam swings around in my lap and faces Becca. "One way to have sex is inserting male part A into female part B. Since you were betrothed, it was explained to you?" She nods her cheeks turning so red they border purple. "Another way to have sex is by inserting either of those parts into your partner's mouth." Becca's eyes widened to saucers. "Eating pussy is a crude way of describing a man orally pleasing a woman" She points to her crotch not willing to say the word to an already shell-shocked looking girl.

"People do that?" Becca asks then slaps her hand across her mouth.

Sam shrugs. "Some better than others."

"Are you still a virgin?" She smacks her mouth again and waves both hands in a no don't answer that motion. "I mean if one has sex with a mouth, are they still a virgin? Not, are you personally a virgin. Since you're not married, clearly you are." She rolls her eyes like it's so obvious. Everybody's lips press together firmly and I can see the stifled giggles.

Sam quirks an eyebrow. "The tongue would be rather freakishly long to break a hymen, but to be honest, most women who have sex for the first time don't have a hymen anyway. Self-love, falls, and even menstruation can rupture it long before," she air quotes, "the wedding night."

Becca looks horror stricken. "Self-love?"

We all squirm, but not Sam. "Masturbation."

Now Becca looks more affronted. "That's… a sin!"

Jacob stands up, stretches and says, "Well that's my cue. Goodnight all." He picks up his stuff. "I'm heading to the security cabin. If anybody has changed their mind about camping, I can drop you off at the lodge."

I'm sure that was for Becca's benefit, but nobody takes the offer.

I tell him to sit down. "Dude! You have a tent, and you can see the cameras on your phone. Stay and camp with us."

We are all grateful for the change in subject, and Jacob agrees to stay. In no time, the banter of sports, work, and women drift up with the campfire smoke.

I look to Becca who smiles and tries to contribute conversationally. I can't help but think that I bet everyone in Becca's life who insists masturbation is a sin routinely relieves themselves.

I love that Sam could answer her questions without shame.

Sam

I wake when Xander lays me on the air mattress. "Did I fall asleep?"

He kisses my nose. "Don't you always?"

I do.

Crawling into the bed next to me, he wraps me in his arms.

"Love, I'm sorry to put you on the spot like that. I just wanted them to spin the notion around in their heads. If they think about it and accept it, just like Morgan has, they will forgive us quickly."

My voice cracks. "You told them you are in love with me."

"I am in love with you. I'm not going to lie. I wanted to come clean right then and there, but I am trying very hard to respect your wishes."

Tears pool in my eyes. "You're in love with me?"

He pulls me tightly to his chest. "Baby, how can you possibly doubt that?" Hooking my chin, he lifts my face and kisses me. It's sweet and chaste and beautiful, until it's not.

The heated kiss develops slowly, building steam before he devours me. It's still beautiful, but it's hot and passionate. He rolls on top of me, which is no small feat on an air mattress. Kissing a sexy trail down my neck, his body inches down the mattress.

"What are you doing?" I ask.

He nips at my shirt as he makes his way down my abdomen. He puts one finger over his lips in a shush and whispers, "I'm going to sniper your kitty. Be very quiet."

Be very quiet? Sweet Baby Jesus, how the heck am I going to be quiet if he is going to… oh, oooohhhh, I bite down on my palm, close my eyes, and let the pleasure wash over me.

A far away sound rouses my curiosity. Not enough to open my eyes. I don't care if it's a bear or a mountain lion, he can eat me when Xander's done, and I'll die a happy woman.

The sound of a heavy-duty zipper causes my eyelids to fly open. It takes a few blinks before I realize what I am seeing. The portable DVD player from our teen years smashed on the floor of the tent, Xander's eyes wide, his lips still wet with me, and Connor's face flashing from shock, disbelief, sadness, and anger. I reach for him but he flinches out of the way.

His eyes lock on Xander and both his fists and jaws clench. Xander begins to rise with a steel gaze of his own. I dress quickly and try to diffuse the brothers before it comes to blows. I'm not successful. The tent collapses as the three of us tumble to the ground. The two boys are trying to make contact, but I'm stuck in the middle. I hear Zack and Morgan yelling and feel the tent grabbing at us. I realize they are trying to free us from the gauzy film and flying fists. I've taken a few unintended hits, and I need them to hurry.

"Morgan, help me, I'm bleeding!"

All the commotion stops. Xander and Connor reach for me in the dark. The tent releases us and after a bit of jostling. I see Morgan backlit by the campfire. Standing up, I wrap my arms around him and the relief overwhelms me. A sob breaks from my chest.

"Where are you hurt?" Morgan asks, his palms take my face to look at me, but he pulls them back when he feels the blood. I can feel the gash at my hairline and I can feel the blood trickle down my still bruised face. I must look a fright because Morgan looks pissed. He whips off his white shirt to clean my face. Jacob appears to my left with a flashlight.

"Samantha, I need you to sit down and let me check you out." Jacob is a nurse. I should let him, but I don't want to let go of Morgan yet. When he gets to the bottom of this, it may be the last time he touches me. I'm carefully pried free from my sanctuary and placed on a log. A first aid kit I hadn't noticed before is open. The smell of antiseptic overtakes the dried leaves and the pine smell of our surroundings.

While Jacob cleans and tends my wounds, the Fisher brothers argue in hushed venom. Shoving starts, ends, and begins again.

"Oh Jacob, I really fucked this up." I knew my relationship with the Fisher Men would be uprooted, but I will never come between the brothers. I had hoped it wasn't possible. I always thought their bond was stronger than ours. The bloodied cotton at my feet tells another story. I'm glad the secret planting of Wonder Woman after all these years prepared me for this moment.

Leaning my forehead on Jacob's shoulder I whimper, "What have I done?" He cups the back of my head to shush me, and I use the moment to silently unlatch the climbing hook affixing his keys to his belt loop. Pulling back from our embrace, I cross my arms to conceal the stolen keys. I lift my free hand to slap tears from my face.

"I've done enough," placing my hand on Jacob's arm. "Will you please intervene?" I shrug a shoulder toward the still hushed but heated argument. Jacob nods and pats my shoulder before joining the Fisher brothers.

I slip into the woods unnoticed and run to Jacob's quad leaving my mess in the dust. I don't have a plan. I don't know my next move. All I know is I need to not be here. They will forgive Xander, and everyone can move on if I remove myself from the equation.

It may be hard, but if I'm honest, the best way to love them is to let them go. I should have stuck with my plan. I should have waited until the others found love. I should go back to New York and wait. Maybe not New York, but somewhere, not here.

Arriving at the cabin I park the quad in the shed and head inside. Packing my stuff is easy since I never unpacked. I owe them a note. They will worry without a note.

Boys,
I love you too much to tear you apart. We are grown-ups now. You don't need me to feel like you're helping your sister,

and I don't need you to walk with my chin up. I'm just a girl you helped once, and I hope you can look back on our time fondly. You will always need your brother.

Jacob,
Your car will be at Nonna's house. Sorry, I took it, but I had to go. I started the car then left the key fob on the rocking chair outside for you.

Slinging my bag over my shoulder, I walk away with one final tear and stiffened spine. I'm doing the right thing, I will not shed anymore tears for the Fisher Men.

CHAPTER 31

She may be your girlfriend, but she's my best friend.

Xander

I shove him back. "Fuck you, Connor. I wasn't taking advantage of her. I told you, I am in love with her. We live together. We sleep in the same bed, and we have been discussing our relationship and how it will affect your friendships with her."

Connor seethes through gritted teeth, "She was asleep and you were taking her clothes off, you prick. Mama raised us better than that."

Zack takes a hold of me as Morgan grabs Connor.

Zack pulls me tighter and whisper yells, "Dude, if that's true, I'm going to hold you down while he kicks your ass, and then we're going to switch places."

"She wasn't sleeping!" I defend.

Connor snarls back, "Her eyes were closed, and we just watched you carry her sleeping body in there." He points angrily at the heap of canvas that was once a tent.

"Connor, think about what you saw. She was naked, my face between her legs, her eyes were closed. I assure you, she was a willing participant, and it wasn't the first time."

Jacob thankfully interrupts, "He's not lying about them being together. Zan knew and arranged for an alone time for them. It's why I asked such pointed questions tonight."

I'm grateful he backed me up, but I can't imagine this secret known by Zan and Jacob is going to bode well with my brothers. Zack and Morgan finally let us go. Zack crosses his arms and glares at me. Morgan's jaw ticks.

It's Connor who speaks though. "How long has this been going on?"

This is not how I wanted to have this conversation. I run my fingers through my hair and blow out a deep breath. "I have always loved her. I have always wanted her. I intend to be her husband someday, but I didn't break the rules. She chose me, she kissed me. She came back from New York with every intention of being with me. She just didn't know how she could choose me and keep you." I lock eyes with Zack. "She wanted to catch the sun without getting burned. She wasn't sure if she could." I glance around making eye contact with each of my brothers. "You answered pretty loud and clear. I will not give her up, so you accept us or you lose us."

I envisioned grabbing my woman and storming off. My goal was to have them watch us leave and debate how terrible it would be never seeing us again. It was a great, if not dramatic plan, but when I went to take Sam away, she was already gone.

"Shit!"

Morgan and Connor checked the lodge. Jacob, Zack, and Becca rode with me to check the other cabins. Jacob noticed the quad in the shed and his car is missing.

I pace and stammer waiting for Jacob to obtain a spare key and let us into the cabin. As soon as the lock clicks, I barrel past Jacob and run up the stairs to her room, calling her name. I freeze in the doorway. It's empty; her bag is gone. I walk into the adjacent bathroom. The smell of her shampoo still lingers in the air, but the bottles are gone. My fists clench. Punching the granite counter, I ignore the pain and catch my reflection in the mirror. My face and eye are swollen and starting to purple.

She must have been so afraid. Now she's hurt, bleeding, and alone. I run downstairs. Jacob stops me at the door. He hands me a note in Sam's handwriting. I always loved her handwriting, but this… this I don't love.

Flinging open the front door, I stomp down the front steps just as Morgan pulls up in his truck. I slap the note in the middle of his chest and yell to Connor as he gets out.

"It's a goodbye. She would rather be miserable than tear us apart." I hop in my Jeep and yell out to whichever brother is listening. "I'm not letting her go. You know how to get a hold of me if you choose to. I'll be with Sam."

I shift into drive but slam on the brakes when Zack steps in front of the car.

He places both hands on the hood and grumbles. "She maybe your girlfriend, but she's my best friend. You aren't leaving without me." He pounds his fist on the hood, swings open the passenger door and drops into the seat before I can protest. In my rearview mirror, I see Connor and Morgan following. I also notice Becca. I forgot about her. Her eyes are wide but her mouth is shut. This must be some crazy culture shock shit show. Frankly, I'm too focused to stop and let her out.

As we get closer to Champagne Falls, the skies open, and we are in the middle of a gnarly electrical storm. The speed limit is impossible, sudden wind gusts nearly blow us into the oncoming lanes. I'm suddenly very concerned about Sam. I scour the roadsides looking for Jacob's Prius.

Sensing my apprehension, Zack grasps my shoulder, "The Prius is lower to the ground and the batteries make it very heavy. She could navigate this storm better in that car than we can in the Jeep."

I nod. I have no idea if it's true, but I hope it is.

As quickly as it started, the storm broke, but it was followed by an unnaturally eerie calm. The skies had a strange green hue. "I don't like this." We pull up to the stop sign on Main street. The streets are deserted.

"What's that noise?" Zack asks looking out toward the park.

Becca leans in between Zack and me, pointing to the dark sky ahead. "Tornado siren."

As soon as the words leave her mouth, we see a perfect funnel cloud disappear.

"Zack, call Morgan. That's really close to Mom's house." I pull over in front of Xanack Ink, "I'm getting Sam. You don't have to go with me."

Zack shakes his head. "I don't have to go? Dude, it's not like a really long ride from the airport. It's a fucking tornado." He knocks his knuckles on my head. "You are of no use to her dead."

I smack his hand away from me. "I'd rather die trying."

He rolls his eyes at me. "Okay, wannabe superhero, drama queen. Might I suggest something rational, like calling first? What if she didn't even go there?" He pulls out his phone and puts it on speaker.

Every ring makes my heart stop, and her voicemail greeting shatters me. He holds up one finger. "You need Morgan's truck. It's heavier than this Jeep."

He types on his phone as he opens the door and lets Becca out. He hands her keys to the shop and instructs her to lock up and stay out of sight.

We climb into Morgan's truck. I delicately ask him to let me drive his work truck into a tornado, like a crazy storm chaser. He answers, "Shut up and fasten your fucking seat belt."

Shifting the truck into drive he speeds down the street. Zack's phone rings. and he answers on speaker.

"I'm in my basement. I'm safe please don't let Xander come here." As soon as the sentence leaves the phone speaker, the funnel cloud disappears again, a ripping sound echoes in the cab of the truck, and Sam's scream is the last thing we hear before silence fills the air.

"Fuuuuuck!" I don't know who yells it, but we all think it.

Morgan dodges fallen trees weaving through neighborhoods. It's a fifteen-minute drive on a good day. The debris makes it a longer drive and we do it in silence. Rolling into Sam's neighborhood, we have to park several blocks away. It looks like a battlefield. We run past fallen trees, overturned cars, and empty plots where houses once stood. The hair on my arms and the back of my neck stands on end and we run faster.

Our steps falter when we turn on the street we grew up on. There next to our childhood home sits a pile of rubble. Her house is gone. My vision tunnels. My limbs move of their own accord. I hear nothing but echoes.

I finally got her. I can't lose her now.

CHAPTER 32

From the Diary of a Casual Observer,
In the wake of the tornado that devastated Champagne
Falls, I hope love and light find you today. Especially
among so much loss.

Sam

In the moments before waking, not quite asleep, possibly dreaming, but aware of the dream. It's a moment of divine clarity. When controlling the path of the dream becomes possible, what the heart truly desires becomes reality with pristine clarity.

I'm normally quicker when I chop vegetables, but I'm slowly slicing cucumbers with deliberate methodical precision. The smile on my face would ordinarily make my cheeks hurt. Smiling is so easy now, it doesn't feel unnatural.

Zack is engaged in a full on light sabre battle with our little girl. "C'mon girl, show Uncle Zack what you're made of. You got this."

Her determined face scrunches. She lunges at him. He jumps out of the way and he snatches her up around her waist digging tickle fingers into her sides. She squeals and kicks and lets giggles that sound like music escape.

"Go home, Uncle Zack!"

"Lucky for you, little girl, my other love is waiting for me." He kisses her head before joining me in the kitchen. "Mom said this is your class roster and sleeping arrangements. Here are access codes to the cabin, she had notebooks and writing materials sent ahead, the Safe Space advocate will be there when you arrive." He flips through the folder of material. "Oh, and since your pussy of a husband can't be without you for three weeks, he'll come up the second weekend."

"I don't talk about your wife, so no calling my husband a pussy, Zachary Michael Fisher!"

He smiles and kisses my cheek. "All three names? Well, aren't you a true Mama Fisher?"

I may not have had the dark beginning, or the life laced with tragedy, but I can be compared to worse things than Nonna Fisher.

Glancing up at the microwave clock, he gathers his things. "Speaking of my wife, that sweet woman can be frightening if I'm late for dinner."

"Pregnancy hormones?" I ask.

"Dare I say, she is worse than you were. Love you seester." He tosses his light sabre to my little girl. "Love you, Padawan." Kissing her briefly, he disappears out the door. Who would have thought a woman could make Zack Fisher jump and clock watch?

I flip through the papers, excited for the next Safe Spaces teen retreat. This cabin is in Nevada. Last season, our retreat was in upstate New York. Teaching teens from abusive households to find therapy in journaling is my second greatest accomplishment. The first one just knocked over a vase of sunflowers with her new light sabre. Uncle Zack's kid is getting drums as soon as he's old enough to bang.

My mom is joining me on this retreat. She teaches jewelry making. Xander sometimes joins me to do art. I shake my head and laugh at how worried I was. It wasn't long ago that I was overwhelmed at the prospect of moving in with my dad after college. I was so concerned the Fisher family would be angry with me for loving Xander. I even wondered if love was enough. I was so prepared to give up on my happiness. How could I not think I was worthy of happiness?

I comfort my little girl. She has my brown hair and freckles but her father's striking blue eyes. Eyes that are filled with tears. She isn't hurt, she's crying because she thinks she hurt my feelings. We have a sweet empathetic little girl. I wrap my arms around her and smooth her hair. "Oh sweet baby, it was an accident."

"I'm sorry, Mama."

"That's step one. What is the next step to apologizing?"

Her little mouth twists and she taps her finger on her chin. Her whole face lights and her shoulders lift when she remembers.

"Step two is asking, 'How can I help?'"

I ruffle her hair. "Very good. Go get the garbage can."

"Uh-oh, what happened?" I turn to the all-familiar panty melting voice of my husband. After all this time, my heart still flutters, and I feel warmth in my soul at the sight of him. I feel my smile widen along with my arms as I make my way to his embrace.

"It was an accident. She already feels bad, and really it's all Zack's fault."

"Ah, so he dropped off your retreat packet?" I nod and kiss him.

"How was your day?" I ask.

"Mediocre until I saw you."

He leads me to the kitchen with a hand to the small of my back and offers to finish the clean-up with our little one.

I finish dinner while Xander showers and dresses. We spend our meal time laughing, reminiscing, and practicing math facts. After dinner, just like his father, Xander thanks me by cleaning up.

Tumbling into bed at night, the weight of the day melts. I fan my shower wet hair over the pillow and put my ice cold feet on Xander's legs making him yelp and grab me around the waist, to tickle me. Our playful roll in bed turns into more rolling, less playing. The tickles turn to grasps, and our mouths connect.

His fingers tangle in my hair as he pulls my body to his chest. His free hand trails its way down my back and firmly grabs my ass. He pulls me to a straddle on top of him. "Mrs. Fisher you are wearing entirely too many clothes." I assist him in removing my nightgown. The devious smirk he gives me every time he sees my boobs makes my lady bits pulse. He is so damn sexy. I lean over to kiss him and I can already feel his erection seeking attention. Smiling into his kiss, my body purrs with my words. "Well hello, Mr. Fisher."

His erection pulses a cool Prince Albert tapping me. "Knock knock." He chides.

Reaching behind me, I grab his length and give it a few slow strokes. He moans, his fingertips digging into my hips. I remove my hand from his straining cock and walk my fingers up his beautiful inked chest, then up further to trace his smooth lips. Leaning in for a kiss, I position myself over his tip. Relief and satisfaction flood me as I slide lower and lower down his impressive cock.

Taking a moment to appreciate the fullness of being fully seated, I throw my head back and savor the feel of my husband. Slowly, I roll my hips grinding, lifting, falling and enjoying every movement. His hands trace up and down my back, tracing my breasts, before squeezing my hips. He guides me to a swifter pace, a deeper angle, and a body quaking pleasure.

As the waves of orgasm plummet my body it's hard to hold myself up. Xander sits up bracing me firmly and rolling me to my back without breaking our connection. We are lost in a tangle of fingers, tongues, and skin. The sensations are intoxicating. Xander leans back on his ankles and slides me up for that exquisite angle I've come to know as his favorite. My vision goes black. In the darkness, I hear his deep voice rumble, "I love you."

I explode in a million satisfied fragments of myself when I feel the swell and release of my true first love. Colton BaddStone was the boy I kissed. Xander Fisher is the man I love. It was always him.

I open my eyes, but it's still dark. Rolling to my side, I feel Xander tracing patterns in my skin. He lifts my arm and writes words. It's a game we used to play. I focus on the strokes; *I love you*, something else and then the letters *O.K.*, last words *wake up*.

Huh? Wake up? I'm not asleep.

Am I?

I flutter my eyes but it's dark. Are they open? I can't move. I try to speak but no noise comes out.

The rational side of my brain knows my happy marriage and a beautiful little girl is a dream. If I didn't know it, I'm realizing it now. The less than rational part of my brain isn't ready to let go. I guess it's time though.

Trying to wake up is like trying to fight my way out of a canvas bag filled with pillows. It's a struggle. Canvas is one of the strongest fabrics, but the slightest tear makes it fall apart. When I finally make my way through the canvas, I find myself standing in a white room with white floors and bright lights. My head hurts, my skin is on fire, and someone is drumming their fingers on my hand. I look at my hand but it's empty. I distinctly feel a hand on mine, but I can't see it. I turn my hand over and startle at a deep far off echo.

"Did you just move? C'mon girl open those pretty eyes."

I grab my head, oh my god it hurts. I feel like I am holding my skull together. I scold myself. *Focus Samantha. You got this.* I concentrate all of my energy on opening my eyes. Normally, I open my eyes to transition from darkness, but my mind is in a room brighter than the room my body is in. My eyelids fly open and I am met with beautiful blue eyes and Xander's face, only it's not Xander.

"Zack?" I ask thorough the rocky desert of my mouth.

He laughs and stands. "There's my bad ass girl." He stands, then sits, then stands again to kiss me on the forehead. "You and Mama are the only people on the planet who can tell us apart."

I look around obviously confused. Zack answers the question I didn't ask. "It was the strangest the thing. You started to groan like you were in pain. You were shaking, your skin got really hot and then that skin writing thing happened."

Oh dear god, I had an orgasm in front of Zack?

"Yes, like that. He motions in the vicinity of my face and chest. I don't need to look, I know I'm red faced. "Xander's eyes got as big as quarters and he darted out to get a nurse."

Oh my god, Xander KNOWS it was an orgasm and not pain. Kill me now. "He left you a note."

Zack raises my arm and sure enough the white letters written in my red skin glow. It reads *everything is okay. I love you.* My other arm reads, *wake up.*

Then everything is okay. His large frame fills the doorway after a small nurse bristles in ahead of him. Despite the poking, prodding, and questions, my eyes don't leave him. He is not only a beautiful man, but this is the face, body, and soul I have always seen as my home. He is my home. I want the dream I conjured.

Silently, I mouth the word, "Hi."

He smiles back at me and the steady beep of my heart monitor picks up in pace. We chuckle. He lifts his chin toward his brother, "Hey, can I have a minute with my girl?"

Zack kisses me on the head before speaking to Xander. "Yeah man, but be sure to save some Sam time for the rest of us." He grasps Xander's shoulder. "I'll let everyone know she's awake and hold off her crazy mom as long as I can."

My mom is here?

"How long have I been out?" I ask.

Xander puts his hands in his pockets and walks toward Zack's vacated chair. "A few hours. You have a head injury. They gave you medicine to reduce swelling and it knocked you out."

"I had a dream."

He flashed a knowing smile.

"I saw my future and I finally know what direction I want for my life."

He sits in the chair next to me and takes my hand. "That's amazing Sam. Tell me all about it." He kisses my knuckles.

"I need to go back to New York." His face falls, and I realize I shouldn't have started with that. I cup his face. "Your girlfriend needs to take a few more classes before she moves back in our home."

His expression is blank. He probably doesn't understand. I run my thumb along his cheek.

"I love you, Xander, I'm coming home to you. I'm going to Skype you every night. You better come visit me when you can, and when I finish, I'll be prepared to build a future with you."

"What about my brothers?"

I shrug, "They can come to visit me, too."

He rolls his eyes at me, "I mean, what if they don't support this." He motions between us.

"They'll get over it or die. I hope they get over it because I would miss them."

His face splits with a glorious smile and he stands to kiss me. His lips fall into me like magnets to metal, and for the first time since waking, I feel like I can breathe.

"Disengage, disengage! Her mother is coming." Connor is out of breath as he appears in the doorway rushing me. "I'm so happy to see you awake. I have to go. I'll be gone for six months."

I wink at Connor. "I'll see you next Tuesday. You owe me a romantic comedy."

He shakes his head. "Dude, that's our secret."

The numerous fits of laughter from the doorway suggest it is no longer *our* secret.

For a tiny woman, my mom has no issue elbowing her way through the enormous wall of Fisher men.

"Oh baby cakes, I am so relieved you are okay." She kisses my face way more than what is appropriate and awkwardly hugs me in that careful not to hurt me way. "Oh, thank goodness Morgan had all the tools in his truck to get you out so fast." Oh great, more awkward hugs and loud mwah sounding kisses. "Why were you even there? Don't you live with Xander right now?" I'd answer her if she stopped kissing and hugging me.

"Dad wasn't home. Is he okay?" I manage to ask.

Nonna pats my hand and smiles her signature eye twinkling smile. "Yes dear, He's certainly fine, he is. Like most folk on a weekday he was at work, Luv."

I grasp her hand with mine. "Nonna, your house?"

"Oh dear," Nonna chuckles. "Yer kind to worry, ya are. But the Fisher home is still standing. It'll be needin' some repair, mind you, but nothin' Morgan can't patch right up. Now don't yer worry yer pretty little head." She gives my hand a final squeeze. "We need to get a move on, Luv. We'll be havin' lots o' neighbors needn' a warm meal and a big hug."

Any person to have been graced with the presence of Mrs. Fisher is a lucky, blessed person. She doesn't love with her whole heart. She loves with her whole being.

Xander stayed behind, but the rest of the Fisher clan left with Nonna. My dad stopped in with his new girlfriend. She is quirky like my dad but unashamed. She's social despite her hang ups. She reminds me of Zan. They are moving in together. Nothing like a tornado to push a relationship to the next level. It did it for me.

In hindsight, I feel foolish. I was so scared to disclose our relationship, that it nearly cost me, Xander. In the end, my boys want me to be happy.

I think Zack is going to take a little longer to be okay with us, but it's clear he's trying. He called me Xander's girlfriend.

Ignoring us will be easy for Connor since he'll be gone for a long time.

Eventually, my mother, who has had her chest draped across my abdomen since she came in, is pried off of me and sent home to sleep. The medications have made me groggy enough to not understand if the time lapses between people leaving are minutes or hours, but it dwindles down to Xander and me.

"I owe you an apology."

He smiles at me. "You do?"

"I do." I nod and meet his eyes. "I put your brothers' feelings before yours. I let it affect decisions about us, and I didn't give us our best chance."

His voice is hollow but not unkind. "You did."

"It won't happen again. If we are going to work out long distance, then there can't be trust issues."

His head drops. "I just got you back."

"Now you can keep me. Let me tell you about the dream I had."

Xander

I must treat women in a way that would make Nonna Fisher proud. As much as I don't want Sam to leave again, I want her dreams to come true, literally and figuratively. I lay the laptop and paperwork on our bed.

While she recuperates from a fractured wrist and a knock to her noggin, I do all the necessary research to set her on her path. She's right, she needs to go back to New York. In just a few classes, she can get the degree necessary to have the career she desires. Starting over here would take her longer.

"I concede, you are going back to New York in January. You'll take two on-line classes beginning in September, but you have to be present for these." I point to the class list.

Mama is on board with Sam joining Safe Spaces, and while they won't be able to pay her in the beginning, I got her covered. Not all rewards are dollars. "You can volunteer at Safe Spaces until you leave, but I insist you take self-defense classes."

She quirks an eyebrow at me but chuckles. "After what happened with Becca, I already talked to Zan about joining her gym and learning mixed martial arts."

Kissing her head, I chuckle, too. "Next time Zack calls you a badass, be sure to show him what you're learning."

Together we work on an electronic calendar. She is going to continue writing and editing, so she can feel like she is contributing to our income. *Like I give a shit.*

I add my appointments and work times. I want her to be happy and if having an income while doing what she loves makes her happy, I'll support her anyway I can.

"I spoke with Zan and Jacob about renting the lodge for writing retreats," she chirps. "They decided if the lodge is used for Safe Spaces, they would donate it, but I can hold writing retreats for authors or other events there for a bargain."

"You want to do that?" I ask.

"Yes, I made a lot of contacts in the writing community. I can offer classes, headline famous authors, and use some of the profit to support my mission with Safe Spaces."

She blows me away routinely. "That's a really great idea."

She nods like a bobble-headed Chihuahua. "Zan said she can work the numbers for me."

For all of Zan's social quirks and brute force nature, she is a mathematical savant. What she offered Sam is huge.

There is an excitement in planning a future with someone, but having someone you love to plan a future that includes you is an indescribable joy.

Sighing, I put my forehead to hers. "It was easy to miss you when I didn't know everything I was going to be missing."

"We already worked out one weekend a month in your schedule to come to visit me. I'll try one weekend a month to visit you."

I roll my forehead across hers in a head shake. "No, you worry about school and homework and coming home for good. I'll worry about visits and skype dates."

"Deal," she rolls her forehead away from mine and kisses my lips softly. Well, if that's not an invitation…

Placing the laptop carefully on the bedside table, I pounce on my woman careful of her wrist. The movement sends the papers scattered on the bed to flight, but I couldn't care less because my mouth is already firmly on hers. My hands travel her tattered body carefully, and I allow her to take the lead in the most comfortable positions for her. I marvel at how lucky I am to be the recipient of this woman's desire.

CHAPTER 33

Where in those multi-races, polo wearing, smiling faces does it say crippling debt, experience required, or death and taxes from here on out?

Sam

Being an adult pretty much sucks.

After weeks of arguing with the admissions office, it is determined, that I cannot go back to school. I have outstanding student loans, and until they are paid I am shit out of luck. I cannot return to school, any school until my $40,000.00 financial obligation has been met.

Hanging up with the admissions office again, I drop my head in defeat.

"No dice?" Xander asks.

"I need to get a job that pays $1,000.00 an hour if I want to start on time."

Kissing my head, he reassures me. "There is no rush, you have a lifetime to complete everything you need to accomplish and I will help you every way I can."

I nod and bury my face in his chest. "It's so frustrating to have all my ducks in a row for once; to have a clear plan of everything I need to move forward, but not be able to afford to do so." I could scream, or cry, or grunt in frustration. Xander's right though, I won't give up. My dreams will just take a bit longer than I expected.

Xander heads out to work and I curl up on the couch with my laptop scrolling the job boards. I have an expensive college degree that I can't afford to pay for. I have a really dynamic plan that will help me accomplish everything I need to. When I step through the other side of this struggle, I am going to make a difference. I just wish it wasn't such a struggle to get there.

Diary of a Casual Observer,

In the wake of tornado clean-ups, a little gossip to offset the drama is in order. Rumor has it that Samantha Reynolds has hooked herself a Fisher Man. That's right ladies, one of Champagne Falls sexiest bachelors is officially off the market.

I didn't realize I had dozed off until I hear Rika's voice on the other side of the front door. She knocks loudly.

"Sam!"

"I'm coming," I yell back.

Setting my laptop down on the coffee table, I yawn and stumble to the door. Rika wraps me in an enormous hug before I can fully open the door to welcome her.

I'm so sorry I wasn't here. I drove by your dad's place and cried when I saw the rubble. I can't believe you were in there.

She pulls my cast to her chest. "You're broken."

"I'll be alright. How was… where were you?"

"The Appalachian Mountains in Tennessee." She pushes past me and heads for the kitchen. "Sit, I'll make popcorn."

I do as she instructs while she tells me about all the charming mountain towns, the gorgeous chalet she stayed in, the picturesque drive, and the motel Abraham Lincoln didn't sleep in, but she did. She plops down on the couch next to me and puts the popcorn between us.

She shovels a mouthful into her face and speaks around it. "Sadly, I had to leave all that behind every day and head into a gnarly remote area to interview a clan of women right out of a horror flick."

"That good?" I snark.

The interviews were disgusting. They have this weird family cult that has a mixture of a few different religions. The head of the family even keeps sacred scrolls that are part bible, part something else altogether.

Each family unit is required to birth at least two girls. One is sent to a similar sect in another state to marry. The other is sent to town to get knocked up. It's how they keep a fresh bloodline without the typical incestual birth defects."

"That's really fucked up."

"I know, right?" Rika rolls her eyes.

"Why were you there?" I ask, grabbing my own handful of popcorn.

"The true crime novel I am writing based on the life of Liam Lancaster. It turns out Liam's grandmother was the sister sent to town to get pregnant. What she got was kidnapped by someone more disturbing than her family."

"Wow." I know Rika's heart is troubled by every stone she turns over, but it will make a spellbinding novel. I'm on the edge of my seat listening to her talk about it.

Glancing at the stack of papers and my laptop on the coffee table she asks, "what have you got going on here?"

"Job hunting," I say flatly. I tell her about all my great plans, the camping trip, the tornado, and my dream. Her face lights with excitement for me, and then I tell her, "I can't afford it."

The lights in her eyes dim. I tell her about my battle with admissions, and the inevitable stall on my happily ever after.

Wrapping me in a hug, she comforts me the only way she knows how. "You'll figure this out, Sam. I have faith in you."

There is nothing to figure out. I am one of many. The sad reality of a college education is that it is slowly beginning to cost more than you can ever gain from it. I hug her back anyways.

Sliding into her phone, Rika begins blaring Stronger by Kelly Clarkson and she yanks me to standing. The impromptu dance party may be her jam, but it can put a smile on my face even when things are grim. While we dance, for just a moment, I let go of my anxiety.

The next song in the playlist is Rachel Platten's Fight Song. We waltz to the slower beginning and jump like little girls when the fight of the song bubbles out of my chest. At the soft ending where her words paint the picture of one tiny flame, Rika spins me and I land in Xander's arms at the explosion.

I didn't hear him come in. I bury my face in his shirt and hug him. "Welcome home My Love."

He smiles and kisses me. "What are we celebrating?"

"We're not celebrating, just taking a moment to forget the stress," I answer.

"I certainly support that." He looks up at Rika and gives her a small wave. "Sam's dad and his girlfriend are coming for dinner; would you like to join us?" He asks Rika.

"No, I don't want to intrude." She says coyly.

Xander flips his hand, "Nonsense. I'm inviting Morgan, too. You can help me cook since Sam is sans two hands right now."

"No!" I blurt. Both heads whip around to look at me. I soften, "I love you Rika, I do, but you can't cook and you know it."

She shrugs. "True, but I can follow directions."

"Is Zack coming?" I ask.

Xander's eyes won't meet mine. "No, he had previous plans."

I nod, even though I know it's a lie. Zack isn't okay with Xander and me. I'm sure he's trying, but he and I are closer than I am with Connor or Morgan. I know he is just trying to figure out where he fits in. If he doesn't come around, He will never figure it out.

Sitting around the dinner table laughing with Morgan, Rika, Xander, Dad, and his girlfriend Moyra. I miss Zack. He would be the life of this party. I clutch the Wonder Woman doll I found in my makeup bag a bit ago. How can I make him see, that we can be okay?

Then it hits me The one place we can go where he has to wish me the best, break bread, and be kind. "Xander, can I bring Rika to Fisher family breakfast on Sunday?"

"Yes!" Morgan and Xander answer in unison.

"What's this?" Rika asks as she makes her way to the table with dessert.

"Allow me." My dad says as he takes the pie he and Moyra brought and begins slicing and serving it.

"I'm taking you to brunch at the Fisher's on Sunday," I explain. "Here's what you need to know." I pat the empty seat she vacated to get the pie. "You are going as my stray. It's a term of endearment for a friend. Instead of saying a prayer you bless the person next to you with a traditional Irish blessing." Rika looks around the table slowly and then back at me. "I'll text you a few, pick one and memorize it." She nods. "The only other thing to know is no use of fowl language or Nonna will make you pay for it." Everyone at the table laughs.

"Be sure to bring about $10.00 in singles, too." My dad chimes in.

"Do you gamble?" she asks.

"Something like that," Morgan answers with a wink.

Throwing her napkin down on the table, she shrugs. "Whatever if it keeps that smile on your face, I'm game. The mopey girl I walked in on is no fun."

'Oh Sweetpea," my dad pats my hand. "Why were you moping?"

Folding my arms on the table, I drop my head into them. "I finally have it all figured out and there is nothing I can do about it."

He laughs. Not just a laugh, but a full-on body trembling laugh. The kind of laugh my dad doesn't do in front of people. "Welcome to adulthood, Sweetpea."

"I don't want to be an adult if this is what it's all about. I thought I'd come home claim my man get a good paying job and live happily ever after. I mean, that is essentially what it says on the college brochure." I throw my hands up in surrender. "You saw the brochure. Where in those multi-races, polo wearing, smiling faces does it say crippling debt, experience required, or death and taxes from here on out?"

Xander pulls me into his lap. "It's okay baby we'll figure this all out."

My dad and Moyra look at one another before he smiles and speaks to me. "I came today to tell you that since Moyra and I are living together, you can have the insurance money from the house when it's settled. The land is yours to re-build or sell. It will take a while for the settlement, but you won't be indebted to your education."

Jumping up, I untangle myself from Xander's arms and dodge the table to catch my dad in a hug. "Oh Daddy, I appreciate that I do, but you worked your whole life to have a home. You should use that money to make yourself comfortable."

Standing up, he accepts my embrace then cups my cheeks forcing me to look at him. "Sweetpea, I worked my whole life to provide for you and some of that time to care for your mother. It had nothing to do with what I want, it was what was best for my family." He kisses my nose. "Nothing has changed. I'm not going to retire anytime soon." He lets go of my face and takes his seat. "I love my job, I solve complex problems, heck I would do that just for fun but my company chooses to pay me for it. I'm going to work there until they make me leave."

We all share a smile and I round the table to sit in Xander's lap. I walk my fingertips up his chest. "I guess I won't have to wait too long."

He kisses my head and speaks into my hair. "You won't have to wait at all."

Pulling back, I look at him confused. "I spoke to your admissions counselor and asked if we paid for your classes in advance could you begin with outstanding loans, she said 'yes.'"

"I don't understand?"

Pushing a stray piece of hair behind my ear, Xander smiles and kisses my nose. "I have enough money in my savings to get you started and when your Dad's settlement is finalized, it should take care of the rest."

I look from Xander to my dad and back with my jaw agape. "I can't take your savings."

He winks. "It's okay, I know where you live."

We both laugh, but I continue my protest. "No, Xander really. I can't take your money."

"Samantha Nikkole! You are starting classes as soon as possible. I'm willing to pay every penny I have to get you back home as soon as possible. Now shut up and kiss me!"

I guess were done arguing. I'm going to remember that line, I can't wait to use it against him in our next disagreement.

CHAPTER 34

How do I give you the blessing to be happy with him, without losing you?

Xander

We look up from our dinner. We both know that knocking can only be Zack. He has such an obnoxious knock. "Jeez man, come in already." I knew he wouldn't let Sam leave for New York next week without fixing things.

His key turns in the lock, and he barges in with all the excitement that is Zack Fisher. "Look, Sam," he says while pacing back and forth and never looking at her. "I didn't know it was yours, I mean it was blocks away, how could I guess?"

"Whoa, honey," she stands and holds her arms out like she is approaching a wild mustang. "What are you talking about?"

He stands as still as Zack can stand starring at the ceiling. His hands are drumming on his thighs. "I was helping with the neighborhood cleanup. I came across it. I opened it to see who it belonged to." He starts pacing again. "I didn't know it was yours, but by the time I figured it out." He stops and turns stone still. "I was hooked."

"Zachary Michael Fisher, what the hell are you talking about?" Her voice is nervous, so I wrap my arm around her waist.

Zack begins pacing again, "I should have stopped when I discovered it was yours, but I read the whole thing."

Sam's face pales. I look between her white face and his apologetic one. I shake my head. "Read what? What's going on?"

Zack pulls a little notebook from the inside pocket of his leather jacket.

"My high school journals?" Sam mumbles.

Zack's head drops. "Yes, I read all of them."

Sam's fists clench. If she was a cartoon character, steam would blow out her ears.

"I'm sorry, but you're a really good writer. I was there and even I wanted to know what was going to happen next."

Through gritted teeth, she seethes. "Those were private."

Zack grasps at his hair. "I know. God Sam, I know."

She crosses her arms. I rub my fingertips up and down her stiffened back. Zack really fucked this up. We were taught better, but still, I've never seen him so upset. I feel for both of them simultaneously.

"I am just supposed to forgive you and move on?" Sam asks with a hint of sarcasm.

Zack looks at her earnestly. His eyes locked on her and for once, he stands perfectly still. Silence is his answer, and I get it. There is no good answer to her question.

A tear breaks the barrier of his eye. Something entirely out of character for Zack.

He chokes but answers her. "You're my best friend. Tell me how to keep you."

I feel Sam break under my palm. I consider leaving them alone to work this out, but I'm not leaving either one of them like this.

"You understand now. I didn't want to risk losing you."

Zack nods, leaning his back on the wall he slides down to sit on the floor. With his elbows on his knees, he breaks into a sob.

"I read what happened to you and my sister. I read about how much you loved my brother and how much you needed us. I understand way more than I did." He rises his tear stained face to hers. "I'm so sorry I made you feel like this."

I nudge Sam. When her teary eyes meet mine, I give her half a smile and whisper, "I'm going for a walk. Fix this."

I nod to my brother. He needs his best friend, and she needs to repair whatever is broken between them. Taking my coat off the back of the barstool, I nod at her again while I slip out the door.

I'm not going anywhere. I'm sitting my ass on the stairs that lead to Zan's apartment. If anyone is storming out of that apartment, I will pick them up and shove them back inside. This gets fixed today.

I cannot imagine my brother reading about Sam's attack. Knowing how she felt, her fear, her hurt, her self-blame, and self-doubt, even cold as steel, hard as stone Zack, had to be shaken. The mess he is right now, it had to be as bad as I think it is.

Sam

The door closes on Xander and I look down at my broken Zack.

"I kept journals as a way of coping. They were private."

He whimpers. "I know Sam. I know better, but I couldn't stop."

"Why?" I asked tilting my head.

He lets out a long sigh. "The first journal I found didn't have your name in it. I read the sweet ramblings of a little girl who was overwhelmed by her parents' expectations of her. I could identify."

I sit down on the floor in front of him and fold my legs. He gives me a grateful smile.

"I read about a little girl dealing with crushes from fantasies of Shia LeBeouf to a ginger haired boy next door. The writing was clearly a child, but so captivating I read it over and over again. The next journal I found was the charts and chronicles of The Fisher Brothers."

I pat his leg when he drops his head. "You knew it was mine then?" I ask.

He nods. "You wrote about me as somebody altogether different. In your journals, I wasn't just a Fisher brother or half of the twins. You got me long before you met me. I had to keep reading because nobody ever understood me. Not even me. I liked who I was through your eyes."

Tears escape his eyes and I lean forward to swipe them. I have never seen Zackary Fisher cry. I know he feels terrible. I want my friend to feel better, but I still feel invaded.

"I thought your dad was cold and unable to care for you. You two are really close and I remind you of him?"

He stands up and begins pacing. "Morgan wasn't your dad, you had a really great dad, Morgan was home. He made you feel like you did before your family splintered."

I nod.

"Connor, was your friend because you lost all of them after the incident. He made you see the difference between love and what was about to happen to you?"

He looks to me for confirmation and I nod.

"I was never darkness to you? You said that the absence of light is just another view. You saw the Zack I was meant to be before…"

Realization dawns on both of us.

He drops back to the floor in front of me. "You know what happened to me when I was a boy. You always knew, and you never once looked at me differently."

I nod while ignoring the single tear that tracks down my face. "I found out when doing unrelated research. I figured if you wanted to talk about it, you would."

"You don't know everything. If you did, you'd understand why I won't speak about it. You'd know why my family needed to help Becca."

"Maybe we will be close enough again one day for you to feel safe enough to share secrets."

He grabs my hands. "Please Sam, please tell me I am not going to lose the only person in my life who gets me. You don't know everything, but you know enough to get me. Xander doesn't even know what you do."

My voice breaks. "You read all of them?"

He drops my hands. "It took me a while to find all of them, but I couldn't stop reading. I hurt too much to feel. I have a steel heart, but reading about your love for Xander broke me. Reading about all the ways he helped you heal. I was jealous of your ability to move on, but I also felt hope. I know how much you needed him, and that makes me feel like an ass."

"Like an ass?"

"The rest of us love you, but none of us love you like Xander does. You love all of us, but not like you love him. I was pissed when the rules were broken. Now, I know I wasn't the one who earned the right to be pissed."

"What do you mean?" I ask.

"We made a pact to do what was best for you. Keeping you out of a relationship with Xander was wrong. It may have been right in the beginning, but not anymore. I let my jealousy guide me. I want to feel what Xander feels, and I resented that I can't. It isn't his fault and it isn't yours. I'm broken. I shouldn't begrudge you any happiness, because I love you girl."

"Oh, Zack." I crawl into his lap. "I love you, too. Don't count yourself out. You are more than capable of love. You just haven't found the girl who makes you feel it."

He releases me from his lap and asks, "are you happy?"

"Happiness is a momentary emotion. I was happy having dinner, happy to see you, unhappy at your news, unhappy at your tears. Whether or not I'm happy is irrelevant, because it will change." I stand up to retrieve two bottles of water from the refrigerator. "I'll answer the question you mean." I unscrew the top on the first bottle and hand it to Zack then sit back on the floor and take a sip of mine. "Finally owning my feelings and being okay with them, figuring out my plans and accepting life may change them, and feeling love as fiercely as I give it provides peace in my soul and joy so deep in my core that momentary unhappiness doesn't shake me anymore."

"Xander does that for you?" He asks sincerely.

"No, I do that for me, Xander helps."

"You are good for one another." He states it flat and simply. It's the truth.

"So we have your blessing?" I ask cautiously.

"You left. You went to New York to sever ties with the rest of us. You tried to let us go. If you had been successful, that would have been the fruition of my nightmares."

He pulls me into his lap and clutches me in a fierce embrace. "Tell me, Sam, how do I give you the blessing to be happy with him, without losing you? I know I hurt you, and you already chose him. Do I even have a chance at redemption?" He grips my upper arms, gives me a small shake. "I will do it, whatever it is you need, but please forgive me and don't shut me out. I can't have you hate me."

I soften and sink back into his chest. "You read my very private thoughts. I'm allowed to be angry."

"Yes, but.." I stop him with my finger placed over his lips.

"In all our years of friendship, how many times have you pissed me off?"

He shrugs, "I don't know, a lot?"

"The offense is worse, but the situation isn't any different."

He pulls me back and stares into my eyes. Hope makes his face glow. "You forgive me?"

"I will. I get to be angry though. I love you Zack and whatever happens, I will always be your badass. I'm yours when I'm angry, and when I'm happy. I'm yours when my heart belongs to your brother. I'm yours when your kids call me Auntie Sam."

His tears spill again. "Zack, I can have my happily ever after, and so can you. We can appreciate everything we have with someone else without losing what we have together." I hold up his pinky finger. "This is the part of you that will always belong to me. The part where we hold the secrets we told, the part where wind therapy was held, the part where you convinced me I'm a badass. You can give the rest of you to someone else. It won't damage this little piece."

He looks down at his pinky and smiles.

"You always paint the clearest pictures with words. This is how you catch the sun without getting burned?"

I nod.

He raises my pinky to his lips and kisses it sweetly. "And this piece of you is mine. Where we keep our secrets, wind therapy, and all of our bad-ass-ery. Xander can have the rest of you." He kisses my pinky again and holds it up for me to view. "But this. This is mine."

We laugh, we cry, and as Xander demanded, we fix us. It doesn't happen in an instant. It probably won't happen completely tonight. After hours of questions, rules, and promises, we will have a plan, and unbeknownst to him, he has Wonder Woman

Xander

"Xander, my love, wake up."

Sam slowly comes into focus. I'm in the stairwell. Still? "Are you and Zack fixed?"

She laughs. "We will be okay. He's asleep in the guest bed. Let's get you in bed, too."

Draping my arm around her shoulder, we lazily walk to the bedroom. "Are you okay?" I ask her when I notice it is nearly morning.

"Yes." She takes my jacket from my hand and helps me pull off my shirt. "Don't get me wrong, I'm pissed and feel violated. He read my very personal thoughts. I'll get past it though."

I unbuckle and slide my pants down. "He loves you. You know that, right?"

She pulls back the comforter and crawls into bed. As tired as I am, I still notice her toned legs stretching from one of my t-shirts. I love that she sleeps in my shirts.

Pulling the comforter over us, I settle her into me. "There has been a lot of hurt in the last few weeks. I, for one, am ready to begin this happily ever after people talk about."

She wiggles her ass up against my cock and I debate how tired I really am. "Remember how we went to Champagne Falls Fest every summer?"

"Who forgets funnel cake?" I ask sarcastically.

Or rides that made her body smoosh against mine.

"I always asked for one thing."

It wasn't a stuffed animal like most girls. Sam always wanted simple things.

"A glow in the dark necklace. I remember. The band used to sell them for a couple of dollars. My brothers and I would each get you one."

"And tease that I was visible from space." We both laugh.

Turning in my embrace she cups my cheek and kisses me sweetly. "I understood that sometimes you need a good break to really glow."

Zack is right, she paints pictures with words.

Curling back into me, her breaths become even on my chest. I know she's tired.

"Sam?"

"Hmm?" she mumbles through a sleepy haze.

"Are we done breaking yet? I'm ready to glow."

CHAPTER 35

As always, my heart races when I see him.

Sam

Talk about deja-vu. Rika and I again are stuffing, pushing, jumping on my bed, and sitting on my suitcase trying to get the latches to meet. Again, we collapse on my bed in a fit of giggles and labored breaths. "I'm lucky you're in New York right now. How would I have gotten that damn thing closed without you?"

"No kidding! Why didn't you mail some of your stuff back ahead of time?"

"I did!" I yell.

The doorbell rings and we both look at the door startled. I don't have the nice spacious apartment Rika and I shared anymore. The foot of my bed is feet from the front door. This is smaller than most hotel rooms, but it was the cheapest lodging I could find. "Who is it?" I ask.

Muffled by the door, his voice isn't any less sexy. "Your future husband."

Bouncing up from my bed, I fling open the door and am met with three handsome blondes. "Wow! I don't know if you all will fit, but do try to come in."

I scoot behind the door to allow as much room as possible. As it always does, my heart races when I see him. They are supposed to be at a wedding. I was going to meet with them later at the reception.

"You all remember Rika?" I peek around the door. "Where's Connor?"

Morgan, Zack, and Xander look back and forth between themselves before Morgan clears his voice and answers. "He's um, detained." The cheeky smiles suggest it's a woman.

"What are you doing here? I ask. "Aren't you supposed to be at the wedding?"

"There was a change in plans. Not our story to tell, but Matt's sister will not be getting married after all." Xander explains.

Poor Rika looks ready to collapse. I know how good looking the Fisher brothers are, but dressed to the nines in suits, they are breathtaking.

"I never thought to ask. It's been a year now. Have you met Connor yet?"

She bursts out laughing, "No, I still haven't met my roommate. It's almost comical." She sighs, "We talk and text. First, it was simple roommate stuff; how things work, do's and don'ts."

I bet that list is crazy long. Connor is something else.

"Then we started playing a where in the world is my roommate game with pictures. Now, he is a trusted confidant, but nope, never met him."

Rika's phone chimes and she bursts out laughing. "Where in the world is Connor Fisher?" She flips the screen around to face us. It's New York, and the scene is familiar.

"Is that…" I shake my head. It can't be. Tourists aren't allowed up there anymore. "It looks like it's taken from The Statue of Liberty."

The photo caption reads, "she's beautiful."

Zack nudges Morgan. "You think he means the girl or the statue?"

We all look inquisitively at the sniggering boys. Morgan clears his throat again. "Um, he left on the promise of a blow job at the top of the Statue of Liberty. She works there."

Zack laughs. Xander slaps a hand over his face, and Rika and I scrunch our noses.

Then a devious smile crosses her lips. She hands her phone to me. "I need a picture with the single Fisher Men."

Xander jumps into action. Oh, it's payback time baby. He makes Morgan pick up Rika bride style, and he makes Zack lean her head back and kiss her Spiderman style. The scene looks like that time Connor kissed me first. He's going to be bummed he didn't stick with his brothers and finally meet her. Well, if the girl on her knees is particularly talented, he might not mind too much.

Rika sends the picture captioned, *Where in the world is Veronica Lang and which one gets a taste of her?* Twenty seconds later her phone rings and we all hear Connor shout, "Don't kiss my brother!"

That gets us all laughing. So much so, that Connor hangs up and switches to text.

Xander pulls my hips to his and whispers in my ear. "I cancelled my flight home so we could drive back together."

"You did?" I ask.

"I did." He nods.

Oh, how I love this man.

CHAPTER 36

Sometimes you need to break before you can glow.

Xander

Pulling the beer bottle up to my lips, I take a long pull and sigh. It has been a stressful couple of days. Obviously, I'm unloading to a virtual stranger. In a bar.

"What started as a strange friendship has proven to become a valuable commodity." I explain, "When my sister Chrissy became friends with Zan, our family inherited Zan's circle of friends. That's where Megan comes in. I sat with her on a plane to Vegas for Zan's wedding, and she's a trip. I was devoted to my *not yet girlfriend* and I have a rule about dating my sister's friends, but she is clumsy, smart, helpful, and hanging out with her is always fun."

"Is she trying to escape her friend zone?" The young woman asks. *Why in the world am I telling her this story?*

"No, actually that's how we got close. She found herself unmarried, pregnant, and in love with a man who isn't Daddy."

"Ouch." The woman admits pushing her blond hair over her shoulder and down her back.

"My family babysits every Tuesday so she can have a date night. We love her little girl." I shake my head, "I'm getting off track." I gulp another drink from the long neck. "Megan is a nurse and the most epic event planner. Ever. I knew this had to be spectacular. Samantha Reynolds deserves nothing but the very best." I point the bottle at the stranger, "and I'm going to give it to her."

"Why are we here then?" The woman asks. It's a fair question.

"She's taking a bath and getting dressed for dinner at the hotel across the street. There is a note on the bed, asking her to come over here." I tap the bar before I look into her big brown eyes hoping she'll agree. The whole situation is bizarre and probably overwhelming for her. Giving her my best schoolboy smile, I shrug and ask again. "So, what do you say, Aurora? Will you help me?"

Her eyes brighten, and tears glisten at the corners. "Thank you for including me. It's the least I can do for him." I hand her the box and kiss her cheek before slipping out of the bar unnoticed.

Megan and I had an elaborate proposal planned, but the sudden cancellation of the wedding had us scrambling from the New York location to the Illinois location. Megan, the pro-planner, and her fiancé Cannon stepped up to make it better than it was before. It's more personal, now. Megan cried when I told her my idea. I fumble in my pocket one hundred times, making sure the ring is still there. I'm nervous. I know she will say yes, I just want her to love it.

Sam

Stopping at this hotel is ridiculous. We are like an hour from home and I'm not that tired. I thought maybe Xander stopped because he was horny. Secretly, I hoped it was the reason. Instead, he filled up the huge garden tub, put out electric candles and dropped in a bath bomb. My postage stamp apartment lacked a bathtub and we both couldn't fit in my shower. I really miss baths. It's the sweetest thing ever.

I sink slowly into the tub expecting him to join me. Instead, he brought a Bluetooth speaker into the bathroom and started the relaxation mix on my phone. "Take your time, Love. We can go downstairs for dinner in a bit." I nod and close my eyes.

Once I am thoroughly relaxed and nearly asleep, I decide I should probably get out of here. I thought, hoped even, I would enter the room to a naked and ready Xander. Instead, he's gone. Laying on the bed is my polka dot pin up wrap dress. I hadn't seen it since Xander ripped it from my scalding tea covered body. Here it is clean, pressed, and on display with a note. Put this on, then check in your purse.

I do as I've been instructed, and since my make-up bag is on the counter, I do a little more. It looks like we have a date. My hair and make-up will be on fleek. My sweet naughty boy. The pale pink thong he laid out for me is now getting damp with excitement.

Once I look perfect, I open my purse, find a note and a glow stick. I open the pale blue envelope with silver monogramming. It's beautiful stationary. The card reads: *It started with a broken window. It was the first crack that let me see you glow.*

A small slip of tissue paper falls out and reads: *Come downstairs, My Love.*

Stepping off the elevator, I look for him, but a man in the hotel uniform hands me a pale blue card. I tear into it like a kid on her birthday.

You looked beautiful that night and a jealous girl tried to ruin you. She has something to say.

I pull it away from my face as if it were a snake, *huh*? Looking up I see the older but still unmistakable face of Ashley Aniston.

"Don't be angry. I've been asking The Fishers for information on you for years. I can never make up for what I did to you, but I'm different because of it." She folds her hands and looks down at them.

"My family had to move, and all the hateful comments really forced me to look at who I was. The thing is, you punished me for a week. You took down the video and months later nobody remembered me. You didn't move to another city, nobody forgot you. I see how much stronger you are, stronger than I ever was." A tear tracks down her cheek.

"I run a Minnesota chapter of Safe Spaces. In addition to domestic violence advocacy, we counsel victims of cyber bullying and cyber stalking. I've made a difference in the lives of hundreds of young boys and girls, it started as a penance, but became a passion."

I'm proud of her accomplishments, but I can't feel anything else for her. So much time has passed, but the hurt still lingers. She doesn't anger me anymore, but there is no more kindness in my heart for her either.

"Anyways," she pulls out a glow stick and cracks it, "from all the breaks I caused, and the cracks in me you found, hundreds of teenagers have learned to glow. Thank you for making me a better person. I'm sorry Samantha, I wish there were better words to explain how much I mean it."

I fumble to put the glow stick she handed me in my purse while I watch her walk away. Taking the video down after a week was the only mercy I ever showed her. She's right; it was a mercy that I didn't receive. Perhaps, seeing the good person she became will change me, but today isn't the day.

The tissue paper wrapped around the glow stick she handed me simply read, *the bar across the street.*

Walking out to the parking lot, I notice it is the best part of the day. The sun has already dipped over the horizon and the sky is painted in pinks, oranges, and violet. The bar is the only thing across the street. It has an Irish Pub feel to it. The name scrolled on the lighted sign reads, The Come Back Inn. I smile at the cute name and make my way across the lot.

The door has a bell that chimes as I enter. It's crowded, but a blond woman catches my attention by waving a pale blue envelope. I make my way to the table for two she is occupying and sit when she motions to the chair.

"My name is Aurora." She holds her hand out and when I shake it she places my hand on her chest. Not going to lie, this is weird. She leaves my hand on her chest, her heartbeat rapid, she opens the envelope and holds the card for me to read. She places her free hand on mine still against her chest.

A long time ago, your heart broke. I believe the cracks made it stretch so there was room for me, too. She is the recipient of Colton BaddStone's heart, and I bet there is still a piece of you in there, just as there will always be that piece of your heart we share with him.

Tears spill from my eyes, and I stare at my fingertips. The heart that nearly burst from his chest when we shared our first kiss is here. Right here. Under my fingertips like it was that day.

Slapping the tears from my face with my free hand, an ugly snot pouring sob escapes me. Aurora hands me a tissue and pulls me to her in a hug. Colton's heart beats against my cheek, and it is just about all I can bear. She takes my shoulders in her hands and pulls back to see my face. "It took a broken boy," she pulls out the glow stick and snaps it, "to give me back my glow." I fall back into a final hug with her.

"Thank you, you have no idea what this meant to me."

She hooks my chin and wipes a tear from my cheek, "You have a really great man who clearly loves you. I hope you found what you are looking for."

I look around the bar and wink. "Not yet, have you got a new location for me?"

Handing me my truck keys, she nods. "I do."

She offers me a tiny tissue paper that reads: *Time to go to the Fisher House. Nonna awaits you in the dining room.*

Hopping in my driver's seat, I peel out of the parking lot giddy with what I am certain is coming. My phone rings and Xander's face lights up the screen. The tips of my smile reach my ears.

"Xander?"

"I'm making sure you are okay to drive after the emotional roller coaster."

"Admittedly, Ashley Aniston was the last person I wanted to see, but Aurora is a beautiful person." I clutch the steering wheel staving off tears.

"She is. Colton's beating heart is going to be a tough gift to top."

I nod even though he can't see me. "I think you've got this."

"Okay, My Love, hang up and drive. I'll see you soon."

"Xander."

"Yes?"

"I love you." Disconnecting the call, I can feel my heart smile and my insides warm. I am fairly certain this is an elaborate marriage proposal and I can't wait to see what's next.

I pull into my Dad's driveway and shutter at the empty lot that was once my Dad's house. Walking to the Fisher house like I did a million times in my younger life is freeing and nostalgic. I walk right in the front door. I'm not the kind of neighbor that requires a knock. The dining room table is covered in manila folders. "Oh, yer here already, you are. Come, come and sit, Samantha. I do as she asks and watch her bustle and fuss over the mess.

"These are me Safe Spaces files. I don't go using computers either. I write all the files in code. Nobody'll be finding any hiders on my watch. No Ma'am, tha' won't."

Sitting next to me she pats my hand. "The most crucial part of helping a family that flees domestic abuse is the first forty-eight hours. That's when they feel guilty; like they have abandoned their loved one. When you have been systematically broken down to thinkin' you're nothin' without yer partner, it's awfully hard to leave. You bet it is."

Opening a folder, she shows me a modern mobile home and a tiny blue envelope. I open it and slip out a card that reads, *The writing workshops you set up in New York raised enough money to get another crisis safe house.*

Nonna smiles and squeezes my hand. "We staff these houses with intervention counselors and they spend the first three days here decompressin' and counselin' before they are placed in a safe house. This may not look like much, but 120 families a year can be getting a fresh start here, because of you." She takes out a glow stick, "All the broken people," she breaks the stick, "will get a chance to glow."

I take the glowing symbol of possibility and hug her tight.

"Aww Samantha, yer do know yer always been me other daughter."

"Yes Nonna, and you have always been a mom when I needed one." I swipe a tear from her cheek. "Where do I go now?"

"There is one more ting you'll be needin' before you become a Fisher. It's time to tell you about our family secret. You may know about what happened to Zack, I'm going to tell you why."

My mouth drops as she explains the not so humble beginnings of her life. She spins a tale of abuse, human trafficking, and kidnapping. Mr. and Mrs. Fisher are the kindest most wonderful people because they have experienced the very worst pieces of humanity. I'm touched and honored to be invited to not only this family but also the family business.

"Where do I go from here?" I ask.

Her smile crinkles her eyes. "The treehouse, Luv."

I've been in Chrissy's treehouse a number of times back when she was Kateri and my best friend, but climbing the ladder as an adult is a little scary. I wonder what the weight limit is?

As I suspected, Chrissy waits for me. "It's my turn."

I hug her tight and take a seat in the bean bag chair that was once my seat. She hands me a blue envelope. I open the card and my chin drops. *Sometimes we can only break so much before we fall apart.*

I look up at my old friend. "Is that what happened to us? Did we break so badly that we couldn't be repaired?"

Climbing out of her bean bag and settling into mine to hold me, she shushes me. "No Sam, we didn't break, I did. I came here every night and I mended all my broken pieces by chatting with a stranger on the internet. I needed someone who couldn't see me to listen. I needed someone who knew how to make me speak. I loved you." She taps my chin playfully, "I still do and always will, but you aren't who I needed. I was too broken to be who you needed. I gave you my brothers, and you gave me the space to work out what I needed to."

My voice shakes with the sob I hold in. "While we healed, we never were again what we used to be."

"I'm sorry, Sam, I'm not who I used to be, and when I finally became comfortable enough in my own skin to be your friend, you had a better relationship with my brothers. I'm okay with that. You need to be, too."

I nod. "I am. I'm happy, and I'm glad you are, too."

Pulling out a glow stick, she cracks it. "When every piece of me shattered, I found a man that could still find my glow. He showed it to me when I couldn't see it myself." She sets it down then takes out another glow stick. "When we cracked," she cracked the glow stick, "My brothers helped you find a whole new glow." She hands me both glowing symbols and explains, "One for you and one for me. My brothers are waiting for you in the make-out spot." We giggle and hug like the little girls we used to be.

I give a final wave as I climb down with more confidence than I had going up. I step around the corner hedges to find three of my best friends. Zack hands me a blue envelope. *According to your diary, this is where we all began. It seems fitting that the pursuit of Sam should end here."*

Morgan takes me into his arms. "I am the guy who takes care of everything, always. When my favorite girl in the whole world was shattered, I needed to take care of her. She shut me out and I couldn't move on. I couldn't think, feel, or eat while she hurt." Letting go of our embrace, he takes my hands. "I fix things and this… this I couldn't fix. You gave me a purpose when I needed one, taught me that not everything can be fixed, and eventually you taught me to find beauty in the broken." He pulls a glow stick from his back pocket. "You encouraged me to polish the damage," he snaps the stick, "and bring the glow to the surface."

Connor takes my hands from Morgan. "Sam I Am," He wipes my tears. "With us, I never saw you as broken." He takes a deep breath. "I like everything just so." I can't help chuckling at his severe understatement. "Everything has a place, everything has to be in its place, my day has a plan, and I don't like change." He leans in and whispers, "I had a hard time dating because I like control." This time HE chuckles at his understatement. "You brought beautiful chaos to my life. You're messy and unpredictable. You give and relinquish control when it suits you, and from the moment I met you, I wanted to be more like you and less like me."

My beautiful Connor, I cup his cheek and kiss him the sweet way he kisses me.

"I was closed so tightly." He pulls out his glow stick, "It took you to find the cracks." He cracks the stick. "Sometimes, I think even I glow."

"Oh Connor, you glow. You glow so brightly, you're blinding. I love you." I wrap him in a tight hug planting kisses all over his face. Morgan puts his hand to the small of my back, so I pull him in to share my frantic kisses like a grandma with a new baby.

"Dude, it's my turn!" Zack pries me from his brothers. He pulls me into his chest and turns his back to his brothers while whispering in my ear. "I used to finger my girlfriend standing here because I saw you watching." I gasp in a breath and slap his chest.

"Zachary Michael Fisher!"

His deep rumble laugh shakes me. "Listen, girl, reading about it made me realize, if my love for you was true, I wouldn't touch another girl. I love the idea of you. I loved the badass girl that wore her scars like trophies. You embraced your darkness, and made it okay for me to love mine." He holds up his pinky finger. I hold up mine and when we wrap them around the other. The tattoo of a heart appears from what is simple lines when we are apart. It's our reminder to one another. This small piece is his, and his small piece is mine. He takes out his glow stick, "I never saw the value in glowing," he breaks the stick, "until you stood out in the darkness."

He kisses my head and whispers again "I read what you did for Morgan. You'll always be my hero for saving his soul." I feel the warmth and embrace of my Fisher Men, well except for one. We have come so far. The jealousy is stifled, and the friendships are as strong as they always were. I thought I would lose them, maybe with wives and kids I will, but not today. Today these three men are the greatest friends a girl could ask for. I wipe my tears with my palms. "I love you guys, but it's time to get my man."

Zack shrugs, "We don't know where he is."

"One of you should have a tissue paper with an address or directions." The three of them look one to another shrugging and smiling conspiratorially.

Placing my hands on my hips I glare. "Are you trying to ruin my perfect proposal?" The smiles vanish. I step forward poking each in the chest as I speak. "Are you interfering in your brother's love life?" Their spines stiffen and Connor breaks the silence.

"He said you should close the distance in the place you did the first time."

I squeal like a sixth-grade girl at a Justin Bieber concert and kiss them all quickly as I bounce and run to my pick-up truck. Turning the key in the ignition, I grip the steering wheel and take one more moment to scream, stomp my feet, and whip my hair.

Time to go get engaged!

I think I blinked my eyes and arrived at Xanack Ink. I don't remember the drive at all. I park my truck, and it is immediately surrounded by women with glow sticks. They all have pale blue t-shirts with glow in the dark lettering that read Cancer cracked us, but Xanack helped us glow. They are all breast cancer survivors. Zack and Xander tattoo nipples on their new breasts for free once a month.

When I open the truck door they all cheer. From the crowd, a blue envelope makes its way to me. I rip it open like a dog with a squeak toy. The card reads: *I tried to make the journey part of the gift, but any journey with you is the sweetest gift.* I hold the card to my heart and hug the nearest woman to me.

She whispers loudly in my ear her words echoing above the chatter, "Last chance to run sweetheart."

Pulling back, I laugh and nod. "Yes, Ma'am, and I'm going to take it." Running as fast as my legs will pump. I sidestep and dodge the ladies until I can fully sprint into Xanack Ink, and I don't stop until I fling open the door of the piercing room throwing myself into the arms of my love, I pepper his face with kisses. "Yes, Yes! Yes, Xander, I will marry you."

I slam my lips almost painfully to his and I kiss him like it's our last. My fingers in his hair, the whole room spinning, I feel the axis tilt of the world, and brilliant colors explode behind my closed eyelids. I consume his smell, his touch, his taste, and when we finally break for air his wide eyes meet mine.

"I didn't ask."

"Right," I pull away smoothing my clothes and for the first time, I take in the room lit with only glow sticks, hundreds of them.

"They don't make enough glow sticks to represent every crack you've filled. Some of you is intertwined into every piece of me." With that, he drops down on one knee. "Samantha Nikkole Reynolds, will you do me the extraordinary pleasure of spending the rest of your days as my partner, my wife, and my home?"

"Yes, yes, yes, I love you, Xander Oliver Fisher!"

"I love you, too." He responds.

I kiss him one more time. "Hey fiancée," I wink. "Take me home."

He lifts me soon to be bride style and does just that.

CHAPTER 37

What a great place for our next beginning.

Xander

I stand next to Chrissy, but I still don't have her title figured out. She can't be my best man because she's a woman. She can't be my best woman, because that's Sam. We decide to stick with the traditional roles, but not the genders they are assigned to.

We stop bantering about our titles when the music starts. It's not the wedding march because that's overdone. Instead, a string quartet plays Perfect by Ed Sheeran. Morgan and Zan walk down the aisle. Zan joins me and Morgan steps over to Sam's side.

Zan stage whispers, "This is so cool, I've never been a groomsman before." Our friends and family laugh, and Chrissy throws her elbow into Zan's arm. "What, I whispered?" she asks.

Everyone chuckles because if I had to guess, Zan learned to whisper in a tight room with a hovering helicopter while juggling chainsaws.

Connor and Rika take to the aisle next. He kisses her head before he retreats to the bride side. Always looking for an excuse to put his lips on a pretty girl. He's going to get in big trouble one day. Rika takes her place next to Zan.

Our friends Cannon and Megan come down the aisle next, followed by their little girl Lia. She is exuberantly sprinkling flower petals like glitter. She blurts out, "Unky Xander, I look boo-ful."

I nod with the collective awes.

Suppressing a laugh becomes more difficult when my big, bad, scary, inked twin brother walks down the aisle alone. He won the right to be maid of honor. I'm pretty sure Morgan and Connor let him win. He embraced his roll like a champ. He threw her a bridal shower, helped her with seating charts, spent his morning at the spa with her, he even helped pick out her dress and took her to all her fittings. He is the best self-titled dude of honor the world has ever seen.

The laughter and sarcasm gulp down my throat in a hard swallow when Sam and her dad step in view. Rows of people stand with similar awe. She is breathtaking. Her skin is glowing. Her white teeth shine through the veil over her face because her smile is brilliant. I am the luckiest man who ever lived.

Reaching the flowered arch where I stand, she faces her dad and he beams with pride. Lifting her veil, he kisses her on her cheek then whispers over her shoulder in my direction. "Remember baby girl, I loved you first. He better treat you like I would."

"Yes, Daddy, you know he's a good man."

"Yes, baby girl, I know." He takes a seat between his girlfriend and his ex-wife, who is already ugly crying. Sam turns to face me, and I nearly lose my shit when Zack bends down, fixes her dress and takes her bouquet so she can hold my hands.

Are you fucking kidding me right now?

Sam grits through her teeth, "Shut it X, he is doing this for me, and you better be proud of him."

I feel all kinds of pride today. Today is a perfect day. Surrounded by my mother's flower garden in the backyard we played tag in, on the grass where we played football and watched the stars, I pledged my love and life to my wife.

When the reception is well underway, the glow stick centerpieces lighting the night, I know a secret spot to sneak off and kiss her privately. After all, we began here, so what a great place for our next beginning.

It's not the end.

EPILOGUE

Rika

My phone buzzes with an incoming text message. Dropping my suitcases in my bedroom, I reach into my purse and smile stupidly with the notification.

Connor: Where in the world is Connor Fisher?
Photo attached

I click on the photo and a shot from the airplane window shows the Grand Canyon.

Rika: Duh! That's the Grand Canyon.
Connor: I went easy on you, eh?
Rika: Heading back to New Orleans, or are you still on the way to Cali?
Connor: Not exactly, I have so much shit going on. My phone is blowing up with family stuff. Sam's fine, I'll call later.
Rika: I'm planning a hot bath and an early night. Call tomorrow if everything is okay.
Connor: You're supposed to take a selfie and let me guess you're in the bathtub.
Rika: For the last time, I'm not sending you nudes. Safe travels.

Connor: Goodnight, beautiful.

I have to shake my head at his consistent flirting.

I feel disgusting after being in a rental car for the last twelve hours. I stink, my hair is a mess, and I ran out of clean clothes on my trip. I was in a tiny mountain town where nobody noticed my stench over the deer urine marking hunting season. I certainly don't feel beautiful. Unloading my suitcases, I separate laundry. If I don't wash some underwear soon, I'm going to have to go commando.

While my clothes go through the wash cycle, I unpack the rest of my bags. Plugging in my cell phone and laptop, I arrange my notes on the desk in my room and begin an audiobook download.

I had a really awful trip. The interviews I did about an abused woman made me sick to my stomach, and haunting images keep creeping into my mind. I make myself a simple dinner, but I can't bring myself to eat it. I'm overwhelmed.

Transferring my clothes from the washer into the dryer, and starting the next and final load, I am relieved that soon I will have fresh clothes. Connor washed my sheets while I was gone. He usually does. I roll my eyes in euphoric bliss at the thought of climbing into clean sheets, in clean pajamas, and sleeping peacefully in my own bed after a long hot bath.

God, I need a bath!

Connor won't be home for another three weeks. He won't ever have to find out. The guest bathroom has a mediocre bathtub at best. The master suite has a jetted tub. After the day I have had, all I want is a long supremely relaxing bath. He never has to know. Cinching my bathrobe closed, I grab my shower caddy and towels, then tiptoe into Connor's bathroom like a criminal.

I run the hot water, drop in my favorite bath bomb, and start my audiobook. The voice of Ethan Woods, my favorite audiobook narrator, pours out of my Bluetooth speaker, and I am almost giddy with anticipation.

Connor is an amazing roommate. We've been roomies for a year now, and we've never met. Oh sure, we text, talk on the phone, and he even sends me postcards, packages, and orders take out dinner for me from time to time. We flirt, and one time after a few drinks, we took things a bit further. We don't talk about that.

Tying up my hair and laying my glasses on the sink, I look in the mirror. I look like Hell chewed me up and spit me back. Hopefully, this bath makes me human again. Slowly, I step into the bathtub and feel the sting of the hot water envelope the bottom half of my body. The smell of peony blossoms relaxes me further.

Connor's travel schedule and mine keep us in different states consistently. He flew to California this morning and is supposed to be in New Orleans this evening. I just arrived from Tennessee. When he gets back, I'll be in New York. It's been our story for an entire year. Opening my eyes, I swipe into my phone and stop the audiobook I started. I'm excited about the new release, but I need Adele in a moment like this. I start my music and close my eyes.

My thoughts drift to my roommate. Admittedly, I may have used his where-in-the-world selfie a time or two for stress relief. He is a gorgeous specimen of a man who is sweet. He gets my motor running with a simple text sometimes. I'm curious if we would have chemistry in real life.

I'm wound up super tight, and I need to change the momentum in my brain. Turning the jets on, I recall the one time Connor and I had a little tequila and an x-rated video chat. I recall it often. That conversation was hotter than a few of my actual sexual encounters. I let out a long soft moan, and reach my hand down to rub out some relief.

My thoughts flood with flashes of his smile from the portrait above the fireplace, his eyes from the last selfie he sent, his lips from the video. The water sloshes around me as I pick up speed and allow my imagination to picture all the things he typed about the delicious mess of sex, beginning with those beautiful lips wrapped around my clit. I moan and jerk with the impending explosion.

"Why are you in my bathroom?"

I scream, and oh my god! He is tilted head staring at me with a sexy smirk.

"I'm naked!"

He nods calmly, "Yes, but that isn't what I asked."

"Get out!" My hands fly over all my lady parts in a last-ditch effort of modesty.

He shrugs and puts his hands in his pockets. "You're in my bathroom, you get out." He leans on the bathroom doorjamb still staring at me with that amused smirk. What the hell?

Connor

My family began the slew of text messages yesterday. My brother in law's sister Piper was attacked. By the time I landed in California, she was in emergency surgery, and now is in a coma. Things are pretty scary and the doctors have suggested family come visit now while they can. Both of my work sites were very understanding, and shortly after landing in California, I got back on a plane heading home.

I was so busy keeping up with the assault by group texts that I forgot to send Rika my where in the world picture. I stopped at a rest area before exiting the highway and sent the Grand Canyon picture. When I found out she was already home, I thought I'd surprise her.

I'm the one surprised. When I heard a man's voice, I thought she was in my bed, with a man. I was pissed. I stormed in my room, but the soft floral scent and empty bed threw me off. Soon I heard music crooning. That must have been the voice I thought I heard. Her plan was to take a bath. Is she in my bathtub?

I hear the jets rumble to life and that confirms it. I change out of my suit and into my basketball shorts and a t-shirt when I hear her moan. Holy fuck, that sounds hot. My plan was to lay in my bed and wait for her to come out, but hearing the water slosh and her sounds of pleasure drew me to the door. It wasn't closed all the way and I saw her. She rarely sends me selfies, aside from the silly faced where in the world pics. The best photos I've seen of her are on Sam's Instagram and her column in the newspaper. Neither do her justice. She's breathtaking. She jumps and I think she saw me. I do the only thing I can do. I own it. I lean on the doorframe and ask her what she's doing in my bathroom. I'm disappointed to discover the jump had nothing to do with me. She is genuinely surprised.

Her flustered words and pink cheeks stir my cock in the most frustrating ways. Her meager attempts at hiding her breasts are adorable. On the famed tequila night, she detailed exactly how she gives head and I have pictured her mouth doing just that, way more than I should. Now that she is naked, on full display, and I see how perfect her lips are, I'm uncomfortably hard.

Despite all the shit I just gave her about getting out, Mama raised a gentleman. I pick up her bathrobe and hold it out with my eyes closed and head turned away. "Here." I hear the water rustle as she steps out and feel the heat of her body in front of me as she slips into her robe.

Opening my eyes, I look at her still flushed face. "I'm sorry I startled you Rika, but hey, I'm Connor." I offer my hand. She glares at me.

"I was naked!" she yells.

"It's just skin." I shrug.

"It's my skin." She steps up on tiptoes and reiterates in my face "Mine!"

I wrap my arms around her, "Look, I really am sorry. I brought dinner and ice cream. Can you be angry with me later? Let me meet you first."

She growls and shoves me out of the way before storming out of my room.

I call after her, "Is that a no?"

I'm answered with a slammed door.

Well, this could be fun.

Check out Rika and Connor's story in:

X-ing Lines
Book II in the Fisher Men series.

Want to learn more about the Champagne Falls Crew?
Check out the Circle of Sanity Series.

Book I. InSanity
The story of the Zan and Jacob

Book II. Sanity's Side
The story of Chrissy (Kateri) and Matt

Book III. Sanity's Sake
The Story of Piper and Ethan

Book IV. Sanity's Edge
The story of Megan and Cannon

In a universe all its own… Rockstar Going Down
The story of Dylan Hart and G.

Rebel is always moving straight ahead with an occasional wobble. After the release of the Four Fisher Men books, she has a Sci-fi Fantasy in the works. Her next romance series, the Textually Ever After series, is well underway with book titles Rock Hard Clock, Kiss My Click, and Ducking Brilliant. Each relationship will begin with an auto-correct or technology failure sure to make you giggle.

All released books are available on Amazon and don't forget to follow Rebel Nicks O'Dey on Facebook, Instagram, Twitter, Goodreads and anywhere else you see her. Except on the street. Don't' follow me in real life, it's creepy.

Made in the USA
Columbia, SC
06 September 2019